Praise for *A Promise Engraved*

A Promise Engraved holds threads of inexplicable heartache, unyielding courage, and daring romance, all woven into the historical tapestry of San Antonio, Texas. Follow the journey of two gutsy heroines, separated by two hundred years, yet united by an intriguing ring. Tolsma delivers a tender story that highlights the timeless truth of the importance of trusting in the light of God's hope even when darkness presses in.

—Rachel Scott McDaniel, award-winning
author of *The Mobster's Daughter*

T0016998

Doors to the Past

A PROMISE Engraved

LIZ TOLSMA

BARBOUR
PUBLISHING

A Promise Engraved ©2022 by Liz Tolsma

Print ISBN 978-1-63609-249-2

eBook Edition:
Adobe Digital Edition (.epub) 978-1-63609-251-5

All scripture quotations, unless otherwise noted, are taken from the King James Version of the Bible.

This book is a work of fiction. Names, characters, places, and incidents are either products of the author's imagination or used fictitiously. Any similarity to actual people, organizations, and/or events is purely coincidental.

See the series lineup and get bonus content at DoorsToThePastSeries.com

Cover Model Photograph: Magdelena Russocka/Trevillion Images

Published by Barbour Publishing, Inc., 1810 Barbour Drive, Uhrichsville, Ohio 44683, www.barbourbooks.com

Our mission is to inspire the world with the life-changing message of the Bible.

ecpa Member of the
Evangelical Christian
Publishers Association

Printed in the United States of America.

DEDICATION

In loving memory of my aunt, Evelyn Tolsma, one
of my biggest fans. Every time I published a book, she
had to have a copy, and she told all her friends about it.
I'll miss your encouragement and support. Love you!

CHAPTER ONE

September 28, 1835

*R*ecent rains that had broken the long Texas summer heat had swollen the Guadalupe River so that it churned and foamed as it roared over the rocks along the bank. After a long day on her now-swollen feet, the water called to Josie Wilkins, sang its siren song, and beckoned her to slip off her shoes so the water might refresh her.

A song she disregarded. Instead, she inhaled the musty scent of decaying leaves filling her nostrils, awakening her. All too soon, she would have to return to the four-room dogtrot cabin and get supper started. Her father would arrive home from his blacksmith's shop in a short while and would be hungry.

As it was, Charlotte would scold her for her skirt hem being muddy. Her stepmother was more ladylike than Josie, much more ladylike. And she didn't hesitate to condemn Josie for her ruffian ways.

She may be only eighteen, but Josie was no longer a child. She'd been in the world, seen and experienced events that many adults hadn't. Her heart would bear those scars forever.

As usual, she swallowed the tears and reinforced the wall around her heart. She fought to keep her head above water so she wouldn't drown. If only she could sleep. Keep the dreams at bay and rest.

She shook the dark thoughts off like dust off a rug. Time flew onward, and home called. Already Father would chastise her for being away from Charlotte too long. If there was a problem with this pregnancy, as there had been before, Charlotte would have no help and no one to send a message to Father.

Before she could turn to head for town, a flash of blue across the river caught her eye. She dashed behind the rough trunk of a large oak tree and peeked around it. Some of the crashing filling her ears came not from the water churning over the river rocks but from men moving through the forest on the opposite side.

Glimpses of red and white mixed in with the blue.

Good thing she had chosen to wear her dark brown gown today. This way she blended in with the tree trunks surrounding her. The Mexican army hadn't learned that lesson so well. Because that's who came stomping through the trees. A horde of them, many on horseback, pulling up short when they reached the foaming water, all dressed in blue uniforms with white sashes and tall white hats with red and blue plumes. Peacocks strutting about the forest, announcing their arrival for all the world to see.

Josie knew that uniform well.

Was Manuel Garcia with them?

A chill swept through her, a hollow emptiness that left an ache in her stomach. She could only pray he wasn't, that she would never have to look into his dark eyes again or endure his large, rough hands all over her, in places they never should be.

Her chest pulsed, her knees went weak, and she leaned against the nearest tree for support, digging her fingernails into the rough bark just to remain upright, reminding herself to breathe, to keep the darkness from consuming her.

Then she forced those memories deep inside, to the deepest part of her, where no one, including she, could find them. Sometimes, like now, they resurfaced and sought her out. But she never allowed them to linger for long.

Remaining behind the tree, she set her focus on the regiment across the swirling water. From the looks of it, the soldiers didn't come on a peace mission. Most held rifles, while a few clasped swords. They were here for a reason. But what?

Tensions had been rising between the Mexicans under the direction of Santa Anna and the Texans, immigrants from America, for some time. Had it truly boiled over into armed conflict?

She blew out a breath. The river would act as a wall for Gonzales for a while, keeping these troops at bay, giving Josie time to discover why they were here, what their intentions were. Too bad she didn't have her colorful embroidered shawl with her today. With her dark hair and eyes, people often mistook her for Tejano—those of Mexican descent born in Texas. The shawl would better help her play the part.

She melted deeper into the forest, its green canopy covering her. On soft, moccasin-clad feet, she crept farther down the river. Though the water was high in this spot, it didn't run as fast, but the forest and undergrowth were too thick for an army to cross here.

She glanced around. The trees surrounding her whispered to her, but there were no other noises. No flashes of color among the green and brown.

Good. No one else was about. Not even an army scout.

Even though the rushing water now covered the rocks, Josie had crossed here often enough that she had memorized where every stone was. Lifting her skirts, she stepped onto the first one, the water swirling around her calves, daring her to remain on her feet.

She met the challenge, her steps sure and secure as she crossed the river. In no time, she was on the other side, slinking into the trees that again provided cover. There were many good things that came from having an Indian girl as a best friend. One was the ability to walk over the forest floor covered with twigs and dried leaves without making a sound.

Another advantage was buckskin. If only she had dressed in that instead of this cotton gown. The hide didn't catch on twigs and thorns. Cotton did. Well, it couldn't be helped. She yanked her skirt from the branch it was caught on and continued on her way, as silent as an owl in flight.

She didn't have to go far before a flash of color caught her eye, the contingent of the Mexican Army that had come marching against their own citizens.

She slowed her pace, even more careful than before not to make a sound, concentrating on keeping her breathing deep and even, close enough now to make out the whites of the soldiers' eyes standing out against their dark skin.

Eyes and skin so much like Manuel's. Eyes she would never forget. Even sleep offered little respite from their haunting depths. Today the memories refused to stay buried. They demanded entrance to her consciousness no matter the force she applied to shoved them away.

Surely the soldiers must hear the pounding of her heart and her ragged breathing.

Several of the Mexicans' horses snorted, their tack jangling as they pranced, eager to be in the fight as they were trained.

Picking her way around trees and scrub, she managed to inch closer to the front line. Here the men would know more about what was going on. Though they may not be able to answer the question that almost burned a hole through her soul, she might glean valuable information from them, like their intentions for marching to Josie's small frontier town.

"They want us to cross that river?" The soldier's voice cracked, as if it had changed not long ago. "I don't think so."

Thanks to Manuel and her time among the Mexicans, she had a pretty good grasp of Spanish.

"We have to obey orders." The first one's companion leaned forward on his horse.

"I hope they don't order us across. I am still not that skilled with my riding. Pedro will lose his footing and send me into the water for sure."

Greenhorns. That was who they had sent against Gonzales. Good to know it wasn't a bunch of seasoned veterans, but that begged the question why they came at all.

She moved away from the river. It was risky to go around the back to the other flank, because she might run into stragglers, but these men had no idea why they were here, just that they were here. As swift as a rabbit, she scampered through the forest to the other side of the troops.

"The water is too high." The deep lines on this man's face said he was more experienced. A veteran, a higher ranking soldier. Here she would have better luck getting the information she needed.

The one beside him nodded. "How are we going to get across and get that cannon? Seems to me we are going to be stuck here for a while."

"Too bad we don't have orders to shoot. How do they expect us to retrieve it if we can't force them?"

"A handful of men?" The scarred one scoffed. "When they see us, they'll tuck their tails between their legs and roll over. They'll beg us to take that cannon off their hands. Besides, it has been spiked, rendering it useless. Only a showpiece to scare off the natives. Santa Anna wasn't stupid enough to give them a weapon they could turn on him."

What they said about the cannon was true. A spike had been driven into the vent hole at the back of the weapon so that it couldn't be used. Since it was almost impossible to reverse what Santa Anna had done to it, the cannon was of no use to the townspeople.

That was all the information she needed. The fact that the Mexicans had come for the cannon was something she had to warn the leaders about. Keeping low and silent, she retraced her steps through the thicket to the river's ford. Her toes would be damp and wrinkled, but it was a small price to pay for the intelligence she would bring the men of Gonzales.

Once she was well away from the river, she hurried her steps into the collection of cabins and businesses they called a town. Most residents also had land allotments—*sitios*—scattered about the countryside, where they spent most of their time.

Before she had gone far, she spotted John Gilbert, hard to miss in his black coat and black hat. As always, the preacher carried a Bible in his hand, even when he was on some errand for his saddler's shop. Her pulse pounded in her ears. Why would he have such an effect on her? Since he was a pastor, better for her to shake away such imaginings.

He was too pure for a woman as sullied as she.

She hurried to catch him. "Pastor Gilbert."

He spun around, a half smile tilting his lips, his eyes a blue she had never seen before and likely never would again, the softness in those eyes such a contrast to Manuel's. Ones that spoke of comfort and peace even as they sent her heart racing. "Miss Wilkins. Always a pleasure to see you. Are you quite well? Your face is flushed."

She bobbed and touched her warm cheeks. No time to give thought as to why they may be so. "I have important and urgent news. Round up every man you can find and have them assemble at our home within the half hour."

He nodded, his black hat slipping forward on his blond curls. "It must be important for you to be in such a state."

Such a state? She studied her muddied skirts, and her face grew warm once more.

John stepped forward and pulled a twig from her hair, causing a tendril to escape the ribbon and brush her warm neck. Best thing to do was to let that comment pass and focus on what was necessary. "Thank you. I'll see you at our cabin in thirty minutes." She turned on her heel and headed in the opposite direction.

When she did peek over her shoulder, John stood with his hat doffed and his mouth a little ajar. Nothing like leaving a man off balance.

She hustled down muddy Water Street, the extra dirt her hem picked up of little consequence to her. She dipped a curtsy to Mrs. Norris and another one to Mrs. Bradley. Both of them eyed her up and down, no doubt taking in her disheveled appearance.

In only a few blocks, Father's blacksmith shop came into view. Before she reached it, the chime of hammer meeting metal rang out.

Heat from the furnace blasted her as she entered. No wonder Father's face was always red, a permanent flush. She couldn't interrupt his work until he finished fashioning the horseshoe.

Then again, this was vital information she was bringing him. It couldn't wait. As soon as he plunged the horseshoe into the barrel of water, she stepped forward. "Father."

He grasped his shirtfront with one hand. "Goodness, child, you're always sneaking up on me. A bad habit you picked up from Bright Star."

Quite the opposite. Bright Star had taught her many good, useful things she had employed numerous times.

Never mind that now. "I bear news. The Mexican Army is camped just down the river a short distance. I saw them when I went for a walk. From what I overheard, they're planning to demand the cannon Santa Anna gave us for protection."

"Santa Anna." Father spit a stream of tobacco juice onto the dirt floor. "That snake of a president-turned-dictator. But the river is high and swift. How did you ever hear them above the roar? Especially without them seeing you." He pulled a blue handkerchief from his pocket and wiped the sheen of sweat from his balding head.

"Well. . ."

"Never mind. I'm most sure I don't want to know."

"I met John, um, Pastor Gilbert on my way here and asked him to assemble the town's men at our house in half an hour. By now, it's likely been fifteen minutes or so."

"Go and warn Charlotte they're coming. I'll be along as soon as possible."

"I love you, Father." She kissed his cheek. Ever since Manuel had stolen so much from her, had ripped her heart from her chest, she never left Father without letting him know how she felt. She never knew when it might be the last time she would be able to do so.

She swept up the street and west two blocks until she arrived at their unassuming dogtrot cabin, the two rooms on one side separated by a breezeway from the two rooms on the other. A wide front porch flanked the entire structure.

When she entered the kitchen, it was cool and dark and empty. She peeked into the bedroom behind it, the one Charlotte shared with Father. Her stepmother sat up in bed with the Bible in her hands. She peered over the pages as Josie entered. "You're a muddy mess."

"Don't fret. I'll clean up any dirt I leave behind. But we're about to be inundated with men. I've called a meeting here in a few minutes."

Charlotte stuck an embroidered piece of cloth into the Bible to hold her page. With a sigh, she pushed back a stray hair, folded back the covers, and rose. Though she showed few visible signs of the coming child yet, the pregnancy had left her tired and sick.

She tottered, and Josie was by her side in a flash. "I can take care of the men. You stay in here and rest."

"I'll be fine. We can't let them come without refreshment."

"They aren't paying a social call."

Charlotte raised a single brown eyebrow. She had been brought up as a genteel southern lady, and that's what she would remain, no matter that she now resided in a cabin on the Texas frontier. "Help me stir the fire so I can make some coffee. I believe we have a few slices of cake left from yesterday. We can cut them smaller and make them go further."

Josie lent Charlotte a hand in the kitchen, setting out plates and forks and cups before men arrived, chatting with each other on the porch.

As soon as things were well under control in the kitchen, Josie wandered outside. There weren't many in attendance, maybe a dozen and a half or so. Was this all they could assemble?

In the group, there was Mr. Cottle, Mr. Martin, and Mr. Almaron Dickinson, a longtime resident of the colony by way of Tennessee. He had the sweetest wife and young daughter. Angelina would make a great companion for Charlotte's little one.

John, a head taller than every other man, blew a sharp whistle, and the group fell silent. Like a clap of thunder, his deep voice boomed over the gathering.

"Miss Wilkins has important news. Let us give her our full attention."

She cleared her throat and straightened her spine to give herself a little more authority. "Gentlemen, we have a force of Mexican troops camped across the river from us."

A din rose from the congregation.

"They're here for our cannon. Santa Anna has decided he wants it back. From the intelligence I gathered, they mean to wrest it from our grasp without a fuss."

"Well, we aren't going to give it to them, worthless as it is. This is a power play on Santa Anna's part." This from an older, paunchy gentleman, Mr. Bateman. Strange that he should be in town today. Usually he was on the *sitio* of land he owned, overseeing his goodly number of enslaved people.

A chorus of cheers arose from those assembled.

Mr. Bateman waved his fist. "If they want it, they're going to have to come and get it."

That might mean the Mexicans would be forced to fire their weapons. Such a prospect sent a wave of goose bumps over Josie's arms.

The citizens of Gonzales were far outmanned.

CHAPTER TWO

September 29, 1835

*T*he deepening shadows of the forest cloaked Josie and hid her from the Mexicans' sight while John and Father approached the riverbank opposite their opponents' encampment. Though it chafed her not to be in the open with the men, if she continued to spy, which she had every intention of doing, she couldn't show her face to the Mexicans. In case of detection, she had to be able to play the part of a Tejano.

Only Manuel would recognize her. When he'd held her in captivity, he'd never allowed her to be seen by other men. She fingered her black shawl, the edge of it embroidered in bright red, blue, and green.

Still, she wasn't about to sit and watch while the men marched to the water's edge. She held to the oak's large trunk, its bark rough against her cheek, but its solidness like a comforting old friend.

The Mexican soldiers mustered along the opposite shore, almost as if they were toys a child had set there in a perfect line, their white pants and white hats brilliant even in the dusky light. Hadn't they learned anything from the American Revolution?

It was quite apparent they had not. They fought in the European manner. This was the Texas wilderness, however, and a place more suited to the guerrilla warfare the Americans had used, tactics that had won them the war not yet sixty years ago.

Most of the men on her side of the river had come from the United States and were familiar with those strategies.

As a chilly breeze rattled the still-green leaves overhead, Josie drew her shawl around herself. The daytime air remained warm and humid, but there was a definite fall flavor to the cooler evenings. Winter would blow in before they knew it.

A sweep of the Mexicans' faces didn't reveal the one that turned her bones to water. She forced herself to relax her shoulders. Perhaps, just perhaps, he wasn't with them.

She touched the bulk of the folded material in her pocket. Mr. Bateman's words had rung in her head long after he'd left and had prompted her to get out her sewing basket, her needle flying through the white muslin. When the time was right, she would slip through and hand it to one of the men up front.

John held his reins as he maneuvered his horse in front of the others, the animal's hooves almost in the water. My, he was striking. If only. . .

But her past was one that would render her forever a spinster. No one, especially the town's pastor, would take a second look at her.

One of the Mexicans, a man who was at least a head shorter than John, also positioned his horse at the edge of the muddy bank.

"Who are you?" John's deep pulpit voice had no problem carrying above the roar of the rushing river.

"Lieutenant Francisco de Casteñada. And your name?"

"The Reverend John Gilbert."

"You are the leader of this ragtag handful of men?" A round of chuckles broke out behind Lieutenant Casteñada.

Josie bit her lip. How dare they come and taunt their fellow countrymen? Each of them on either side of the river were citizens of Mexico, after all. They shouldn't be fighting among themselves when fierce tribes of Indians and dreaded diseases threatened them both.

She slipped from behind the tree. Careful to keep low, she wove her way through the handful of horses the few men on this side possessed.

John continued his tête-a-tête with Lieutenant Casteñada. "Our leader isn't presently here. I'm standing in his stead. What is it you want from us?" Although they already knew, confirmation from Lieutenant Casteñada's lips would solidify her credibility as a spy.

The Mexican gripped his reins to steady his horse as it snorted and side-stepped. "I will speak only to your leader."

Josie slipped between two horses, motioning for Almaron Dickinson not to give her away.

"Then I am the leader. Tell us why you've come. Perhaps we can settle this peacefully."

At John's declaration, a bubble of laughter expanded in Josie's throat. Their pastor was a pretty good actor in his own right.

Lieutenant Casteñada glanced at each man beside him before returning his attention to John. "We have come for your cannon. The one Santa Anna gave you back in '31."

"Oh, that useless spiked weapon you provided us for defense against the Indians?"

When the men around her tittered, Josie joined in with her own mirth.

John leaned forward in the saddle. "We buried it in a peach orchard. If you want it, you will have to come and get it."

This was Josie's cue. Careful to keep her head down and out of sight of the other side, she came alongside Father and handed the fabric to him. He smiled, and she faded into the back. Father unfurled the material and waved the flag. Onto the white background, Josie had sewn a black star, a cannon, and the words COME AND GET IT.

Even from this distance, Josie couldn't miss the way Lieutenant Casteñada's face reddened with the taunt. He didn't like the bitter taste of those words, did he? John could speak such things because they were already aware their opponent didn't have the authorization to fire on them.

At least for the time being.

If word got back to one of the commanders or to Santa Anna himself, those orders could change at any time.

"We will get that cannon back." The lieutenant leaned forward over his chestnut horse's withers, his face reddening. "One way or another, we will get it back."

Father passed the flag to John, who held it in front of himself. "This is our answer. If you want it so much, you're going to have to come and get it." With that, John wheeled his horse around and led the small group of Texans away from the river and to the military plaza at the far western edge of the settlement, just a block from Josie's home. She ran the short distance to catch up to them, pins loosening from her hair as she did so. Yet another reason for Charlotte to take her to task.

When John rode into the center of the plaza, the men quieted, just as if he had strode up the church aisle to the pulpit.

"Hey, preacher." Charles Mason, lately arrived in the colony and one of the few men dressed as a soldier, called in a strong enough voice for the entire company to hear him and well beyond. "There's just one problem."

"Say what you have to say, Mason." Father was never hurried, never ruffled. He was the calm amid the storm. He always had been.

"The problem is that there are what—eighteen of us? And how many of them?"

Hundreds, by Josie's count. A slogan like COME AND GET IT was stirring, but that wouldn't take them very far. As soon as the river receded, the Mexicans would cross it, and the few farmers, ranchers, and tradesmen of Gonzales wouldn't stand a chance against the well-trained and battle-tested Mexican Army.

Another round of murmuring rippled through the men.

"Reinforcements." John spoke the word in his firm, preacher-like manner. "We don't have to fight this alone. While Gonzales proper may not have many men, just think of those who live in the outlying areas. We can call them in."

"But how long before Lieutenant Casteñada takes matters into his own hands and finds a way across the river? Or starts firing on us? Or sends troops around our flank?" Mr. Bateman wiped beads of sweat from his bald head.

John remained unflustered, other than taking off his hat and stroking his curly golden hair before placing his hat back on his head. "The river should hold them at bay for at least a few days. We'll get Moore in here to lead us, but in the meantime it is imperative to get word to the settlements in the Austin colony. I can ride east. Who will go southward?"

Josie's heart raced faster than a mustang across the plains. There was no greater rush in the world than riding her mount as hard as possible. She had always relished the one book Father owned other than the Bible, a leather-bound volume filled with fantastical colored pictures and even more fantastical stories of knights and damsels in distress.

But she would be no fair lady in need of rescuing. The ground underneath her feet almost vibrated with the anticipation that a major event was about to occur, one she had to be part of. She came alongside John. "I'll go."

Before he could answer, Father did. "That is out of the question."

She resisted the urge to stomp her foot. "You have no better spy than me. Without the information I gleaned, you wouldn't know they had no intention of firing their weapons."

"And what if they catch you out there?" Father's voice quavered, so unusual for him. Then again, he had lost her once already to the Mexicans.

She couldn't deny the roiling of her stomach, but she quelled it and infused her words with as much confidence as possible. "I easily pass for Tejano."

"American, Tejano, Mexican, it doesn't matter. You are a woman. That fact alone puts you at risk." John shifted, his saddle creaking underneath him.

Perhaps he knew, perhaps they all did, what had happened to her when she was gone, though no one dared speak it out loud. Instead, the townspeople gave her wide berth when they met her on the street or in the store or even in church.

This, however, was a mission she must participate in. Perhaps while she was out she would meet some Mexicans or Tejanos who might give her the answers to the questions that plagued her like a swarm of gnats. That was why she had to ride.

She tugged on her gown's long sleeve. "And if two men leave? What kind of situation does that put the women and children in? Then it will be sixteen against one hundred and fifty."

John slid from his horse, his already dirt-caked boots plopping on the churned, muddy ground, his reins still in his hand. "You do beat the Dutch, Miss Wilkins, but I am not about to put a woman in harm's way."

Father came beside her and patted her shoulder. "Why don't we discuss this at home? We could all use some supper." He turned to the crowd. "Shall we reconvene at the church in two hours? By then we'll be refreshed and perhaps will have had some time to reflect on the matter at hand."

Though Josie huffed, she followed Father the two blocks toward home. While he stabled his horse, she assisted Charlotte in reheating the stew from dinner and sliced the bread she'd made the day before. By the time Father entered the kitchen, wiping his boots on the rag rug by the door, Josie had the table set and the water poured.

Father said a quick prayer, and then he filled Charlotte in on what had transpired that afternoon.

Josie allowed her spoon to clatter into her bowl, earning a scowl from Charlotte. "You have to let me go, Father. You know I'm capable. What holds you back?" Though she attempted to keep her words from sounding whiny, they did, especially when she knew the reason. She picked up the salt cellar and sprinkled some on her food.

A certain darkness overtook his green eyes, a cloud that covered him from time to time. The lines in his face deepened, and he turned from a relatively young man into an old one in an instant.

She had plucked a heartstring she hadn't intended on touching. "I'm sorry, Father. I know you worry, but in truth, Mother and I didn't so much as leave the cabin that day." To soften the blow, she grasped him by the hand. "It can happen anytime, anywhere, even if Charlotte and I stay here. Please, don't be frightened for me. Let your head rule the day, not your heart."

Although the thought of running into Manuel sent prickles up and down her arms.

"But you are my heart." Father cleared the huskiness from his throat. "I lost so much that day. I never want to lose that much again."

Tears clogged Josie's air passage. How awful it must have been for him to come home and find his wife and his infant daughter dead and his fifteen-year-old daughter missing. For over a year, he had believed her to be dead as well.

"I know, Father, I know. Every night I pray we never live through anything that horrible again. Pastor Gilbert would tell us, though, that we have no guarantees in this life and that we must entrust the ones we have into the Lord's hands. That is why I want to be able to live whatever days God has ordained for me to the fullest. You have placed me into His care."

Charlotte dotted the corner of her mouth with her napkin. "I don't approve at all of a young lady galivanting through the wilderness on her own, and I can't see how you could, George. Josephine is a different sort of young lady. And I don't mean that as a compliment."

Josie strained to keep herself in her seat. "I have skills that most of the rest of us, men included, don't possess, skills I learned from some of the best Indian warriors around. And you know I won't be happy unless you give me your blessing."

Charlotte stabbed a potato with her fork. "She might go even without it and leave me here without her. That is just the time something will go wrong with the baby and I'll need to get a message to you."

Father harrumphed.

"Father, please. You know I possess the capabilities of completing this mission. And you also recognize the wisdom in not sending out too many men. They're needed here for the town's protection."

"What about yours?" He lifted the napkin tucked into his collar and wiped his mouth.

"Wherever I am, there is inherent peril in this world. Much as I know you would like to, you can't protect me from every danger."

"But I would rather not send you into the heart of it."

"It's nothing more than a simple jaunt through the countryside. A hop and a skip between *sitios*. A Sunday ride."

Father shook his head and rubbed his clean-shaven chin. "If I allow you to do this, you must promise you will take the utmost care. Avoid contact with anyone, if possible, and carry my rifle with you."

Josie jumped from her chair and kissed Father's cheek. "Thank you."

"I said *if* I allow you to go. Before I make my final decision, I need some time to mull this over. I will render my decision in the morning."

This might prove to be the longest night of Josie's life.

CHAPTER THREE

SAN ANTONIO

Present day

*W*hy did we have to pick such a hot day to do this?" Paula Lopez swiped her forehead.

Kayleigh Hewland shot her friend a narrow-eyed glance. "Your face isn't even red. And it's not hot. It's just ten in the morning."

"That's the other thing. You drag me out so early on a Saturday. I should still be sleeping."

Kayleigh laughed. "You love it, and we both know it." She continued her way down the pedestrian mall lined with shops, bright *papel picado* with their snowflake-like cutouts strung overhead, crisscrossed between buildings, flapping above them in the light breeze.

Nothing could beat a Saturday morning spent at Market Square among the vendors and the hawkers with everything for sale from trinkets to antiques to food. Even this early, the mouthwatering odors of frying meat and cinnamon filled the air. All the week's stress washed away when she stepped into this sensory extravaganza.

Kayleigh and Paula made their way to one of the first booths set up inside the market. The proprietor, her dark skin wrinkled and toughened by many years' exposure to the fierce Texas sun, showed a semi-toothless grin as Kayleigh and Paula examined the rings, necklaces, and earrings she had for sale.

Kayleigh picked up a pair of sterling silver arrow-shaped earrings. "Do you make everything yourself?"

"Not all of it. Some are antiques or interesting pieces I come across."

Paula slipped the matching bracelet on her wrist. "What do you think? I kind of like it."

The same thing happened every week. Paula complained about having to get up early, complained about the weather, complained about how hungry she was, and then ended up buying more than Kayleigh. But that's why they made such a fabulous pair.

"Get it if you want it." Kayleigh fingered a group of gold bracelets.

"You'd rather have a ring."

That's why Paula was Kayleigh's best friend. They got each other.

Once Paula completed her transaction, they moved to the next booth. Paula nudged Kayleigh in the ribs. "I've waited long enough. You promised to tell me all about your date last night with Jake."

"Ugh. Don't remind me."

"It went that well, huh?"

"I almost had to use the emergency call contingency plan."

Paula chuckled. "You know I'm always there for you."

"Thanks. I appreciate that, but I think I'm done with that dating app. Nothing but creeps. Time to sit back and let God."

"Suit yourself. By then, Mr. Perfect will probably be on his honeymoon cruise with some gorgeous blond."

"A chance I'm willing to take." This conversation needed to go in a different direction. "Look. There's the horchata stand."

"What I dream of every Friday night." Paula struck off in the stand's direction, her dark, curly ponytail bouncing as she moved.

Kayleigh followed in her wake. Before she caught up to Paula, though, another stand caught her eye. This one was nothing but rings, all standing in their black felt holders, shining, beckoning to her. Paula would find her. Kayleigh needed to see these. Now.

She stepped into the three-sided tent that flapped in the slight breeze and scanned the offerings. What a paradise this was. She slipped on a square-cut ruby in an art-deco band. Nice, but not quite her. Next she found a blue, green, and pink opal ring in a delicate filigree setting. Still not anything she would wear much, if at all.

And then she spied it. She sucked in a breath, her heart missing several beats. It was simple. Rather unadorned. The band was gold but tarnished with age. The black stone in the middle had a streak of yellow-green running through it. A memory sparked in her mind.

"They call that a cat's-eye ring." The gray-haired man manning the booth moseyed toward her.

"It's beautiful." So much like the one Mama used to have. Her most cherished possession.

"Try it on."

She slipped it onto her middle finger. The fit was as if it had been designed just for her. A squeal escaped her lips. What if it was Mama's ring? What if she'd found a small piece of her past?

No. The chances of that were just too great.

"Aha." Paula came up behind her, white horchata in hand. "I knew by the squeak it was you. What have you found?"

"Look at this." She wiggled her fingers in front of Paula's face. "Isn't it gorgeous?"

Paula scrunched her eyebrows. "It looks kind of old and beat up, and it's just black." She picked up the opal ring. "I like this one much better. Look at all the colors in it."

It was true. The ring wasn't flashy, and it must have had a hard life. But something about it spoke to her. She was drawn to it, maybe because it resembled the one Mama had and brought back flashes of Mama's smile, her lilting voice, her gentle touch. There were more memories that she resisted visiting in the middle of the busy marketplace.

She stared at it more closely. There was a small chip on the edge. In a vague recollection she remembered Mama talking about how it wasn't perfect, just as no person was perfect.

Could it be? What were the odds? "No. This is the one I want." She turned to the seller. "Where did you get it?"

"I bought it off a man years ago before I specialized in rings. He said he needed the money, so we made the swap. I put it away and forgot about it until just a couple of weeks ago when I found it cleaning out my shed."

Kayleigh's heart tripped over itself. The man who'd sold the ring to this vendor could be the man responsible for her parents' deaths.

"I even had it up on the internet, but no bites. Several times I've thought about throwing it out."

"Oh no. I'd like to buy it."

Paula pulled on her arm. "Are you sure you don't want this opal one?"

"No. How much?"

"Well, since it's not the prettiest thing and didn't cost me very much, I'll give it to you for twenty dollars."

In a flash, Kayleigh reached into her purse, pulled out a crisp twenty-dollar bill, and handed it to the man.

"Do you want a bag for that?"

She shook her head. "I'm going to wear it."

"Have a nice day, then. And thanks."

"Before I go, do you remember who sold it to you? What he looked like? Maybe even his name?" Dare she hope?

"Oh, it was twenty years ago or so. I can hardly remember what I had for supper last night. Sorry about that."

She pulled her business card from her cross-body bag. "If you remember anything about him, anything at all, please let me know."

The man peered at the card, then at Kayleigh. "This sounds important."

"It is."

"I'm not going to get in trouble for it being stolen or anything, am I?"

"No. Just please, if you think of anything, call me. Text me. Day or night."

He raised his eyebrows and his shoulders at the same time. "Sure thing."

When they were out of the man's earshot, Paula turned to Kayleigh. "What was that all about?"

"It looks just like my mama's ring. What if whoever sold this to that guy is connected to the case?"

"Oh honey, that's wonderful and awful at the same time."

"I'm not getting my hopes up, but it's the first crack in the case in twenty years. Any shred of hope is better than none."

Kayleigh and Paula spent the rest of the morning wandering the other stalls and shops around the market. During the entire time, Kayleigh fingered the ring on her hand. It was as if it had always been there. Or had come home at last.

Finally they settled under a bright red umbrella at a table outside their favorite restaurant. While they waited for their meal, Kayleigh examined the ring.

"You haven't stopped staring at it all morning."

"I can't tell you what it is about it, but I love it. Like I said, my mama, my birth mother, had one very much like this. When she died, she was wearing it. The man who killed her ripped it from her finger before he ran away like the coward he was. Is."

"Wow, no wonder you were drawn to it."

"It's beautiful in its simplicity."

"You aren't a frou-frou girl, that's for sure. Let me see it."

Kayleigh slipped off the ring and handed it to Paula, who turned it over and over and examined it on every side. Then she peered at the inside of the band.

"Oh Kayleigh. Look at this!"

CHAPTER FOUR

September 30, 1835

*C*hariot's hooves pounded beneath Josie as she raced her muscular stallion across the open expanse, the sky spread out like a blue curtain above them, the emerald grass a carpet in front of them. She had undone the pins in her waist-length hair and let it flow freely behind her, the wind rushing at her face. This she loved. This she lived for.

Father's approval of this assignment had freed her from her dull life with her demanding stepmother.

No saddle meant that she and Chariot could move as one, each reacting to the other's signals. Josie only needed to apply slight pressure to Chariot to speed him up or lean back a little to slow him down.

The sun warmed her back and Chariot's black flanks. Her cheeks would be red, and Charlotte would scold her, as Mother would have done, but she would withstand a moment of disapproval for this unparalleled exhilaration that surged through her.

This was her place, her home when she couldn't be home. Her Tonkawa Indian friend, Bright Star, had taught her to ride. Ride like this, free and unfettered. For a moment in time, she could forget all that had happened in the past and what might happen in the future. Only this moment existed. The rushing air blew all the bad, the awful, the terrible away and cleansed her better than five bars of soap and ten tubs of water.

Chariot's slowing brought her from her thoughts, and she sat straighter on his back. He was wiser than she, since they had a goodly amount of ground to cover today. It would benefit neither of them if she wore him out before they completed their rounds.

Already they had visited several scattered farms in the area, sounding the warning, calling all able-bodied men to arms, urging them to be ready to defend the little town against the menace of the Mexican Army.

Father was right. The Mexicans had spoken about not firing on the townspeople, but they could change their minds after meeting the town's resistance. The men of Gonzales had stood up to them. There was no telling how their overlords would react. They needed every man and every weapon they could muster to stand up to Lieutenant Casteñada's force.

Her heart lightened as she approached the next cabin on her route, the home of her friend Hortense and her new husband, Franklin Nash. Soon she slipped from Chariot's back and into Hortense's arms.

"How good to see you, dear friend." The fragrance of onions and bacon drifted from Hortense.

"And you too." Josie released her friend from the embrace. "You look like married life agrees with you."

A pretty pink palette colored her cheeks. "I highly recommend it. You should try it someday."

"I doubt anyone could capture my spirit. Or my heart." Only John. And that was nothing more than a fantasy.

"Not the way you race about the prairie like you do, that's for sure." Hortense led Josie inside while Franklin tended to Chariot.

"I'd offer you tea, but I know you enjoy your coffee. And it's a good thing we have a cow now, so you can add your cream."

Once Hortense had the coffee brewed and a slice of peach pie on a plate in front of Josie, the two sat back and chatted about Hortense's new role as a wife and how she loved having her own home to tend.

Perhaps Charlotte was right. Josie would never find a husband if she didn't tame some of her wild ways. But they were what defined her. She refused to give up herself to become a missus.

Franklin ducked through the door, tattered hat in his hand. "I won't interrupt you ladies and your visit, but I smelled that coffee, and it drew me like a magnet."

"Of course, darling." Hortense went to the stove to pour her husband a cup. "Although we must already be an old married couple. It used to be me who drew you like a magnet."

He came behind her and enveloped her in an embrace, kissing her cheek. "You always will, my dear."

Josie squirmed in her seat. "I'm glad you came in, Franklin." At her words, he stepped away from his wife. "Unfortunately, this isn't a social call, and I must be going soon." She filled them in on the situation in Gonzales and their need for men to be prepared to defend the cannon.

Franklin rose. "Of course I'll do my duty."

Hortense also rose and flung herself against her husband's broad chest. "Please, don't go." Tears shimmered on her fair lashes. "It's been but a few short weeks since our marriage."

"And I want to provide a safe place for you and any children God may bless us with in the future. We shouldn't have to live in fear of Mexicans or Comanche or anyone." He turned to Josie. "Give me a few minutes to gather my supplies, and I'll ride back to town with you. You should have an escort."

Why did no one believe she could take care of herself? "I'm not immediately returning to Gonzales, as I have a duty and obligation to inform as many as possible. The militia is gathering at the military plaza."

"But I can't leave you on your own."

"I've come all this way by myself. Don't worry. I will be fine."

Hortense sighed. "Get used to it, Franklin. Josie has been a free spirit from the day I first met her."

"Father loaned me his rifle, and I know how to use it."

"You shouldn't be in a position to have to use it."

"I doubt I will. Say goodbye to your wife, head to Gonzales, and I'll be there in no time." Josie downed the rest of her coffee and stood, giving Hortense a long hug. "When this is over, I promise to come and spend more time with you."

"You had better." Hortense affected a pout but finished with a laugh. "Godspeed. Stay safe."

"I will. You know I, of all people, am not careless nor reckless. With my knowledge of Spanish and Indian, I get along with everyone."

"Just promise me you'll be careful. I don't even like the thought of you in that town with a possible battle looming."

Josie wouldn't put words to it, but she would rather be surrounded by others amid a firefight than alone in a cabin in the wilderness. That was when the Mexican had come for them. Mother and her sister, Laura, were dead. That despicable man had taken her alive. At least on horseback, she had the chance to outrun anyone who would confront her.

She would never, never permit anyone to use her in such a manner again. She would die first.

Before long, she was astride Chariot once more, waving goodbye to her red-eyed friend. "God keep you safe." She shouted, but the wind carried her words away.

She finished the rest of her stops in short manner, alerting a good number of men to the situation in Gonzales and securing their promises to come to the town's aid. Tired of Santa Anna's antics, most of them, in fact, were eager to participate.

At last she was able to turn Chariot toward Gonzales. The sun perched on the horizon, and the air held a damp chill that foretold of the coming winter. But more than that, the atmosphere around Josie, around everyone in Gonzales, around all those she had spoken with, was thick and heavy. A weight on her shoulders. One she couldn't shake.

When she neared town, she led Chariot to the river to drink. Though the foamy water still ran fast, the flooding and raging had subsided to a small degree.

The big dark horse Josie led by the reins whinnied and nickered, tossing his head. "You're like all the other men, aren't you? Too used to your freedom that you want to fight over one small cannon."

Chariot snorted in return.

She stood back and allowed the majestic black animal to lower his head and lap up the water. Overhead, birds sang in the trees, their leaves green for the time being. Soon they would blush color and tumble to the ground. For now, she drank in the peace and solitude of the area.

Chariot broke off his drinking and lifted his head, his ears perked. He'd heard a noise. Josie went to him and stroked his wiry mane. "Shhh. You're fine." Her hands trembled, and Chariot must have sensed it, because he tossed his head and nickered.

A cracking of sticks and twigs came from behind her. "Oh, you goose, it's just John come to play a trick on us." It wouldn't be the first time he'd done so. She called over her shoulder. "Very funny, Pastor Gilbert. You may have startled me before, but I am wise to you this time."

The man who emerged from the thicket wasn't her fair-skinned, blue-eyed friend. Instead, the man's hair was dark and curly, and though sturdy of frame, John would have dwarfed him. He was dressed in the blue uniform of the Mexican Army and held a rifle in his hand. A scar cut across his face. One she was very familiar with. "*¿Por qué estás aquí sola?*" His deep voice rumbled.

Manuel. Somehow he'd discovered a ford across the river.

Josie pressed her back against Chariot, though he sidestepped. "I'm not alone. My husband will be back here in just a minute."

"Senorita Wilkins, you cannot fool me. I saw you here that first day, and I watched you with the Texan troops the other day. I even watched you this morning as you rode out of town. You see, my dear, I am always watching you." He stepped toward her.

At some point, he had suffered a broken nose, which now gave him a crooked, uneven appearance. "I like a little bit of fire in a woman. Come across the river with me. We can rekindle our romance."

Josie gagged. What they'd had, if anything, was not romance but violent force. By this time, he was almost straight in front of her. Close enough that she could smell the tequila on his breath, her stomach churning. She couldn't press herself any closer to Chariot.

Once before, he had stolen her from her home. Then she had been an innocent youngster.

Now she was older and wiser. She knew what this man was capable of, what he had already done, and what he was willing to do again. She had run out of room to make her escape. "I will never go anywhere with you." Her words were shaky, just like her entire body.

"*Ningun problème.* I like the privacy we have here better."

She couldn't take a breath. Even if she could scream, no one would hear, not out here, not with the men of the area drawing battle lines a few miles downstream.

Her throat burned. There had to be a way out. She wouldn't allow him to hurt her again. Not ever. Not until her dying breath.

She reached behind her, the cool metal of Father's gun a sweet slice of comfort. Could she draw faster than him? He readied his own pistol, his hand hovering over it.

No chance that she could shoot him. She had been foolish and hadn't withdrawn the weapon first thing, as soon as she had heard him approaching.

"There is going to be a battle, you know." He stared at her with eyes so dark she couldn't distinguish his pupils.

All she could do was nod, even though her intelligence the other day had told her the Mexicans weren't ready to fight. Unless they had changed their plans. Perhaps she should have listened to Father and stayed behind. That way she could have spied more, listened better to the battle plans their foes had drawn.

"It will be a great and glorious victory for Santa Anna."

"Don't be too cocky. The Bible says that pride goeth before a fall."

He now was nose to nose with her, his hot breath on her cheek, sending a shiver down her spine. "When we win, I will have the ability to take your life. Or to save it."

Her pulse pounded so hard in her ears she almost missed what he said. What was clear was the venom in his voice. That was unmistakable.

Venom she had heard before, on that awful, fateful day.

From behind her came the cocking of a gun. More Mexicans? *Please, God, no.*

She was trapped.

There was no way out.

CHAPTER FIVE

Present day

*K*ayleigh leaned over the café table where Paula held the cat's-eye ring. "What? What is it?"

"It has an inscription."

Her blood pumped a little faster. "What does it say?"

At first, Paula squinted, then she shook her head. "I don't know. I can't quite make it out."

Kayleigh's curiosity got the better of her. "Let me see." Paula handed over the ring.

Worn by time and years and the fingers of many women, the engraving was difficult to decipher. Impossible, really. Just like Paula, Kayleigh squinted. "I can make out a few letters, but that's all. Oh, this is frustrating. Now I really want to know what it says." Mama hadn't mentioned an inscription. Then again, Kayleigh had been so young, even if she had, she might not have remembered.

"You need a magnifying glass."

Kayleigh raised an eyebrow. "Like I carry one of those in my back pocket."

"What if we take a picture of it and enlarge it?"

"Have I ever told you how brilliant you are?" Kayleigh snapped a couple of shots to get the entire engraving. Then she pulled them up on her phone and zoomed in.

That helped a great deal. Though the letters were quite worn, Kayleigh could now make them out. *Fe/JG2JW/MAR36.*

Unfortunately, that meant nothing to her. She studied the engraving for a while, trying to make sense of any of it. In the end, she had to admit defeat. It had her baffled. She handed her phone to Paula. "See if you can decode this. You read plenty of mysteries. This might as well be in Greek for all I can read it."

"I'll have a crack at it." Paula examined the picture, biting the inside of her cheek. As the laughter of children, the din of conversations in both English and Spanish, and the squeak of the waitress's shoes on the tile floor swirled around Kayleigh, several long minutes passed.

At last Paula handed the phone back. "Beats me."

"Now what am I supposed to do? I have to know what this is all about." Had to know if this had some tie to her birth family.

The server brought them their lunches and scurried away. The restaurant was crowded today.

Paula sipped her lemonade. "I'm intrigued too, but I have no idea how to go about figuring this out. All those hours of reading have done me no good as far as becoming a detective. I'm always surprised at the end. It would be cool to find out though."

Kayleigh's phone picked that moment to ding with a text message. Work. Her job as a refugee coordinator took up a great deal of her time. In fact, it was unusual that she had gone without any interruptions this morning. Saturdays were her days off, but that often didn't mean anything. "I gotta go. They have a ten-year-old boy they've brought in from the border, and he's really scared. All alone, from what I'm getting."

"Aw, that's terrible." Paula motioned for the busty red-haired waitress to bring them boxes.

Once Kayleigh had her food tucked inside the Styrofoam container, she hugged Paula. "Same time, same place next week?"

"You're going to kill me, you know? Sleep is important to a body."

"Go to bed earlier on Friday night. Maybe by next week I'll have figured out the ring's engraving."

Kayleigh hustled to her silver SUV parked in the lot next to the market. Thankfully, traffic at noon on Saturday wasn't bad. The hour-long drive left her plenty of time to think about the ring.

And that inscription. What could it possibly mean? The first part was *Fe*. She wracked her brain. *Fe. Fe. Fe.* Then something from high school chemistry triggered. Wasn't *Fe* the chemical symbol for iron? It had been a little while since those days, but from what she did recall, that was it.

Why, though, would someone inscribe the chemical symbol for iron on an old ring? That didn't make any sense.

Just before she arrived in the small town of Karnes City, she turned right and traveled down a country road for a couple of miles before she came to the Karnes County Residential Center. When she exited her vehicle, she couldn't miss the laughter from a group of children playing in one of the facility's three courtyards. She made her way into the brick building that might have blended in with its rather dull, brown surroundings except for the bright blue covered entrance with a red-tiled roof.

Though the building was huge, she'd been here enough to be able to make her way to the intake area. In the crowded room, Spanish enveloped her like a hug from long ago. Women and children occupied every one of the blue plastic chairs grouped in threes and mounted on black metal brackets. A refrigerator stood on one wall, but it was a little boy sitting underneath a rainbow painted on another wall that caught her attention.

He sat bent over, covering his face, his shoulders heaving. One of the women from ICE pointed Kayleigh in the boy's direction. This was the one they had called her about. It might have been any of the children, many alone, many of them with dirty, tear-streaked faces.

She took a seat beside him. *"Hola. Me llamo* Kayleigh. *¿Cómo te llamas?"*

He peeked at her through bony fingers. "Elias."

"It's nice to meet you, Elias. This place can be kind of scary, can't it?"

He nodded, his brown eyes large in his small face, his hoodie pulled up so it almost covered his head of thick, black hair.

"Is your mother here?"

He shook his head, a fresh round of tears dampening his cheeks. "She told me to be strong, to be a good boy, and make a good life for myself. Then she sent me away with a group of people. We have been walking for many days. Once we crossed the river, they left me by myself. A border guard found me and brought me here, but I want to go home."

"Where is your home?"

"Mexico. Mama was afraid I would be killed or be part of a drug gang. But I will be good if I go back. I promise. I promise." He sobbed, wiping his face on his already-dirty hoodie.

She gathered him into her arms and allowed him to cry it out. At just ten, to go through what he'd been through in his life, tore her apart. At least her memories of that time were hazy and fuzzy. His would be clear and strong.

She smoothed his hair away from his dark face. In her arms, he hiccupped. "What is going to happen to me?"

She handed him a tissue from her purse. "I'm not going to let anything bad happen." Though with the overcrowding at the facility, it would be a difficult promise to keep. "You will stay here for a while. Do you have any family in America?"

Elias unzipped his hoodie. Inside of it, written in black marker, was a name and a Florida address. *"Mi tío."*

"Muy bien. Probably in a few days, they'll send you to your uncle."

Though he nodded, he didn't smile, and his eyes remained large. Likely this was all too much to take in.

Elias fingered her ring. *"Esta hermoso."*

"Gracias."

"Can I have it? Maybe it will bring me good luck."

"I'm afraid not. In here, it will only get you into trouble." Having any sort of valuable would make him a target for the older, more ruthless children.

He would have a hard enough time as it was. She well remembered.

CHAPTER SIX

*F*or two nights now, Kayleigh had lain in bed wide awake, the ring heavy on her finger. Tonight she touched it and twisted it even as she tossed and turned and twisted herself in the sheet. Every time she glanced at her phone, the time had barely moved. The background music of traffic in front of her condo didn't lull her to sleep as it usually did.

When her lids grew heavy and fluttered shut, the thought of the ring jarred her awake. It tortured her and tormented her, almost like the band of gold from *The Lord of the Rings*. She might as well be Bilbo Baggins. Perhaps Elias was wrong. Perhaps it didn't bring good fortune but bad karma.

Not that she believed in such a thing.

She lay on her side, one hand over the other so that she touched the ring, could hold on to it, almost as if she were holding on to Mama. Ears alert to every noise, her muscles were taut. She'd been wrong to think that it might help her to sleep. Sleep would never come easily to her again.

Though she had a new place, one that Jason, her stalker ex-boyfriend, knew nothing about, she still startled at every sound. The air conditioner kicking in. The natural creaks of the building. The neighbors coming home from a night out.

Being in a secure building before hadn't stopped him. How he'd been able to get into the complex that night, she would never know, but she'd tripped over him as she closed her door behind her and left for work one morning, her heart tripping along with her.

That had put her over the edge. The love letters he sent to her, the flowers delivered to her office, the phone calls at all hours of the day and night had rattled her, but when he'd shown up at her place and was within feet of her all night, that was the last straw. The police had arrested him, but he'd served his two-year sentence. The other day, the police had informed her that he was now out of prison.

No piece of paper with a restraining order written on it would stop him.

She held her breath almost every moment, expecting him to show up at the office or in the parking lot or at her house. Anywhere, really.

It was as if time had marched backward, and it was two years ago when she was as timid as a fawn in the woods. The old fear of what he might do next had hit her like a sucker punch to the chest.

She must have dozed off, because a noise on her porch jolted her awake. Not a loud noise, but a scratching sort of sound. For a short while, she lay statue still, not daring to breathe.

There it came again. She should have moved into a building that allowed large attack dogs. A pit bull would come in handy right about now. In the morning, she would talk to the condo president about allowing her to have one.

That didn't do her a bit of good now. The scratching came again, the sound of it irritating every nerve in her body. Good thing she hadn't gotten rid of that baseball bat she kept between her bed and the nightstand. And good thing she'd broken the record for home runs her senior year of college. It wasn't a division one school, but D3 wasn't bad.

She could still swing a bat hard enough to hurt someone. As she slid from underneath the covers, she grabbed the bat. The cool tile floor underneath her feet sent goose bumps up her skin, even as the sound came again. Definitely from the porch, definitely real and not a product of her imagination.

She crept from her room, the bat in one hand, her phone in the other. In a moment, she would decide which one she would use. Maybe both. She could text 911 and then use the bat to hold off the would-be intruder until the police arrived.

There it came again. She clutched both items in her hands so tightly, it was amazing she didn't break either one of them. Her ears rang.

The scratching continued. With shaking hands, she unlocked her phone and tapped on the messages icon. It was hard to type a message with one hand, but she managed to compose one.

The sound again. This time followed by a faint mewling, one that grew stronger by the moment. She didn't send the text.

When she turned the venetian blinds open, she released a breath. All the tension drained from her body as she stared down at the orange tabby cat clawing at the sliding door. "You crazy kitty. You almost got yourself knocked over the head. How naughty of you to scare me like that."

She opened the door to shoo him away, but he made a break for it, dashed around her, and planted himself on her sofa. She sat on the opposite end from him so she didn't scare him away. "What's wrong, buddy? Is someone after you too? Don't worry. It's safe here. You'll be fine."

He purred in answer to her.

Since she was already wide awake, she might as well stay up. She filled a bowl with water for the cat, the ring on her finger catching her eye as she did so. She could get some work done, but the inscription haunted her. So even though the clock in the microwave proclaimed it to be four in the morning, she poured herself a glass of Diet Coke, sat at the kitchen table, and opened her laptop.

MAR36. That could refer to a date. She googled March 1936. Floods in the Northeast and Canada. That was the biggest news in the US. Most of the rest of the historical happenings had to do with Hitler invading the Rhineland. None of that made sense. How would a ring that had to do with Europe end up in a Mexican market in Texas?

She sipped her icy cold pop. Sweet and fizzy, just the way she liked it. The cat curled at her feet, warming them, and fell fast asleep.

If it was a date, likely it was personal to someone and would mean nothing to her. If the entire inscription was a code between two people, she may never figure out what it meant.

Was Papi the one who had inscribed it to Mama? Probably not, because the letters were worn and difficult to read. They had been very young when they had died.

It would drive her crazy until she knew what it meant. That's the way she was. She couldn't start a crossword puzzle without seeing it all the way through. She couldn't paint one wall without painting the rest of the room. Once she started a project, she had to finish it.

Mom told her she was driven. Paula told her she was obsessive.

Next she searched for Mar 36. That yielded plenty of strange results. A type of drainage system. A 36-inch tall Del Mar vanity at Home Depot. A 36-foot catamaran for rent in Cancun, a home for sale at 36 Cresta del Mar, one for sale at 36 Mar Del Way, and one for sale at 36 Vista Mar. Nothing that might be tied to the ring in any way, shape, or form.

She twisted her hair around her finger. Mom might yell at her for doing it, but she wasn't here to see. While Kayleigh downed about half her insulated cup of pop, she stared at the computer screen. She scrolled through search results and images. Even maps.

Nothing.

Perhaps a jeweler might be able to tell her more about the ring's origins. That could give her a clue as to where to look next. Some possible direction to go in, at the very least.

She managed to get a little bit of work done before a run, a shower, and breakfast. There was a strip mall not too far from her complex that was home to a jewelry shop. She passed it every day on her way to work but had never been inside.

When she arrived, she swung the glass door open, the bell on it jingling as she did so. Quaint.

No one was about. She strolled by glass cases, the diamonds inside winking at her like stars in the night sky. On the back counter, next to a cash register, there sat a bell, the kind you tapped to make it ring. So she did.

"Just a minute." The deep voice came from a back room.

"No hurry." Kayleigh gazed at the gold crosses lined up in the case underneath the register.

Not more than sixty seconds later, a man who couldn't be more than thirty, with a tattoo of a cross on his forearm, stepped from the back room.

"Oh." The word slipped from Kayleigh's lips.

"I'm sorry."

"No, it's just. . ."

"I'm not what you expected. And I promise you, I'm not here robbing the place."

"I never thought—"

"Just joking." He flashed a grin, a small dimple in his whiskery right cheek. "What can I do for you?"

Kayleigh wriggled the ring from her finger. Already she missed the weight of it. "I bought this at the Mexican market on Saturday, and I was wondering what you can tell me about it. Also, there's an inscription on the inside that has me baffled."

He peered inside. "Hmm. That is a difficult one to decipher."

She showed him the picture of the inscription on her phone.

"I thought MAR36 might be a date, but there isn't much that happened in March of 1936 that makes sense with the ring. The man I bought it from said someone sold it to him about twenty years ago."

The jeweler studied the ring for a few more minutes, turning it over, peering at the picture of the inscription once more. At last he leaned on the counter and directed his attention toward her. "This is a cat's-eye ring."

"That much I knew."

"It's a very nice one, with the black quartz and that green-yellow vein running through the middle of it, though the stone does have a small chip."

"It was the yellow vein that caught my eye."

"The gold work is simple but well done. But if MAR36 is a date, I don't think it refers to March of 1936. This ring was probably crafted in the late 1700s or early 1800s."

"What?" Kayleigh's mouth fell open. "I would never have guessed it was that old."

"There are different types of cat's-eye, and people have been using it for thousands of years. It's found all over the world."

Kayleigh studied the long-haired man up and down. "You're quite the fount of knowledge."

"History nerd, if you must know."

She would never have pegged him that way. "Then I guess I came to the right place."

"That you did."

"What can you tell me about the inscription?"

"That's a good question. I'm not convinced MAR36 is a date. It could be almost anything. Fe is the symbol for iron, but this is gold. Probably a high carat, I'd think—18 or even 24. That's what they used then, so I don't think that's what Fe means. I have to admit, I'm baffled."

Kayleigh slumped. "I was really hoping to get some answers."

"It's very interesting. If you'd like some help figuring it out, I'd love to give you a hand."

Now she straightened. "Really?"

"Sure. I'm Brandon Mullins, by the way." He reached out to shake her hand.

She shook it. "Kayleigh Hewland. Good to be working with you."

"Do you mind if I take a few pictures of it? And get your contact information? Then I can do some research."

"Sure." When he returned to the back room, she wandered the cases filled with sapphires, rubies, and emeralds set as rings, necklaces, and bracelets. Very beautiful stuff. Maybe Brandon had designed some of it. If he had, he was quite talented.

She reached the end of the display and glanced out the door. A dark, hooded man bent over her car, peering inside.

Her stomach went cold.

Perhaps last night's noises weren't just the cat.

Perhaps Jason, her stalker, was at it again.

CHAPTER SEVEN

September 30, 1835

*A*s Manuel stood in front of Josie and the snapping of twigs came from behind her, every part of her, from her limbs to all her insides, trembled. She had forgotten the most important lesson Bright Star had taught her. Like two sisters, they had traipsed through the trees, always quiet, always stealthy, always alert to their surroundings.

Never let them hear you, never let them see you, never let them smell you.

Wise words when hunting deer or buffalo. Wise words when attacking other tribes. Wise words when away from town on your own.

But now that she'd been separated from her friend for a few years, she had forgotten the lessons Bright Star had taught her. If she hadn't forgotten, she had at least become careless and didn't always implement them.

Manuel came closer. Bile rose in her throat, and she swallowed it back into her sour stomach so she wouldn't vomit onto his white pants.

Not again. *Dear God, not again.* She would rather die. Prayed He would take her right now.

When Manuel reached his filthy hand with broken fingernails to touch her, she recoiled. Chariot sidestepped, giving her a little breathing room. Manuel closed that distance in no time, the trap clamping around her once more.

"You are mine. Don't ever, ever forget it. I took you once before. I have every right to take you again. You belong to me. No matter what, you will never be free. Even when I'm not with you, I will haunt you. I will make sure you never forget me."

Manuel reached out again, his hands hot and dry and rough against her smooth skin. He caressed her cheek, trailing his touch down her neck.

She screamed, an Indian holler she'd learned from Bright Star's brother, a young warrior.

Manuel slapped her so hard that the sting of it blurred her vision. "You will do as I say. You know what happens if you don't." He spoke through clenched teeth, the words seething.

A moment later, before she'd had a chance to catch her breath, a cold, hard object pressed against her stomach. He cocked his pistol.

Her weak knees wouldn't hold her up much longer. Especially not with the way the world around her spun. She swallowed hard.

He leaned in, the pistol digging into her midsection as he kissed her behind her ear.

Though she gagged, she summoned every bit of strength inside of her and kneed him in the groin.

"Ah!" He doubled over, the gun still trained on her. "You little vixen. Do you know what I do to those who disobey me?"

Before she could turn to sprint away, something—no, someone—crashed through the woods, bursting through the thicket.

"Get out of here." A deep voice. A wonderful, throaty, deep voice.

John.

Manuel turned around, but by that time, John had his rifle pointed at the man's head.

"I said to leave. Unless you want to be the first casualty of this battle."

"This senorita invited me here." Manuel's voice was a good deal higher than before.

John's face flushed as red as a Texas sunset. "I won't ask you again."

"Your lady friend is a temptress. I'd watch out for her if I were you." Manuel straightened, groaning, then limped away and disappeared into the woods.

Josie's knees collapsed, and she clung to Chariot's reins for support. A moment later, John was at her side, holding her up. She stared at him. He wasn't a vision but was truly here.

He opened her canteen and offered her a drink, which she downed. Her throat was more parched than she had realized. "How did you know I would be here?" With shaking hands, she handed the canteen to him.

"Did that brute hurt you?" John studied her from head to toe, returning his gaze to her. For a moment, his glare was hard, but then it softened, as did his voice. "Oh Miss Wilkins, how he could have spoiled you. How he could have hurt you. The thought sickens me."

Tears burned at the back of her throat because of her shame. He had already spoiled her. If John knew, he wouldn't be so kind and gentle with her. He would turn his back on her.

"I'm fine. Truly. Thank you for rescuing me." Because either she would be dead or Manuel would be.

"I've been back from my rounds for a while. When you didn't show up, I had a feeling where I might find you. I never dreamed of discovering you in the position you were in."

"Please, I beg of you, don't tell Father. He will never allow me out of his sight if you do." Even Father didn't know about Manuel and what had happened when he had killed her mother and sister and kidnapped her.

John turned in a small circle before facing her again. Here she was asking a minister of God to lie for her.

"I won't tell a falsehood."

"We'll tell the truth. I was out here on my way home and stopped to water Chariot. Father knows I cherish the peace and quiet of this grove." She peered at the man in front of her.

John bit the corner of his lip. "If he asks a direct question or if the information becomes necessary for your safety or that of others, I will inform him of this encounter."

"I understand."

He held up his hands, his eyes narrowing. "On one condition."

She slumped her shoulders. Always there were conditions. "What?"

"That you stay close to home until this skirmish is over. Just for your father's peace of mind. He won't be an effective soldier if he has to worry about you and Charlotte."

"I hate promises." She toed the ground.

"Why?"

"I have such a difficult time keeping them."

His laugh, like a distant roll of thunder, cascaded over her in waves. "At least you're honest."

"Thank you for not telling Father. You understand how precious my freedom is to me."

"I don't know if I understand, but I sympathize. I can't imagine what it was like for that freedom to be snatched from you when you were kidnapped." He grasped Chariot's reins, and she strolled beside him as they returned to town.

She shook her head. "That's not what I meant. I'm talking about the freedom I had when we lived closer to the Indians, when they were my friends. I had freedom to roam and freedom to run and climb. Things I could never do as a white girl, raised to be a proper lady."

"I can see how you would find that restrictive."

His voice held neither approval nor disapproval. How was she to figure out what he thought of it? Of her?

She couldn't sort out this swirling inside.

※

October 1, 1835

Overnight, a small tent city had sprung up in Gonzales. Even from her home on St. James Street, the odor of frying bacon reached Josie as the sun peeked above the horizon. The din of men coming awake filled the air, thick with excitement and anticipation, as thick as the fog that had settled over the area.

Father had joined the men at the encampment, proclaiming it was his duty to be with them. They would never be able to protect the town if they weren't unified. That's what he said.

This morning, as she sat at the breakfast table with Josie, Charlotte pushed the eggs around her plate. "I'm worried for the men."

Josie sprinkled some salt on her eggs and forked them into her mouth, chewing for a moment. "I'm not, at least not anymore. You should see how many responded to our plea for help. The town is overflowing with volunteers from outlying areas. We may not have fancy uniforms like the Mexicans, but we do have spunk and spirit and plenty of guns to scare them away." One man in particular would hopefully run all the way back to Mexico City. Maybe even farther.

"Oh, I hope there isn't a fight. I don't know why you are so interested in all of this. You should be home sewing your trousseau instead of gallivanting about, urging these fine young men to fight their own countrymen. I don't see why they don't just give back the cannon."

"There won't be any battle. Remember, they don't have orders to fire on us."

After breakfast, while Josie washed the dishes, Charlotte went to the other room to make the bed. She was back a moment later, a piece of white fabric in her hand. "Your father must have forgotten this. He told me he was proud of it and wanted to fly it, though I don't know why he would want this crude thing."

Josie would be the first to admit that her sewing skills weren't what they should be. Still, the insult stung. No matter. If Father was proud of it, he would have it. "Once I've cleaned up here, if you don't need me for anything, I'll go to the camp and take it to him." Josie dried her hands on her apron. She jumped at any chance to be out of the house and out from under Charlotte's thumb.

"That is something you could do to please him."

In no time, Josie had her bonnet strings tied underneath her chin and had set off for the encampment. Today's weather was bright and sunny, and Charlotte's warning about freckles still rang in her ears, though right now they had much more to worry about than sun splotches.

Men bustled about the camp, the just-arrived Captain Moore shouting orders at the scraggly militia. Horses whinnied and boots tromped on the ground as the men drilled and paraded.

She didn't need much time to pick Father out of the assembled fighters, his hands around his weapon, his head high, his steps precise. Beside him was John, every bit as proud and disciplined as Father. He kept his eyes forward. Did he even blink against the harsh sun?

For a while, she stood and observed the goings-on. If the unforeseen happened and a fight did break out, this ragtag bunch of farmers-turned-soldiers would be as prepared as possible. Life on the frontier required it. They weren't all that different from the militiamen who had fired the first shots of the American Revolution in Lexington, Massachusetts, just sixty years past.

Finally, Captain Moore called a break, and the men scattered. A few moved to an open area to practice target shooting. The reverberations stung Josie's eardrums. Father, however, came to her side. "Is there a problem with Charlotte?"

"Oh no. I didn't mean to frighten you. She is quite well. I came to bring you this." She unfurled the COME AND GET IT flag. "You forgot this when you left yesterday."

"We'll fly it proudly. Thank you."

John joined them, his strides long and sure, a weapon in one hand and his Bible in the other. "Thank you for that. We were wondering where it had gone."

Her stomach fluttered. "Now those Mexicans will know that we aren't giving up that cannon no matter what."

A flash of a blue-coated man on horseback, a tall, white hat on his head, a red feather stuck in it, cut off their conversation. Josie had brought that flag at just the right time.

Lieutenant Castañeda, the Mexican commander, had come to pay a visit. *"Buenos dias, señors."* He sat tall, holding his reins loosely, his dark eyes scanning the area. Probably scouting for the cannon.

"Buenos dias." John strode to meet Lieutenant Castañeda. "To what do we owe the pleasure of this visit? I hope it is to inform us that you have given up this idea of taking away the very cannon Santa Anna gave us for our own protection."

"Indeed not."

Captain Moore, who had arrived last night, sat astride his mount and joined their group. "Then you have no reason to be here."

"You would dare defy your president? The man you swore your allegiance to when you arrived in this colony?"

"That man is not the same one we agreed to follow. That man led a republic. This man leads a dictatorship. In good conscience, we cannot give our cannon to someone who might very well turn it on us." Captain Moore gripped his rifle tighter, his knuckles turning white.

"He would never do such a thing."

"There are plenty of things we thought he would never do."

Father unfurled the flag. "This is what you can tell your commander. If he wants that cannon, he is going to have to come and get it himself."

"Be reasonable. No one here wants a fight."

"Then why did you come for the cannon?" Captain Moore stood with arms akimbo.

"Santa Anna commanded me."

"And you will follow that despot to the ends of the earth?" John's voice boomed across the camp. As sudden as quiet falls after a summer storm, so sudden was the quiet that enveloped the area. Even the horses stilled.

Captain Moore shot John a why-did-you-say-that look, then redirected his attention to Lieutenant Castañeda. "That doesn't answer my question as to why he would have need of it."

"I don't question." Lieutenant Castañeda stared at his hands. "I obey orders." Now he gazed at the soldiers in front of him. "And I suggest you do the same. Santa Anna is in no mood for any trouble with the colonists."

Father still gripped the flag. "He begged us to come live here."

"Just do as I say, and all will be well. I will send three of my men this afternoon for the cannon." Lieutenant Castañeda wheeled to leave.

Josie managed to exhale for the first time since the Mexican soldier had crossed the river.

The river that no longer raged and so no longer afforded them the protection they had been relying on. She shivered and drew her shawl around her shoulders.

"If you send anyone for that cannon, they will be met with resistance." Captain Moore followed Lieutenant Castañeda, who now pulled to a halt. "As you see, we are prepared to fight for the right to protect our homes and our families not only from the native peoples but also from a government that doesn't respect that right."

"You should never have been allowed to come here. You aren't used to our ways but to your American leniencies. This is not America. This is Mexico, and you need to respect its leader."

Josie sidled closer to Father, who waved the flag over his head. They were in a no-win situation. Lieutenant Castañeda would never leave without the cannon, and the men of Gonzales were never going to give it to him.

John pointed to the banner above Father. "If you want that cannon so much, you and your men are going to have to come and get it and face the consequences for doing so. Do not test us. Do not try us. We refuse to back down."

That's just what Josie was afraid of.

CHAPTER EIGHT

October 2, 1835

*D*arkness pressed on Josie, the weight of it crushing her chest. Pain, pain, nothing but pain. A scream reverberated. Her scream. What was going on? Why so much pain? Why was she screaming?

The pain tore through her midsection once again.

"No te preocupes. Todo estará bien." The female voice was soft, lulling, but did nothing to dull the pain.

How was she not to worry? How was everything going to be fine when she couldn't figure out what was wrong?

A cool hand smoothed back her hair. As suddenly as it had started, the pain subsided. For a split second, an infant gave its newborn cry. Then utter silence. An oppressive silence that threatened to suffocate Josie. *"Ayúdame! Help me!"* Her screams died in the heavy air.

A soft rustling of skirts told her she wasn't alone, even though she lay in a dark room in which nothing was visible. *"Ayúdame. Por favor."*

"I'm here." The soft, feminine voice soothed Josie.

"I heard a baby crying. It was my baby, wasn't it?"

The silence stretched for several moments.

"Wasn't it my child?"

"No. Your child is dead." The words were as chilled as spring water.

"You lie. That was my child crying. Mine. I want my baby. Give me my baby." Josie attempted to sit up, but the woman pushed her down by the shoulders.

"Don't go anywhere. You are too weak."

Then again came the piercing wails of an infant. Not just any infant, but hers. Though it had just been born, she recognized its cries. "You can't keep me from my child. Give him to me." Again she struggled to come to a sitting position.

"Your baby is dead."

With a jolt, Josie woke up, the bedsheets tangled around her, sweat coating her body. She rubbed her eyes. The dream had returned. The nightmare that had plagued her for eighteen months.

If only it were as simple as a nightmare. In reality, it was more a memory than a dream.

A memory she revisited almost every night.

The bedroom door flung open, and Charlotte appeared in the entrance, a candle glowing in her trembling hand. "What was that screaming all about?"

Yes, her throat was sore. She must have been yelling out loud. "Just a nightmare."

Charlotte clucked her tongue. "Always a nightmare with you—waking me up when I need sleep the most."

Josie grasped the bedsheet. "I'm sorry."

"Maybe if you talk about them, they'll go away. The rest of us could get a decent night's sleep for once."

"No. It's fading. I'll be fine in a moment. Go back to bed."

"You have more nightmares than anyone I know. My mama would say that's the signal of a troubled mind at the least and insanity at the worst."

A breeze from the open door flickered the candlelight. "I have no need to rehash them. If I forget about it, I'll be able to go back to sleep."

Charlotte turned. "Well, don't have any more."

"I won't." Did Charlotte believe these horrific dreams were within her control? If only she could stop them.

"Good night then."

Darkness descended once more as Charlotte left with the single candle. No moon shone through the glass window. No stars brightened the sky.

Though Josie had assured Charlotte that she would be able to sleep again, that was far from the truth. As the crickets chirped outside her room and a coyote howled in the distance, she lay wide awake, replaying every aspect of the nightmare.

Over and over again she'd had this dream. The one in which her baby cried, even though the woman told her that her little one hadn't survived.

Except that it was no dream. It was as real as the bedsheets she clutched in her fists.

If that was the case, then where was her child? Had something been wrong with the infant, and that's why they told her the baby had died? When she insisted that she had heard a child's cry, they told her she was *loca*. Out of her mind because of childbirth.

But she wasn't. Deep down in her mother's heart, she was convinced her child lived. Her soul should know these things. True, she was a young mother. True, she had never laid eyes on her child. True, she didn't even know if she had birthed a boy or a girl.

Those were undeniable facts. Another undeniable fact, at least to her, was that her child was alive.

The baby would be eighteen months old now. Eighteen months without its mother. Eighteen months without the love and nurture it needed and deserved. That's why she had to find her baby. They needed each other.

For the rest of the night, she stared at the dark ceiling above her. If she chased away every thought and concentrated as hard as she could, her little boy's laughter rang in her head. Or maybe it was her little girl's giggles echoing off the walls. She could almost, almost hear the child calling for her. What good was life if she and her baby weren't together?

As soon as the first rays of pink and orange daylight filtered into the small bedroom, Josie rose and dressed in a simple white gown with bright red trim and covered her shoulders with a dark shawl embroidered with red, blue, and yellow thread.

Eighteen months ago, she had allowed the midwife and Manuel to whisk her newborn away without giving her so much as a glance at the child.

She allowed her hair to flow freely, so long it covered her entire back. Her skin may be paler than most Tejanos, but in every other way, she appeared as if she might have been of Mexican descent. And while the men were preoccupied today, she would use the opportunity to search for any kind of clue about her missing child. Not her dead baby, but her missing child.

Thankfully, as usual, Charlotte slept until well after sunrise. As soon as was proper to pay a call, Josie slipped across St. Matthew Street to the Cain home. All sat still and quite in the town. Today no children played in the muddy streets or on the patches of green grass. No women slipped to and fro about their business, tending to their gardens. The dogs didn't even dare bark.

Though the sun was warm and strong, a brief shiver shook Josie's limbs. She steeled herself and wiped her sweaty palms on her gown. If she was going to follow through with her plan, she couldn't have any qualms, couldn't give in to a fit of nerves.

Not long after Josie rapped on the door, the middle-aged Mrs. Cain opened it, the flour streaked across her face reminiscent of Indian war paint. Mrs. Cain stepped over the threshold and towered over Josie, who stepped backward, while the older woman stared at her down the slope of her beakish nose.

"Goodness, child, why are you dressed in such garb? If one of our dear soldiers catches sight of you, he'll shoot you on the spot. Why on earth are you out and about at all, Miss Wilkins? I know your father told you to stay put. He told all of us women the same thing. Is something wrong with Charlotte?"

What about this woman turned Josie mute? She couldn't form a word. Instead, she shook her head.

"Then out with it. I don't have all day to stand here waiting for you to find your tongue."

If she were to follow through with her plan, she had to have Mrs. Cain's cooperation. The thought was enough to wrest the words from her lips. "Can Charlotte stay with you today? I have to go out."

"Out? Where in the world are you going out to? Don't you know there could well be a battle fought today?"

On the contrary, she was all too aware. Too aware of what might happen to her if she did what she had in mind.

But she wouldn't allow herself to wonder any longer. The strange fluttering in her midsection told her that the answers she sought lay just beyond the river.

No matter how her stomach roiled, no matter how her hands shook and her legs trembled, no matter how unevenly her heart beat, she wouldn't back away. She had to discover the truth once and for all. Otherwise, the nightmares that plagued her might just consume her.

"I know what's going on, Mrs. Cain. I have an important message to take to my father, and I daren't leave Charlotte alone for even a few minutes. Father is frightened for her health after the loss of her first baby when she was by herself. In fact, I have already been gone too long, and I'll catch a scolding like I did the other day. I see that you are busy, but if I brought her here, she wouldn't be any trouble. She's busy with knitting and sewing for the baby, and later she's likely to want to lie down."

"Goodness. Is it going to take all day for you to deliver a message? Which, by the way, I can't believe your father would approve of. There has to be a boy who could take it for you."

Josie clamped her mouth shut. She had said too much, had tipped her hand. Questions were the last thing she wanted. At the moment, she didn't know how she'd explain to Charlotte or later to Father when he found out she'd left her stepmother, but that was a problem to be dealt with when it rose to the top of the deck.

Even though Mrs. Cain hadn't given her consent, Josie wasn't about to give her a choice in the matter. She backed away toward the porch steps. "Thank you so much. I will deliver Charlotte in a short while. I appreciate this favor and assure you that I will repay you." By this time, her feet had touched the ground, so Josie bobbed, spun around, and strode across the street and around to the front of her own cabin.

Only to be met by Charlotte, arms crossed over her chest.

"Don't ask me, Charlotte. I don't want to have to lie to you. Just go spend the day with Mrs. Cain. Please. For my sake and for Father's."

"What are you up to? You are dressed as a Tejano. What is it you have in mind?"

"I don't want to have to leave you alone, but I will if you refuse to go." Josie held her breath, waiting for Charlotte to call her bluff.

Instead, Charlotte turned inside, and Josie followed. While her stepmother dressed, Josie prepared a light breakfast. They both ate quickly, though Josie mostly pushed her griddle cakes around on her plate.

"Whatever is going on has you as nervous as a hen with a fox stalking the coop. Tell me right now what is in that brain of yours."

The long-festering secret begged to be lanced, but Josie wouldn't be able to stand the pain of it. No one knew what had happened while Manuel held her captive. By the time Bright Star's brother Running Deer had rescued her, no traces of her pregnancy remained. No visible signs, anyway. Her heart would forever be scarred. "I wish I could. I long to, but it's not possible. You wouldn't understand."

Charlotte reached across the table and grasped Josie by the hand. "You do nothing more than mope all day. Such blue moods surely aren't good for me or for my child. I wouldn't tell a soul."

That may be the case for a moment, but before long word would get out. Charlotte wouldn't be able to hold her tongue for long and would tell Father. Because John and Father were so close, he would confide in the young pastor. And John would never look at her the same. Soon the entire town would shun her, and she would be the village's pariah for the rest of her days.

She wrested herself from Charlotte's grasp, scraped back her chair, and gathered the breakfast dishes. "Are you almost ready to go?"

With a sigh, Charlotte gathered her knitting supplies. "Your father isn't going to be happy when he finds out about this, which he surely will."

No doubt about that.

Soon she had Charlotte safely ensconced at the home of one dour-faced Mrs. Cain and was mounted on Chariot, headed through Gonzales to the river ford.

Like an expectant mother biding her time until her labor pains began, so was the town of Gonzales. An uncertainty had gripped its citizens, and their unease was palpable. You could almost taste the tension in the air and feel the fear creeping like a weed into the hearts of the handful of women and children.

Too long holding their breath like this might strangle them.

Though the waters continued to swirl, they were lower at this place, not far from where the Mexicans camped. Still the river rose to Chariot's knees, which is why she'd had to bring her trusty, sturdy stallion. Once across, she hobbled him and continued on foot, creeping through the trees until she arrived at the Mexicans' camp.

Or what was left of it. They must have moved farther downstream. All that remained was muddy ground, trampled grass, and two wagons carrying supplies.

CHAPTER NINE

*J*ust two wagons stood lonely sentry over the now-abandoned Mexican camp, their horses harnessed to them but their drivers nowhere to be found. In the not-too-far distance, the jangling of harnesses and the thumping of hoofs told of the Mexicans readying themselves for the standoff over the cannon.

The trees around Josie held their breath.

Her focus was on those two wagons, the wood that comprised them dark with age. All she had to conduct her search. And what clues would those yield? Surely Manuel had taken his personal belongings with him. There was nothing here but emptiness.

The same emptiness that dwelt in her soul every minute of every day.

It hadn't been worth leaving Charlotte alone with Mrs. Cain. It wasn't worth the explanation she would have to give Father.

Then again, she had to search. She would never know what information she might stumble on until she gave it a try. She wouldn't have survived Mother's murder, her own kidnapping, or the supposed death of her child if she was one to give up.

Before she stepped from the woods, she scanned the area. Perhaps the wagon drivers were with the troops. Perhaps they had gone off on some other mission, whatever that might be. Whatever the case, they weren't around. As a wide-eyed doe watched her movements, she moved into the clearing, both of them alert to each other and their surroundings.

One of the horses snorted, and she petted his muzzle. "There's a good boy. I'm not here to hurt you. It's okay. If you stand still for me and don't take off, I would appreciate that."

The horse calmed at her words, and within minutes she was lifting her skirts higher than was seemly and climbing over the wagon's tailgate. A canvas stretched over the top, so the interior of the bed was cool and dark, and it took her eyes a few moments to adjust to the dimness.

Pots and pans nestled inside several crates. She moved one to the side to discover salt and pepper. There was also a barrel of flour. This must be the cooking wagon. Though Béxar was close enough that the men could have carried hardtack and nuts with them to sustain them for a few days, this discovery proved that they were digging in for a long siege of Gonzales.

They were prepared to remain until they had that cannon, a fact worth noting to Captain Moore when she saw him next if no skirmishes occurred between the two sides in the meantime.

An ax, several bedrolls, and a few spare blankets, and that was all the wagon contained. Nothing personal. Nothing pertaining to Manuel.

She hopped down and moved to the next wagon. Here were barrels of gunpowder and other items used to make bullets, and even a few spare weapons. The traveling armory, from the looks of it.

Nothing of any help or personal nature in here.

In the distance came the boom of a cannon followed by the crackle of gunfire. Josie jumped, her throat tight. The battle they had been anticipating had begun. Neither side had backed down.

"*Vamanos, vamanos.*" The voice came from just outside the wagon Josie occupied. Her stomach sank. Even dressed as a Tejano, she shouldn't be in here. She had to get out before they discovered her.

But how? Where?

The voices approached, shouting orders to move out. As they came ever closer, Josie dove behind a barrel, just fitting in the narrow space between it and the side of the wagon bed.

In the dim light, a glint of gold caught her eye. She picked up the object. A cat's-eye ring, the stone black with a yellow-green streak down the middle. The wagon tilted and creaked as the driver took his seat. He yawed to the horses, and the wagon jolted forward.

As did Josie's heart, and not from the sudden movement. She peered at the ring.

The one that had been Mother's. There was no doubt about it. The gold work, the slight chip of the stone identified it. Mother's ring.

When Manuel had murdered her, he'd ripped it from her finger, laughing, jeering, sneering at Josie. Now she clutched it in her fist, clinging to it. Oh, to have a piece of Mother back. No matter what, she would never let it go again.

Why would Manuel leave it in the open like this? He had wanted it so much he murdered Mother for it. Now he left it just lying around?

No matter. At least she had found it.

Around them came men's shouts, all in Spanish. "Fall back. Don't anyone fire. Just fall back."

The wagon circled around, and still clutching the ring, Josie lifted the heavy canvas. The Mexicans in their blue and white finery scattered like mice before a cat. In their haste to get away from the advancing Texans, they almost tripped over each other.

Captain Moore led the charge across the river, after the Mexicans, John and Father right beside him, both tall and proud in the saddle. The men they led wore no uniforms. Some of them had donned gray shirts with white straps crisscrossed over their chests. A few of them stood out in bright blue shirts. Some had slouch hats pulled down almost over their eyes. A few wore no hats at all.

Among the last of the retreating Mexicans was a face Josie would never be able to forget. The ruddy darkness. The bulbous nose. The almost-always narrowed eyes and bushy brows.

Manuel.

He turned, raised his gun, leveled it at John, and fired.

An instant later, John shouted and grabbed his shoulder. He leaned over and clung to his horse's mane, sliding from his mount to the muddy ground.

Josie stifled the scream that begged for release from her throat. She had to get out of here. Had to get to John.

The wagon picked up speed. Soon they would be going so fast that there would be no way out. She grasped her skirts in preparation for jumping. When she did so, the ring slipped from her hand and clattered to the wagon's floor. It rolled out of sight.

No! No! She couldn't lose it again. She turned to peer out the back. Father had leapt from his mount and was attending to John. Him or the ring? Which one?

By the time she located it, she might not be able to get out of here without snapping her neck.

She glanced backward, caught a glimpse of gold, then back at John. If she didn't retrieve it now, she never would. It would be lost to her forever.

Stumbling as the wagon hit a rut, she moved toward the ring and scooped it up. This time she placed it on her finger and then moved to the tailgate.

She swallowed hard, inhaled, and leaped from the moving wagon, landing with a thump that jarred her entire body, her teeth clattering in her mouth. As the Mexicans with their wagons pulled away, Josie kept her eyes forward. Steeling herself to fight off the wave of tears that threatened, she wound her way through the woods toward her horse, leapt on Chariot's back, and raced toward John.

Father and Captain Moore were with him.

By the time she reached him and slid from her horse, a ring of red spread across the shoulder of his pale blue shirt. She knelt beside him in the mud, dampness seeping through to her knees. "John, are you all right? Please, tell me you're going to be fine."

"I must be dead and in heaven." He moaned. "I hear Miss Wilkins's angelic voice, but she can't be here."

Father came to her side and pulled her shawl from her head, her hair tumbling out and falling over her shoulders and down her back. "Josie. I expected better of you. You've disobeyed me."

"You can scold me later. Right now we have to take care of John so he doesn't die."

John moaned again. She motioned for Father and Captain Moore. "Let's get him to our house and pray that he survives."

Because life without John would be as bleak and stark as trees in winter.

Father and Captain Moore lifted John from the mud and hoisted him between them. The fighters behind them had scattered and likely had turned for home now that Gonzales was secure. The men settled John in the saddle, though he slumped over.

He couldn't ride to town like that. He'd slide right off Mack's back. Josie shook her head. "This isn't working. He's not strong enough to sit in the saddle by himself. I'll ride with him and watch over him."

Father nodded his consent and gave Josie a hand to mount. With a great amount of care not to hold too tight and make John's pain worse, she hugged him from behind and secured him. As she pressed on the wound to stem the bleeding, she nodded for the men to head toward the house.

They made slow time, Father riding his horse and leading Chariot, John's agony increasing every moment. "Don't let me go."

"I won't. But you have to do your part. The last thing I need is for you to faint. I'm not sure I could hold you up then."

"Tell me why you were so close to the battle."

She couldn't tell him the truth. She never would. He, of all people, no matter how good and godly he was, would never understand, would be the first one to shun her. Once word got out about what happened to her, no one would want her to be part of polite society.

If they found out about her recurring nightmare, they might think her crazy. No, better to keep that part of her past in the past. Buried.

But was her child in heaven with the Lord? Or did that child live? If her baby was in glory, wouldn't she know? However keenly she felt the child's loss, it would be tenfold if the little one were dead. Wouldn't it be?

She shuddered at the memory, the dream so vivid and real. Not only the sound of her baby's cries but also the odors of fried onions and a woman's perfume. The rough blanket as she clutched it. It was as if she were back there again.

But it wasn't true. She kept telling herself that over and over again. "The battle handed me the perfect opportunity to conduct a little spy mission."

"That's why you're dressed as a Tejano. And I'm getting blood all over your white dress."

"Don't worry about that. I'll scrub it well, and it will be as good as new."

But would he? She pressed all the harder, her hand now sticky with his blood. If only they could move faster, but that was impossible to do without injuring him further.

Over the years her family had spent here, he had become an integral part of their lives. He was a wonderful pastor, able to move a congregation with his passion and obvious love for the Lord. He was compassionate to those who were hurting, and hardworking, often making calls late at night or burning his candle low to prepare a sermon. From their house, his was visible, and when she'd go to the porch when she couldn't sleep, light would be flickering in his window.

"Charlotte?" His voice was soft and breathy.

"Don't you scold me for leaving her alone. I got Mrs. Cain from across the street to watch her. I'm glad I came, and I would do it again if I had to."

"What did you find out?"

She repositioned him in her arms, as the right one had gone to sleep. Though she was by no means a dainty woman, he was a heavy load to carry. One she carried with a great deal of care. "Not much, unfortunately. Only the teamsters were there with the wagons. Everyone and everything else was gone. I searched the wagons to no avail. One held supplies, which they have plenty of. The other was of arms and ammunition. That they also possess in abundance."

"Should have blown up their gunpowder."

"Now isn't the time to be giving me that idea." She chuckled. "Besides, there wasn't time. I saw that man shoot you, and I had to get to you." She glanced at the ring on her finger.

"Anyway, the battle is over, and we won. Think about that. We get to keep our useless cannon, and the Indians—and dare I say, the Mexicans—will stay away from us. You can keep holding your services without worrying about being arrested."

Though they had to pledge to become Catholic to become Mexican citizens and claim their land, many continued to practice the Protestant faith at risk to themselves and their livelihoods.

John's only answer was a moan as Mack stumbled.

"Can't you go any faster?" Josie shouted to Captain Moore who led Mack as well as his own horse.

"We are moving at top speed." Captain Moore tightened his grip on the reins. "How is he doing?"

"Fading. Likely in shock from losing so much blood." Josie's arms shook as she fought to keep John upright. "Come on. Stay with me. I told you that you can't faint like a woman. What kind of impression would that make on me?"

This time John didn't acknowledge what she said. A vise gripped her heart, impeding its beating. Her arms trembled from holding him. "Hurry! Please, hurry!"

CHAPTER TEN

Present day

Kayleigh scurried down the walk along the river, trying to hurry. If she didn't get moving, she'd be late for her meeting with Brandon. That's what she was calling it. A meeting.

Even at night, San Antonio's Riverwalk was a colorful place. Red, blue, yellow, and green lights strung from trees and across pedestrian bridges reflected off the shallow water while flat-bottomed boats with colored LED lights around them floated past. Even the umbrellas at the various restaurants' outdoor tables glowed in bright primary colors.

No wonder this was one of Kayleigh's favorite places in the world. The aftermath of a Minnesota blizzard could be beautiful, like glitter tossed over the snow and glinting in the sun, but it couldn't compete with the vibrancy of these colors and the people of this place.

She should take a picture and text it to Mom, but then she would ask why Kayleigh was here and with whom, and then she'd have to explain about the ring and Brandon and how he'd texted asking to meet her. As soon as Mom heard Brandon's name, she'd jump to all kinds of conclusions Kayleigh would rather she didn't.

Breathless, Kayleigh arrived at the restaurant only to have the hostess tell her Brandon had yet to make it. She signaled for the waitress to take Kayleigh to a table on the upper-level balcony.

So she settled into her chair, kept her phone beside her on the table under an umbrella peering over the water, and twisted the ring on the middle finger of her right hand as she waited for Brandon.

He hadn't said what he wanted to discuss. Perhaps he had figured out the mystery of the ring. Maybe this was a date. Kayleigh squirmed. For the time being, singlehood was good. That's what she proclaimed to boy-crazy Paula. She had a busy and fulfilling job, a good church, and great friends. At this point in her life, she didn't need more.

She'd make that clear to Brandon. If he ever showed up. Now it was ten minutes beyond the time he'd said he'd meet her. So where was he? She leaned over her phone to unlock it and swiped up for the home screen. No messages from him.

The waitress came by with a basket of warm tortilla chips and two kinds of salsa and refreshed Kayleigh's Diet Coke. It was bad for her, but if she had one vice, it was her penchant for the drink.

Another ten minutes passed, during which time she consumed more chips than she should have. Great. Brandon had stood her up. Well, she'd pay for her Coke, leave a generous tip because of all the free chips she'd consumed, and forget about him.

After she had paid her bill, she made her way to the inside of the restaurant to return to the street level. Something shiny caught her eye, a certain talent Paula told her she possessed. As she straightened to proceed, she bumped into someone. "Ope. Sorry."

"Well imagine bumping into you here."

Brandon.

"Were you on your way out?"

"I figured you'd stood me up."

"Yeah, sorry I'm late. Just as I was about to close, a customer came in. Isn't that always the way it happens? Anyway, he took his time perusing the merchandise and walked out half an hour later without purchasing anything. And I'm rambling. Hello."

If only he weren't so charming, she could stay angry with him for making her wait so long, but he was, and she couldn't. She waved away the explanation. "Don't worry about it."

"I should have texted, but I didn't want to take the time. Again, I apologize."

"Work happens. I should know. My job is 24/7. I may be officially off duty, but that means little when I'm needed."

"Should we ask to be seated and start over again? Or have you already eaten? I didn't think I was that late."

"You weren't, I haven't, and yes, let's start over."

They returned to the table Kayleigh had previously occupied. She fingered the edge of the menu, even though she'd decided long ago what to order.

The waitress came by and took Brandon's drink order. He was a straight Coke drinker. Maybe he could redeem himself.

He closed his menu and set it at the edge of the table. "Tell me what you do."

"First you have to share with me what, if anything, you've discovered about the ring."

"Fair enough. And not much. Nothing more than what I already knew.

Cat's-eye rings have been around for thousands of years. They're made from chrysoberyl, the traditional gemstone for cat's eye. The line down the middle is called chatoyance. It's actually an optical phenomenon. The band of reflected light moves just beneath the surface of a cabochon-cut gemstone. Often they're thought to bring good luck. Sorry if that was boring."

"Quite all right. You're passionate about your job. The man I bought it from said he got it from someone who needed the cash."

"That's an interesting tidbit. Did he say anything else about it?"

Kayleigh shook her head, her curls bouncing with the motion. "That was it." She wasn't ready to share with him what she suspected about the ring's previous owner, that he could be the man who killed her parents.

A little while later, once the waitress set their food in front of them, before he partook in his meal, Brandon closed his eyes and bowed his head. Oh, she should have done that. She did go to church, but sometimes the busyness of the day overtook her, and she often didn't eat meals at a table.

The aromas of cumin and chilies tickled Kayleigh's nose and sent her mouth to watering. One bite of the crispy chicken flauta, and she was in heaven. "This is my favorite restaurant on the Riverwalk."

"One of mine too." Brandon took several forkfuls of his enchiladas, the melted cheese stringing out as he raised the food to his mouth. He sipped his Coke and leaned back. "You never answered my question about your job."

"You assume I have a job. Perhaps I'm a wealthy heiress who spends her entire day at the spa."

"Ah, but you admitted you have a demanding job, and a woman with a boatload of money wouldn't buy rings at a flea market."

"Busted." She wiped her hands on the napkin in her lap. Flautas were finger food, at least to her. "I'm a refugee coordinator for the state of Texas. I deal mostly with unaccompanied minors entering through Mexico, though many come from Guatemala, Honduras, and other Central American countries."

He raised an eyebrow as his fork clattered to his plate. He caught it just before it bounced onto the floor. "Really?"

Great. Another soul who didn't understand what her work involved or why it was so important. It always raised her hackles, and she sipped her pop to fortify herself. He didn't know her background and what had happened to her birth parents. "Regardless of your politics, they're helpless in all of this. Their parents send them, and they come. We try to place them with family they already have in the States." But they weren't always successful. Just ask her.

"Hey, I didn't say anything. I don't know you enough to judge you."

Now she was the one to stare at him out of the corner of her eye.

"That came out wrong. Let's move the discussion to a different topic, okay?"

She nodded and continued to munch on her flautas. After she finished one, she leaned back in her wrought-iron chair. "Well, since turnabout is fair play, what got you into the jewelry business?"

"It was my dad's store, my granddad's, and his before him. As the fourth generation, I couldn't allow the tradition to be broken. It must be a gene we all possess. I grew up in the back room, watching my dad and granddad work. Dad took early retirement and handed it over to me."

"My dad was a Realtor in a Minneapolis suburb. Not much to pass on there." Besides, she'd always had this yearning to discover her Hispanic heritage, hence the move to Texas.

"I thought I detected an unusual accent. I could never live there. Too cold."

She chuckled. Not like she hadn't been told that a time or a thousand. "You get used to it, especially if it's all you know, but I do appreciate not having to shovel snow here. That's certainly a bonus."

"You're tougher than me. Give me the Texas heat any day of the week."

"I'm getting used to it, but enough about the weather." That's not why she'd agreed to meet him. "Tell me again why you don't think *Fe* in the ring's inscription stands for iron. Because that was my thought, and I haven't come up with anything different."

"Because the band and setting of the ring is made from a high karat of gold, and because the periodic table of elements wasn't created until 1869."

"Then that's definitely out. But what could it mean?"

"I was hoping you could shed a little light on that. What have you come up with?"

"About as much as you. When I googled MAR36, all I came up with was vanities from Home Depot and real estate listings. Not anything likely to be inscribed into a ring. And since the engraving is rather worn, I would say it's been there a pretty long time."

"Very astute observations. Well done."

"So where do we go from here?"

"I'm just not sure what to tell you. I guess we'll have to do some more thinking and searching. Perhaps you could go back to that person who sold it to you and find out what else he knows about it. Maybe he wasn't telling you everything."

"That's a great idea. I think I will."

Just then, Kayleigh's phone rang. One peek at the caller ID, and her stomach sank. Work. Of all nights to get a call from them. Maybe she could handle it without having to go in. "Hello?"

"Ah, good, I caught you." Lila, her boss, sighed. "We have a situation, and I think you might be the best person to handle it. It's that boy Elias that you dealt with a couple of weeks ago. You know we haven't been able to locate his family, so he's been placed in temporary care. The problem is that he won't eat or speak or anything. The foster parents are beside themselves. Could you come?"

Her throat tightened, and she pushed away memories of that awful day and the equally horrible weeks that followed. "Of course. Text me the address, and I'll be right there." She hung up and glanced at Brandon, giving him a sheepish grin. "Work."

"I figured that."

She grabbed her purse from the ground beneath her feet.

"Where are you parked? At least let me walk you to your car." He threw some money on the table and stood.

"Really, you don't have to. It's not far." Although, after the incident at the jeweler's, it would be kind of nice to not have to go to her car alone.

"I insist. I may look like a ruffian, as my mom would call me, but she did raise me to be a gentleman."

"And I'll pay you back for dinner."

"Again, not necessary."

Heaven forbid he think this was a date. It wasn't, was it? "I insist."

Together they sauntered toward the parking garage where she had left her SUV. He didn't question her along the way, and she didn't engage him, too lost in rehearsing what she would say to Elias and how she would get him to respond.

All the experiences she could draw on.

They reached her vehicle in a few minutes. As she unlocked the door, she turned to him, the wind having mussed his long, sandy hair. "Thank you. I appreciate all you've done for me."

"You're welcome. We'll keep in touch."

That was cryptic, but she didn't have time to analyze what he might mean by it. Instead, she slipped behind the wheel. After the few minutes it took to input the foster parents' address into her phone, she pressed the button to start the car.

Nothing.

She tried again.

Same result.

"Come on, Daisy, you can't quit on me. I need you."

"Talking to someone?"

The voice at her window sent her jumping so high she almost hit her head on the ceiling.

CHAPTER ELEVEN

*S*omeone knocked on the window. "Hey, what's wrong? Won't your car start?" The man's voice sent Kayleigh's heartrate into the dangerous zone.

She turned toward the man and giggled when the wind mussed his curls and she caught sight of his cross tattoo. She opened the door so she could hear him better. "I'm so stupid. For half a second, I thought you were someone out to get me."

Brandon furrowed his forehead. "I've been here the entire time. It's only been a few moments since you got in the car. Are you okay?"

"I'm fine. Just fine." No need for him to know about the man at the jewelers or about her past that made her jumpy. "Do you have any jumper cables?"

"I make a really bad guy. No jumper cables."

Kayleigh laughed again, this time with more mirth behind it. "I don't think that of you. Mom is always telling me I need cables, and I never get around to buying any. You know, it's not something you put on your grocery list or your Christmas list, though every year Grandpa threatens to get me some for my birthday."

"You should. I should too. But that's not helping you right now. I'm just a few aisles over. Let me give you a ride."

She bit her bottom lip. She didn't know Brandon that well. Not much at all, really. For all she knew, he could be a serial killer wanted in seventeen states. She could almost read the headlines now. WOMAN GETS IN CAR WITH STRANGER; BODY PULLED FROM RIVER.

"I'm a nice guy. I promise. Or if you're uncomfortable, I can call a taxi."

That would be the smart thing to do. Deep in her heart, though, came a stirring, a belief that she could trust Brandon. *Don't let me be wrong, Lord.*

"If you don't mind."

"I wouldn't have offered if I did."

She grabbed her oversized purse, the one she kept her files in, and a bag with toys and games to help calm children and help her make a connection with them. "All ready."

They made the short trek to Brandon's black truck. It was so high, she had to climb onto the running board and use the handle to lift herself inside.

"Quite some ride you have here."

"Not necessarily designed for short people."

Her height was the bane of her existence. Both of her parents were tall and kept everyday items on shelves she couldn't reach. Now that she was on her own, she could arrange her kitchen and the rest of her condo just how she liked it so that she didn't have to struggle to get what she needed.

In no time, they were zipping through the streets of San Antonio. She still had the GPS pulled up on her phone, and the voice guided them through the city toward Terrell Hills, one of San Antonio's suburbs.

"Am I allowed to ask why you got called away tonight?"

"One of the unaccompanied minors I've been working with is struggling. I'm going to see if I can talk to him and help him feel more comfortable in the home he's been placed in."

Brandon nodded. "What got you involved in such work?"

While the question was innocent enough, she wasn't about to share the details of her life with him yet. "I feel sorry for these kids. Can you imagine being ten and sent away from your home, making a dangerous trek on foot with strangers, then arriving in a new country where you don't understand the language? And being taken into custody and held in a detention facility?"

Brandon tapped the steering wheel. "I never thought about it quite like that."

"Many people don't. I'm not making a political statement one way or another about the situation at the border, but you must admit that the children are innocent. They didn't ask to be sent away from their families to a country where no one wants them."

"I promise to ruminate on that."

The voice on her phone told them to turn into a subdivision filled with spacious, well-maintained homes on large, manicured lots. Of course this was culture shock to Elias.

In the end, she didn't need the GPS to know which place she needed to go to. On the front step of a white stucco ranch-style house sat Elias, covering his face. As soon as they pulled into the driveway, it was clear his shoulders shook as he cried.

No sooner had Brandon put the truck in park than Kayleigh slid from the seat, plopped to the ground, and hustled to Elias's side. From the large front window, she caught sight of a couple standing with hands clasped, watching Elias with eagle eyes.

Good for them for allowing him to grieve while keeping an eye on him. She nodded to them, then turned her attention to Elias.

First off, she had to find out what was bothering him. *"¿Que pasa?"*

The boy peered at her, wiping the moisture from his eyes, his face still crumpled. *"Todo."*

"It can't be so bad that everything is wrong. Aren't the Cliftons nice to you?"

"*Sí*, they are fine. They bought me some toys, and I have my own bed."

That was a luxury to many of these children. "They haven't hurt you, have they?"

"No. They are very nice. *Me gustan los dos.*" Elias shuffled his feet encased in a brand-new pair of sneakers so white they almost blinded her.

"I'm glad you like them both, but you miss your parents, don't you?"

He nodded, his mouth twisted. "I want to go home." The words were low and soft.

"I know how hard this is for you, not understanding what's going on. When I arrived in this country, I was all alone."

Elias turned to her, his mouth agape. "You were?"

"*Sí.* The food was different, I didn't understand the language, and I was scared about what was going to happen to me."

"That's just how I feel." Tears threatened to spill from his golden-brown eyes.

She bumped his shoulder. "It's okay to cry, to let out your feelings. I won't tell anyone."

With that permission granted, Elias allowed the floodgates to open again and the tears to pour down his thin face. She gave him the time he needed to mourn, handing him tissue after tissue from her purse. Another item she'd learned to carry.

Poor Elias. He'd lost his home, his culture, and his parents. That was quite a bit for a young boy.

All the time Elias sobbed, Brandon sat in the truck, his focus on them. Elias's foster parents also kept vigil at the window. Many minutes passed before his tears slowed, then stopped, leaving hiccups behind. From her bag, she pulled several more tissues for him to blow his nose.

"*Gracias.*"

"*De nada.* Sometimes talking helps us feel better."

"Did it help you when you first came? Besides, I didn't know you were like me."

Their situations were quite a bit different, but they shared the common thread of aloneness. That bonded them and formed a pathway for her to reach the boy. He was, after all, just a child who had likely seen more than his share of poverty and violence. Possibly even death. "For a long time, I didn't talk to anyone. I acted like everything was fine even though it wasn't. Finally, I opened up to a counselor at school, one who spoke Spanish, so I was comfortable sharing with her. She helped me so much."

"Will you listen to me?"

"Always, but you have Senor and Senora Clifton to talk to as well. They'd really like to help you as much as they can. You have to let them know how you're feeling so they can make it better."

"But you know what it's like. They don't."

"Then let's start with me. Tell me about your life in Mexico."

So he poured out his story about his five brothers and sisters at home, how they had to walk every morning to get water for the day, how he had never had meat until he'd come to this country. It was a luxury his family couldn't afford. But they had fun and laughed when his parents weren't too tired from scraping a living out of the ground. They played made-up games together at night.

Then he told of how his cousin had said he was going to America and if his parents paid him some money, he would take Elias with him to their uncle's house. His parents gave almost every penny they had only for his cousin to desert him soon after beginning the trek. Another group found him and let him stay with them, but they too left him on his own once they reached the border.

"Why would my parents send me away? Didn't they love me?"

She embraced the now dry-eyed child. "Just the opposite. Sending you away ripped out their hearts. There isn't a moment they don't think about you and pray for you, but they love you so much that they want a better, safer life for you than they can give. They did this because you mean that much to them, because they believe in you. You're going to grow to be a great man and do great things."

"Can't I go home?"

"I don't know." They couldn't ship him over the border like they did adults, but she empathized with his loneliness. "For right now, you stay here and study English and go to school and learn as much as you can. Talk to the Cliftons and let them know how you're feeling. And you can always speak to me. I'll leave my phone number."

"Will they let me use their phone?"

"Let's go inside and talk to them about that. I'm sure they will."

"Okay."

After Kayleigh spoke to the Cliftons and got Elias settled, she returned to the truck where Brandon sat fiddling on his phone. He smiled when she opened the door and climbed in. "I speak Spanish, and I couldn't help but overhear what you said to that boy."

"Oh."

"I didn't mean to, and I hope that didn't violate any privacy policies."

"As long as you don't say anything to anyone else."

"You were great with him. I just don't get how their parents send their children here alone."

"You probably heard as well that I came here as a child?"

"I did."

"And. . ." She held her breath as she waited for his answer.

"You were just a child caught up in circumstances. But I do have a question."

"You know, it's getting kind of late, and I don't want to talk about it. Would you mind taking me home? I'll call a tow truck to get my car." That was one subject about her life she didn't care to discuss with anyone but her closest friends.

"Sure." He started the engine and pulled from the driveway.

A song come on the radio that she loved, so she turned up the volume, in part to keep the conversation to a minimum. They spoke about the music and bands they liked and what concerts they'd been to in their lives.

Once back in the city, he dropped her at her condo. "I had a nice time tonight."

She opened the door. "I did too. Thank you for dinner." She reached into her purse for some money to pay him back.

He touched her hand. "No. I meant what I said when I told you there was no need. It's my way of apologizing for being so late and for not solving the ring's mystery."

"Not necessary. Perhaps it'll remain a mystery forever, but it's driving me batty. I'm the kind of person who, once she gets a hold of a bone, doesn't let it go."

"I'm the same way. I'll lie awake tonight trying to decode the inscription."

She slid from the truck. "If you come up with anything, text me, because I need to know who owned this ring."

Once she did, she might just know who killed her parents.

Then that person could be brought to justice.

CHAPTER TWELVE

October 2, 1835

*J*osie grappled with the fact that Manuel had tried to kill John, not in the heat of battle, but on purpose. To get back at her, no doubt.

High astride Mack, Josie held to an injured John with all her might as Captain Moore led the horse away from the battle. The dank odors of horseflesh, blood, and sweat churned her stomach.

A half a lifetime must have passed before the town came into view, the brown of the dogtrot houses broken by the vibrant reds and pinks of late summer roses blooming around them.

"Almost there, John, almost there. Just hang on for a couple more minutes." Josie glanced down at him. The red stain had grown on the course of the trip.

Then they pulled in front of their cabin, the neat rows of corn and beans and cabbages that Charlotte and Josie had planted behind it, the blooming plants with medicinal properties in the front.

When Captain Moore reached for John, she released her grasp on him, then rubbed her aching arms before sliding down from Mack's back herself. By this time, Charlotte and Mrs. Cain had arrived.

"What happened?" Charlotte wrung the handkerchief she clasped in her hands. "He's covered in blood. I do believe I am going to swoon."

Let Father tend to Charlotte. Josie's attention remained fixated on John. "Get some water boiling, then bring the brandy and those sheets we ripped into bandages."

By this time, Father and Captain Moore had John situated in Father and Charlotte's big feather bed. Because John's shirt was already ripped, Josie had no qualms about tearing it further. Father returned with the bottle of brandy not long after Josie had exposed the wound, and Josie doused John's injury with it. Then she went to the kitchen where the pot of water boiled over the fire.

One good thing that had come from her time with the Indians was the knowledge she'd gleaned about herbal medicine. More than once, it had come into good use. Now she put her knowledge to work for John. She chose yarrow and made a poultice of it before returning to the sick room.

"John, can you hear me?

His eyelids fluttered open. Good. He hadn't passed out. "I have a poultice here. It's good for clotting blood, so I'm going to apply it to your wound. I just don't want to hurt you."

With a clean cloth, she wiped away the red seeping from the wound. It didn't appear to be deep, nothing more than a flesh wound, but there was no point in taking a chance. She set the yarrow wrapped in cloth on his shoulder.

When she did so, he screwed up his face.

"I'm sorry."

"It's fine. I know you only mean to help." He repositioned himself and winced.

"Let me." She moved the pillows about until he nodded.

"Thank you. You are a good nurse and friend."

She warmed at his compliment but balked at his use of *friend*. If only it could be greater than friendship, but he saw her as nothing more than a good acquaintance. All for the best. She had to keep that in the front of her mind.

Soon his eyelids grew heavy, and pain and exhaustion carried him away to sleep.

She emerged from the bedroom to discover Father and Charlotte sitting at the table, cups of coffee in front of them, both giving her glares that would have burned holes through trees.

Father motioned for her to sit. "You have some explaining to do. What possessed you to go out during a battle? You could have been hurt. Or worse. Look at what happened to John. How could I bear to lose you? You are all I have left of your mother. When I laid her in the ground, I swore to her to do all in my power to find you, bring you home, and keep you safe for the rest of your days."

"And you did. But that was well over a year ago. I am no longer a little girl." So much had changed her in that long, miserable year Manuel held her. When Running Deer had found her, she wasn't the same Josie she had been. Instead, she was deflowered, tainted, and broken. "I went to do some spying."

"In the middle of a battle?" Father raised one eyebrow. "What useful information could you give to us then? That is assuming you could march up to one of us and let us know what you found. No, you were needed here."

Charlotte colored at Father's words, and a pang struck Josie's heart. She had run off, and Charlotte could have needed her. Her first pregnancy had not gone well. In the end, though, Josie had been in the right place. "I found Mother's ring." She slipped it from her finger and held it out to Father.

He widened his eyes. "You did? How? Where?"

"In a Mexican wagon filled with gunpowder and everything needed to make bullets. It was there behind a barrel. Whether Manuel lost it there or placed it there for safekeeping, I couldn't say."

He took it from her and examined it over and over. "That's the ring. Oh, to have it again." He handed it to Josie. "I can't wear it, so I want you to have it. Remember your dear mother and tell your children and grandchildren about her."

She slid it onto her finger, the weight of it solid and comforting. Almost like Mother was here with her.

A quiet moment stretched between the three of them. Then Father cleared his throat. He scraped back his chair, and the heavy footfalls of his boots closed in on her. Soon he held her by her shoulders. "I'm just thankful no misfortune befell you today. A ring is a material possession, no matter the memories associated with it. I would rather gaze into your face and see Mother there than to have the ring and not be able to see her reflection in you."

"I was careful. I have no intention of ever being taken by them or anyone ever again."

"Your actions today could have resulted in just that outcome. Nothing is more valuable than a human life. Nothing is worth it."

Father was right. This had to do with a human life. The one of her child. More than anything, she had to know if that child lived or not.

"I mean it, Josie. How could I ever stand it if I lost you too? Please, for my sake, promise me you'll stay safe." His voice was harsh, but his eyes were soft and a little teary.

Charlotte pushed back her chair. "I believe that's settled now. George, I could use more wood for the fire. Josie, help me finish this stew. Perhaps when John wakes up, he'll be ready to eat some."

Father left to fulfill Charlotte's request, and Josie went about setting the table. Charlotte stood at the stove, stirring the meat and vegetables in the pot. "I can't believe you went out there. How could you be so…?"

"Brave? Foolish?"

"I know you want to help the men of this town, but there had to have been more to it."

Josie shook her head so hard, she gave herself a headache. "That's all."

"You can't bring your mother back."

"This doesn't have anything to do with her."

"Be honest with yourself." Charlotte replaced the pot's lid and turned to Josie. "It isn't until you face whatever is haunting you that you will have true peace. You have to have it out with God before you can heal."

Bless Charlotte for wanting to help, but she was expecting a baby. Each day that she blossomed a bit more, a bit more of Josie died. She prayed the baby would be born strong and healthy. At least the mother would be well cared for during her pregnancy. Loved and pampered.

Josie hadn't had that.

Before dinner, she peeked into the bedroom to check on John. He slept, which was a good thing. Sleep promoted healing more than anything else. By the time supper was finished, though, he had awakened, so she brought him a bowl of stew. His nap revived him a good deal.

"How are you feeling?"

"Thanks to your doctoring skills and that poultice, so much better. I'm grateful for your care."

"You are welcome anytime. I watched this happen, you know." She filled him in on her scouting expedition, including finding Mother's ring, and was rewarded with the same scowl as Father's. "It was awful seeing you get hit. Especially since that man aimed at you on purpose. The Mexicans weren't to fire at all. That's why they fled. But because you came to my rescue, he singled you out and ignored the command."

"It is not your fault. And really, I'm fine. Nothing more than a graze. It doesn't bother me all that much now that you're done pouring whiskey into it and putting poultices on it."

She took his empty bowl from him. "I'm just glad you and Father are home safe and sound. Now that the Mexicans are gone, life will settle down again." Perhaps now that she had the ring, it would stop the nightmares that plagued her.

He touched her cheek, very soft and fast but enough to send a shiver skittering down her spine.

"While we should be thankful that no one lost their lives today, I'm afraid this little skirmish was just the beginning of something bigger to come."

She wrinkled her forehead. "What do you mean?"

"The men were talking even before the battle. None of them came to Texas to live under a dictator like Santa Anna. Most came for the land, believing they would reside in another republic like the one they had left. They aren't happy, but they aren't about to give up and return to the United States, and they aren't about to let the Mexicans run roughshod over them either."

"Do you mean there could be war?"

"Very likely. Another war for independence like the one in 1776."

She gasped.

War might give her more chances to spy on the Mexicans, more chances to find out what happened to her child. But if Manuel fell in battle, she may never get the answers she sought.

And if John fell. . .

She couldn't even contemplate that.

CHAPTER THIRTEEN

October 10, 1835

After the battle, life in Gonzales did not return to normal, especially not for Josie. Sure, women once again went about their daily tasks, tending to their children, cooking meals for their families, making purchases at the general store. The familiar, sweet incense of smoke combined with the tang of decaying leaves as fall approached.

But that ring and everything it symbolized haunted Josie's nights. Her dreams doubled in their frequency and intensity. Today she tried to distract herself by offering to take Father his lunch, so, basket in hand, she set out from the house. The militia hadn't disbanded after the skirmish but had stayed put. Even the two-block walk to the military plaza proved the changes to the little town. All she had to do was to step out of her door, and the din of men's voices, the clang of swords, and the neighing of many horses reached her ears.

This was no longer a ragtag bunch of men come to defend a town and protect its cannon. This was the Texas army.

Instead of men marching together, practicing hand-to-hand combat, or shooting off their long rifles, she found them gathered in the plaza's center, words flying like a swarm of angry bees.

Some of the men were the same who had chased off Casteñada after the battle, the ones who had first answered the plea for help that John and Josie had brought. New recruits, faces Josie didn't recognize, had swelled the troops, even though about a hundred of the original men had left after a message came that the Mexicans were threatening the town of Victoria.

At the head of the gathering was John, using his preaching voice to be heard over the cacophony of voices, each one raised a tick higher than the last. Try as he might, he couldn't maintain order among the troops.

Mr. Bateman, short and swarthy, stood beside John. "I appeal to you all, gentlemen, to make me your commander. Am I not one of the oldest settlers of the DeWitt colony?"

Winslow Turner, his chin off-center from the rest of his face, waved his hand above the crowd. "Why should we? What kind of military experience do you have?"

"What kind of experience do any of us have? We all fought in a battle, so that's something for us."

"Captain Moore at least has experience fighting the Waco and Tawakoni tribes." This man, unfamiliar to Josie, his face tanned like leather, slapped his woven straw planter's hat against his knee. "That's why he should be our commander. At least this confrontation wasn't his first taste of fighting. You are lily-livered enough to run off at the first volley of shots zinging past you."

"How dare you?" Mr. Bateman roared. "You didn't answer the call until the Mexicans had retreated. How can we trust you to lead us in battle if you can't even be on time?"

More yelling ensued from every sector of the camp. Josie approached John, who shouted for all he was worth. He would have no voice left to preach on Sunday. "Gentlemen, gentlemen, let us all be reasonable. How will we be able to fight the Mexicans if we can't maintain the peace between us? We are on the same side." Though they usually listened to him, no one paid him heed. The bickering continued, spreading like a prairie fire through the assembly.

Father, able to peer down on each man there, whistled sharp, piercing. Enough to bring a hush over the men.

Now John could be heard. "We must proceed in an orderly fashion and maintain unity amongst ourselves. Let us find three worthy candidates and put it to a vote."

Shouts erupted, the troops all yelling for their candidate. It was nothing short of anarchy.

Josie wove her way through the encampment until she reached Father. After he acknowledged her with a single nod, he whistled and once more gained the soldiers' attention. "We are hungry, and that is causing our irritability. I say we dismiss to partake of the noon meal, clear our heads, and discuss our choices. We will reconvene at four o'clock for the vote. At that time, we will have a commander to lead us against our Mexican tyrants."

A great cheer erupted, crashing like thunder. Appealing to a man's stomach was always a good choice to bring any argument to an end. Eager for their suppers, the men broke into groups and scattered throughout the camp.

Josie held out the basket she had brought. "Charlotte sent you some dinner. There's enough in here for you too, Pastor Gilbert."

He toed the ground, his eyes downcast, a deep frown on his face. "I'm not hungry. Thank you though."

Father took the basket and rummaged through its contents. "Fried chicken." He smacked his lips. A moment later, Father was savoring Charlotte's cooking.

While Father dug into the meal with a great deal of relish, John slunk away, disappearing into the crowd. "Excuse me, Father. I'm going to go after him."

He raised his eyebrows in response.

Let him think what he wanted. She had known John long enough to sense when he wasn't himself. On soft, fleet feet, she hustled after him, dancing around the campfires that had just been lit for cooking.

If she knew John at all, she knew where to find him.

Out of habit, she crept through the cottonwood thicket without making a sound. Through the thinning leaves, she spied him, kneeling in front of a large rock on which he had placed his Bible. Not the big one he used for preaching on Sunday but a small one that could slip into his pocket.

For a while, she stood in reverent silence, offering up her own prayers for wisdom for John. Being the colony's spiritual adviser, and an illegal one at that, was no easy task. He finished his supplications and rose, rubbing his shoulder where the Mexican bullet had grazed him. Thank goodness they were not well made and did little damage.

Now she moved forward, making as much noise as possible, even though doing so went against everything her Indian friends had taught her.

John turned and nodded. "You always know where to find me."

"That's because you always go to the same place."

"So I make it easy for you to track me." He gave a crooked grin, one that no less lit the dimple in his right cheek.

She shrugged and tugged the sleeves on her gown. "I can read in your face that you are troubled."

John picked up his Bible from the rock and placed it into his jacket pocket. "Nothing slips by your notice."

"I have been told I'm a rather good listener." She settled on the rock between them.

He circled it before facing her once more and blowing out a breath. "The men are about to mutiny. Either that or leave altogether. Here I believed myself to be a leader in this community, in the entire colony, but I can't even rally troops to our cause."

"That's because you are a man of peace, not war. You preach reconciliation with God and with our neighbor."

"That makes me weak in their eyes." He scrubbed his face, including his long sideburns.

She rose and went to him and touched his arm, her heart aching for him. He took his responsibility to his flock to heart, so much that it weighed down his shoulders. "Not weak. Just not a military general."

"Not even a military private, I'm afraid." He gave a wry laugh.

"Is that truly the mantle you wish to wear?"

He glanced at the trees overhead, the leaves on them rattling in the gentle breeze. "I suppose not. But how can I keep them here until they resolve who should lead them into the next battles?"

"So there are to be more?"

"Yes. This incident proved to them that they are weary of the Mexican yoke on their shoulders. Santa Anna hasn't been true to his promises. He is a dictator, and the Texans won't stand for it."

"That alone should hold them here."

"Some, perhaps, but many are eager to return to their land and to their families."

"Then maybe they aren't cut out to be part of the army."

He shrugged. "You might be correct. But then we'll need fresh recruits. We won't be prepared for the next battle. There is no doubt that it will be bigger and more intense than this little skirmish. This was merely a prelude to what is to come."

Josie shuddered. She had witnessed enough bloodshed and death in her life. How much more would she be able to stand?

Now it was John's turn to touch her arm. Even though his fingers brushed her long sleeve, it still warmed her from the inside out. Innocent enough, but yet. . .

"I understand that none of this can be easy on you."

"It's not, but at the same time, it is part of life, isn't it? You served in the army."

"As a chaplain to the men who were keeping the peace between the settlers and the Indians."

"One thing you have never told me is where your family is. You mentioned your mother had passed away." One thing they had in common.

"When you speak about bloodshed, I am one who is accustomed to it." His voice cracked. Again he rubbed his face, lines that weren't there a moment ago now fanning from the corners of his eyes. He carried a heavy burden.

"Please, allow me to help you."

Though his smile wasn't fully genuine and didn't reach those blue eyes of his, at least it was a smile. "I don't speak of it to anyone, and I ask for your discretion."

"On my honor, I won't breathe a word of what you tell me."

He nodded his head the slightest of bits. "After Mother went home to the Savior, Father was lost without her. He never recovered. I discovered his body in his office. Self-inflicted gunshot wound."

Josie gasped. "Oh Pastor Gilbert, I am so sorry."

His blue eyes shimmered, and he swallowed hard. How she ached to go to him and comfort him, but that would be unseemly.

"Every time I close my eyes, the scene replays itself in my head." He shook himself, as if sloughing off the memories. "But good came from it. The incident drew me closer to the Lord, for it was only to Him that I could flee and find comfort. It solidified my decision to become a pastor."

Imagine him having a secret so heavy as that. Perhaps he wouldn't shun her if he knew of her circumstances. Then again, he was innocent in what happened. She was not. "I will pray for you, that the dreams that torment you will cease." How well she understood them.

He straightened, signaling to Josie that the topic was closed. "Come. We should get back. I only pray that when we meet for the vote in a few hours that most of the men will still be there and that the one we elect will be a good leader."

With John leading the way, they departed the sanctuary of the copse and returned to the town, now swelled with men come from the surrounding area. Their quiet little village was anything but right now.

After a quick check on Charlotte, who was napping, she followed him to the military plaza, which hummed with activity. Here and there, men continued to debate who their leader should be. Though the ranks had thinned a bit, more men rode into the encampment.

Exactly at the top of four o'clock, Father whistled for the men's attention. Once he had it, he turned the platform over to John.

"Men of DeWitt colony, we stand at a critical juncture. Many have agreed that the time has come to shake off the heavy weight of Santa Anna's foot on our necks, but we cannot be successful in that venture without a strong leader. I am not that man. We must come to some kind of agreement before we fall to pieces and accomplish nothing."

When John stopped for a breath, far in the distance, Josie picked up a sound. A reverberation in the ground. Horses' hooves pounding. Because she was at the back of the crowd, she managed to slip away and dash to the edge of town.

There on the open prairie rode a large contingent. She stood and held her breath as they approached. At last she could make out their shapes, dark against the still-bright sun. No tall hats indicative of the Mexican Army, and no Indian ponies to suggest Comanche or Apache.

She turned and sprinted to the military plaza. Men shouted in an attempt to be heard over others. Pure chaos.

She may have missed a few years with Father, but he had taught her one thing. How to whistle. Mother had hated it and so did Charlotte, but from time to time it came in handy. The one she gave was just about as loud as Father's.

All attention focused on her, the stares of the men boring into her from all sides. "Hold off on that vote. I believe we have another contingent about to arrive. Wait to see who is with them and what their opinion is."

The men turned to the horizon. They shaded their eyes to better see the approaching party. In short order, a tall, slender, graceful man with a wide, knowing gaze rode into town.

And all the men cheered.

CHAPTER FOURTEEN

October 25, 1835

The candle on the table flickered in the slight breeze that blew through the chinking in the cabin, casting shadows that danced on the walls. As it was almost bedtime, Charlotte had allowed the fire to burn low, and a chill seeped through the cracks. Rain pattered on the roof, a background to Father's intoning the Bible passage. Josie and Charlotte sat at the kitchen table with him, steaming cups of coffee in front of them.

> *The Lord is thy keeper:*
>> *the Lord is thy shade upon thy right hand.*
> *The sun shall not smite thee by day, nor the moon by night.*
> *The Lord shall preserve thee from all evil:*
>> *he shall preserve thy soul.*
> *The Lord shall preserve thy going out and thy coming in from*
>> *this time forth, and even for evermore.*

Josie warmed her hands on her cup, then lifted it to her lips and sipped, the bitter brew jolting her from the lilting words of the passage. Psalm 121. The traveler's psalm. "Father, are you trying to tell us something by reading that?"

He closed the leather-bound tome and pushed it to the side, casting glances first at Charlotte and then at Josie. Even in the dim light, Josie didn't miss the creases in his forehead.

Charlotte held him by the hand, a rare display of affection between the two. "Whatever you have to say, don't worry about me. I'm fine."

He nodded. "As you know, Stephen Austin has been drilling the troops and training them since he arrived earlier in the month."

When he had ridden into town, the entire village had cheered for this leader who had helped colonize this section of Texas and who had fought with the infantry, a man with both military and organizational experience others here lacked. Also a man who, after having been imprisoned in Mexico City, had no love lost for Santa Anna.

Within days of arriving in Gonzales, he had appointed four captains and called for reinforcements. The village women often went to watch him train the troops, the ragtag bunch of men learning how to march as a unit and how to quickly reload their weapons.

He was the well-respected leader the men had been crying for.

Charlotte nodded. "Go on."

"The time has come for us to move and begin the fight. Austin is bringing us to Mission San Francisco de la Espada, closer to where the Mexicans are at San Antonio de Béxar."

"Oh George, that's so far away." Charlotte's words warbled. "Are you sure you're ready? He has only been working with the men for a few weeks."

Josie slid to the edge of her seat, twisting the ring on her finger. Father had taken it from her for a time without explanation. It was good to have it back where it belonged. "So he is going on the offensive against Santa Anna?"

"Exactly. General Cos is marching toward San Antonio de Béxar. Austin says this is the time to tighten the noose around the necks of the Mexicans there."

"I'm concerned about the men's preparedness." Charlotte brushed imaginary crumbs from the table.

"We do lack a large stockpile of ammunition and a great deal of training, but we must act now while the troops are still excited about their victory here and have the will to pursue the matter. Time is of the essence. Charlotte, if you're up for the trip, I would like you and Josie to come with me to the mission. You will have protection there and be near me so I can keep an eye on you."

They may not hug or kiss in front of others, but Father and Charlotte cared deeply for each other. Especially because of what happened with Mother, Father was protective of his new wife. As for Josie, she had to restrain herself to keep from jumping up and kissing Father's cheek. There she would be closer to the Mexicans. She could do a little spying and a little searching at the same time.

A slight grin crossed Charlotte's face. "I don't wish to be parted from you. Without the men here, the town will be vulnerable and open to attack from both the Mexicans and the Indians. I agree it is best we all remain together."

"That settles it then. Pack a few things, just what is necessary. We shouldn't be gone long. At least I pray we aren't."

Josie prayed this would be her chance to find the information she so desperately sought.

What a sight the Texans were as they rode toward Mission San Francisco. The only weapons they carried were Bowie knives and long-barreled flintlock rifles. Most wore buckskin, some new, some yellowed with age.

Wide-brimmed sombreros topped some heads while others sported beehive hats and still others wore coonskin caps with the striped tails trailing down their necks. Large, sturdy American horses strode beside smaller Spanish ponies. The one unifying aspect was that instead of canteens, they all carried Spanish gourds.

In front of the column rode a man on a half-broke mustang carrying Josie's COME AND GET IT flag.

Amidst it all, Charlotte bounced in a small wagon that Josie drove and Chariot pulled. He wasn't used to the job but settled into it. Thanks to the recent rain, the animals didn't kick up dust. They could be grateful for God's small graces.

This was their third day traveling. Other women and children, including Almaron Dickinson's wife, Susanna, and his daughter, Angelina, had joined them on the trek. By now, most were tired and sore and wanted nothing more than to stop moving and bed down in a comfortable and safe place with a roof over their heads.

John rode up beside Josie. "How are you ladies making out?"

"I'm fine." She tipped her head to the back of the cart where Charlotte slept on a pallet of blankets. Her stepmother was wan. "For her sake, we need to get to the mission as soon as possible."

"We'll be there shortly. Some of us are riding ahead to the Concepción Mission to scout out a place for the encampment as there isn't enough room inside the walls for all of us."

What she wouldn't give to be part of the scouting mission, to be of more use than driving the cart.

John chuckled. "I can see by the way your eyes are lighting up that you'd like to come with us. Your Father said he would drive for a while if you want to go."

"More than anything." Her heartbeat kicked up a few notches.

"Then unhitch Chariot, and let's be on our way."

Not too much later, John, Josie, and several of the captains that Mr. Austin had appointed were winding their way through trees, their canopies of leaves shading them, the branches rustling in the breeze. Here the soft forest floor hushed the horses' hooves and stilled Josie's hammering heart.

Whenever life was too much to bear, especially after Mother was murdered and she lost her child, Josie sought refuge in the trees. This was her sanctuary through her time with the Mexicans. At sixteen and heavy with child, she spent all her spare time in the forest, pleading with God to right her life.

He hadn't listened.

But still she came, the place a balm to her soul through all the sorrows she'd suffered. And now it steadied her breathing.

She followed John astride his chestnut mare. The pastor she had known in Missouri was an old man, at least to her child's way of thinking, with thin gray hair and a stooped frame. John was anything but. Broad-shouldered, straight as an Indian's arrow, well-muscled, prepared for battle.

Yet vulnerable.

And that did nothing to keep her heart in a steady rhythm.

Instead, she focused on the path ahead, here and there littered with brush. After traveling for a while, the group broke through the trees to a prairie, the sky now blue and brilliant above them, an expanse that stretched from one horizon to the other.

At the front of the group, Jim Bowie kicked his horse's flanks and spurred him to a gallop. The others followed suit. A tingle surged through Josie as Chariot's hoofs pounded over the ground, the wind tugging at her hair tucked underneath her bonnet. To let it flow free would be wonderful but not practical.

They passed in front of Mission San Francisco de la Espada where Mr. Austin would stay and where the scouts would return for the night. Stone walls encompassed it. For the inhabitants huddled inside, it was a hedge of protection against a host of enemies. Josie and the rest of the team kept riding. Every now and again they picked their way through a thicket, their horses enjoying a respite from their runs. At one point, they crossed a stream and both man and beast drank from it.

Once again on the prairie, another mission came into view, the twin towers of its church rising into the azure firmament. Josie pulled alongside John. "Which one is this?"

"Mission Concepción. We aren't far from San Antonio de Béxar and the Mexicans at all."

As if to punctuate and validate his words, a blast from the town's cannon sent Josie jumping in her seat and put Chariot on alert, but it did no real damage. One more cannon shot sounded, and then peace settled once again.

A slow grin spread across Josie's face. "We are positioned perfectly for a battle. And it appears the citizens of Concepción are prepared for one."

John nodded, the tail of his coonskin cap bobbing with the motion. "Where do you suggest we make camp, my lady?"

The other men pulled up, and they formed a circle, the horses prancing and pawing at the ground. From her vantage point, Josie surveyed the area. Trees behind the mission and in front of them. Between the trees, prairie and a river. A small one, not fast and swift like the Guadalupe, but a water source nonetheless.

The river boasted a horseshoe bend. She pointed. "That might be a good place. The stream is a source of water, and the trees provide good protection. If need be, the soldiers can climb down the banks and keep their heads low. That makes it a good strategic position."

Jim Bowie nodded, his saddle squeaking as he shifted positions. "Very good, for a woman." He kept his voice even and his face expressionless, so it was impossible to say if he meant his words as a compliment or a subtle disparagement.

Sometimes she and Bright Star would go out with Bright Star's brother, Running Deer, and he would teach them a warrior's ways, pointing out such things to her. When she made an astute observation, he praised her and said she would have made a fine warrior. If it weren't such a forbidden thing, she might have fancied Running Deer as a suitor. Just a young girl's silly dreams. Still, he would have protected her from Manuel, and that would have made all the difference in her life.

"So that's where we'll set up camp then and wait for the Mexicans to make their move." John's voice jolted her from the past to the present once again. The captains got to work on designating areas for each of their units, the advance troops arriving a short time later. Most of the army remained at Mission San Francisco de la Espada. Soon the quiet of the place was broken by the neighing of horses and the shouting of men. Boots and hooves trampled the grass.

Across the river and through the thicket, Josie spied movement. A blue coat. A flash of a white hat. Red plumes.

Mexican scouts.

Her pulse pounded in her neck.

"Pastor Gilbert." She had dismounted and led Chariot to where John was setting up tents. Instead of returning to San Francisco tonight, with such a good position, they had decided to claim it.

He turned to her, and she pointed across the river. "Mexican scouts. They know we are here."

"I suspect the booming of that cannon alerted them."

"Is it such a good idea to stay here?" If the Mexicans planned to attack this small band of soldiers before Mr. Austin and his reinforcements arrived, they might find themselves in a great deal of trouble. Perhaps, after years away from her Indian friends, Josie was losing some of her skills. She would have to be more careful and think harder about all possibilities.

"You didn't know they would figure out so fast that we were here, that they happened to have scouts in the area at the same time we did." John's voice was as calm and steady as ever, but a single creasing of his brow conveyed his worry.

"If I had seen them sooner. . ."

"They weren't prepared to show themselves just then and probably didn't intend to make us aware of their presence. In fact, I'm sure they didn't. See, they're terrible spies. This will give us time to send for Austin and for him to get here as soon as possible with those reinforcements."

"I'll ride back right now. Chariot is strong enough to make the trip."

"Give me your ring."

She snapped her hand behind her back. "No. What do you need it for? It's precious to me."

"Miss Wilkins, have faith in me. I will give it right back to you."

Have faith in him. Over the years, various people had asked her to have faith in them. Father said to have faith that he would keep them safe. He didn't. Mother said to have faith that the Mexicans who came wouldn't hurt them. They did. God told her to have faith in Him about all manner of things. He hadn't proved His trustworthiness regarding any of it.

John stared at her, his gaze penetrating to her very core. He must be able to read her doubts, to sense her hesitation. Her chest rose and fell faster. If he could read her, he would discover what she kept hidden in the vault of her heart. A place so tender, so raw, that no one was allowed in there. Not even her.

Each time she tried to enter, the pain was so sharp that she couldn't venture too far into that cave of memories before the darkness consumed her. Frightened her out of it.

If John got in there, it would all pour out and leave her emptier than she had ever been. She would be nothing. So she turned away, rubbed the ring's smooth stone, and yanked it from her finger before spinning around and handing it to him.

He turned to leave.

"Wait." She grabbed him by the arm. "You promise you'll bring it back?"

He tried to yank from her grasp, but she held firm to him. "I promise. Have faith."

"Why do you need it? Already Father took it from me, and now you're asking for it."

"Don't question me. It's better you not know."

"I demand you tell me." She stomped her foot but once. She was acting like a little child. John understood the importance of the ring, where it had come from, though not the entire story. He wouldn't be so cruel as to keep it from her. "I'm sorry. That was petulant and immature."

"I should have explained that I'll bring it right back. Get Chariot ready to go. By the time you mount, I'll return your ring."

As always, John was true to his word. Just as she swung herself onto her stallion, he returned with the ring and handed it to her. "Tell Mr. Austin what your father told me, that this ring was used by the Culper group during the Revolutionary War."

"Why does he need to know that?"

"He'll understand. He's smart and well educated. Now go. Godspeed. Ride as fast and as hard as you dare. And whatever you do, don't lose the ring."

CHAPTER FIFTEEN

*A*fter rolling out of bed at a ridiculously early hour, Kayleigh made a run to Karnes County Residential Center and was in her car on the way back when her phone rang. She pressed the button on her steering wheel and answered it.

"Oh Kayleigh, thank goodness I was able to get a hold of you." On the other end of the line, Lila was breathless. "I got a call from Tina Clifton this morning."

After zoning out while traversing the back roads, Kayleigh came fully awake. "What happened?"

"Elias ran away."

"What?" Kayleigh almost swerved off the street. She forced herself not to get too worked up. Surely he had just gone outside for a while or to a friend's house or something of the sort.

"She woke up this morning, and his bed was made and all his clothes were gone, along with the little suitcase they had bought him."

Oh no. She gripped the steering wheel with all her might. "He was desperate to get home. He wanted to go back to his family."

"Whatever the reason, we need to find him as soon as possible. Tina has already alerted the authorities, but we thought maybe you had an idea where he might be."

"Not a clue. Listen, I'm on my way back from Karnes County. I'll be there as soon as I can. He's in real trouble, not knowing the language, not knowing who to trust."

"I know you pray, Kayleigh. Do that now. We can use all the help we can get."

"Already praying."

That's just what she did the entire way back to San Antonio. Of course, once she hit the interstate, an accident ahead created a traffic jam. Since she turned off the radio to focus on praying, she had missed the report and was caught in it before she'd had a chance to find an alternate route.

She sat and swiveled between stewing and talking to God while she crawled along. She called Paula and asked her to pray. Though she tried Brandon's number to ask him to do the same, she got his voice mail and left a message. Just when she didn't think she'd be able to stand another minute of it, her heart pounding in her chest, her left foot tapping on the floor, the bottleneck eased, and traffic moved again.

At last she arrived at the Cliftons' house. Poor Tina was on the front lawn, calling for Elias, pacing so much she'd have no trouble getting her steps in on her tracker today.

All around the block sat black-and-white police cars, their blue and red lights strobing even in the bright light. One of the officers stopped her, and once she explained to him who she was, he let her pass. She parked in the Cliftons' driveway.

She had just released her seat belt when Tina ran to Kayleigh's car, pouncing on her the minute she stepped out. "Do you have any idea where he might be? When you were here the other night, did he mention going anywhere?"

"Only that he wanted to go home. I reassured him this was a good place to stay and that we were doing everything we could to take care of him."

Tina swiped a tear from her dark skin. "While I made supper last night, we talked about his family. I thought it would do him some good to talk about them, perhaps ease his loneliness and help me to understand him better. Looking back, that wasn't such a great idea."

"You did nothing wrong. It's good for the children to let their feelings out and to remember those who love them. They should never forget."

Mom had done her best with Kayleigh, to help her remember Mama and Papi, but even though she was five when they crossed the border and she lost them, they were only shadowy figures in her mind. She didn't have any pictures of them or any mementos. Only the murky haze.

She couldn't even recall the sound of their voices. That was the worst part of all.

She shook away the memories so she could focus on Elias. A tall, older officer approached her and queried her about what she knew about the boy. She answered all his questions. "He just wanted to go home, and that's understandable."

The cop peered at her over the top of his bifocals. "You comprehend a great deal about these circumstances."

"I do work with these children as my profession, and I have for almost five years." Unless he required her to reveal more, that's all she would say on the subject.

Thankfully he just nodded, asked a few more questions, and took Kayleigh's information in case they had any need to speak to her further.

Tina strode around and around the yard until her husband arrived home from the airport where he'd been about to take off on a business trip. When he scurried up the drive, she ran into his arms, and he held her for a long while.

Kayleigh had witnessed that kind of love between her parents. Both sets of them. That much she did remember. Through thick and thin, both couples stuck together. Though Paula encouraged her to finally find a man—like her very single friend had any right to demand it—Kayleigh wouldn't settle unless she found a love like that.

A love that held each other in the sweltering hold of a bus as it careened across Texas.

Wait a minute. Wait. A spark lit in her brain. "We talked about the bus." Kayleigh spoke into the air, but it stopped Tina's sobbing, and she glanced up from her husband's shoulder.

"What do you mean?"

"When I was here the other night, we talked about the bus, how he and I both took the bus here when we arrived. If that's how he came, that's how he would leave."

Tina's eyes widened. "But how would he get there?"

"I have no idea."

"He doesn't know which direction the stop is." Dan Clifton shook his head.

"I know. I know. But it's the only thing that makes sense."

The officer who had questioned her made a beeline in her direction. "The bus?"

"I just thought of it now."

"Isn't there a stop a few blocks over?"

Tina's mouth dropped into an O. "That's the one commuters take into the city. We never use it, so I didn't think about it, but Elias did comment on it when we went past it the other day."

The officer was already on his way to his patrol car, followed by Tina and Dan, with Kayleigh hot on their heels.

The ride to the stop wasn't long, and it was especially short with the lights flashing and the siren blaring. Everyone moved out of their way. Kayleigh clung to the seat of the Cliftons' car, the scene all too familiar to her. *Focus, focus.*

She released an audible whoosh of air when she spied a tiny figure huddled underneath the shelter at the corner. His little shoulders shook. As soon as the officer stopped the car, Tina and Dan jumped out. Kayleigh hung back. It was best if Elias didn't become too attached to her. He needed to think of Tina and Dan as people he could trust.

Especially if Kayleigh wouldn't be able to reunite him with his family.

She slid from the seat and stood beside the patrol car while the officer and Dan and Tina spoke to Elias, ready to help them interpret or do whatever else was needed, though the Cliftons spoke fluent Spanish and were capable parents.

As she stood there, she rubbed her arms, her throat closing little by little until she could hardly breathe. Why this reaction, and why now? She'd helped many unaccompanied minors over the years and never had so many memories surface. Before this, she'd been able to separate the past from the present.

"Kayleigh?"

At the voice behind her, she startled, clutching her chest and leaning against the patrol car so her weak knees didn't collapse. "Brandon. You just about scared the stuffing out of me."

He shrugged and raised his eyebrows. "Didn't mean to do that. I was on my way to meet you at the Cliftons'. Your message sounded frantic. I was driving by and noticed the commotion and then saw you over here. What's going on?"

She explained the situation to him, and several times he touched her arm.

"I'm so sorry to hear this."

"All he wanted was to go home. What ten-year-old wouldn't want to stay with his loving parents, no matter their financial circumstances?"

The officer approached them, a smile across his face. With it, he was more grandfatherly and less stern. "Thanks for all your help, Miss Hewland, and for the tip. He wouldn't have gotten far because he had no money with him, but since he's not familiar with the culture, it was dangerous for him to be out here anyway."

"Thank you for everything you've done. We all appreciate it."

"I think we're about ready to go. We can finish at the house."

She pulled herself away from the car. "It's not far. Is it all right with you if I walk? I'll be there in about fifteen or twenty minutes."

The officer nodded, and a minute later, he and the Cliftons drove away, Elias snuggled against Tina in the back seat.

"I'll walk you to their house." Brandon locked his truck and slipped his keys into his pocket.

"You don't have to do that."

"You look as though you could use a friend."

"That bad, huh?"

"I didn't say that, but unless I miss my guess, this incident has you shaken."

While time alone to process what had happened would be nice, so would spending time with Brandon. "Thank you."

For the first block, they strolled without saying a word. They came to a park, the squeak of rusty old swings filling the air as children pumped their legs, soaring ever higher into the sky. Oh, the freedom that had filled her when she'd figured out how to make herself fly like that. Adrenaline still raced through her at the sight.

She'd imagine she was flying to heaven to be with Mama and Papi.

"Let's have a seat." With gentle pressure on her back, Brandon led her to a shaded green metal bench a little distance from the playground. A brook babbled behind them.

Kayleigh twisted the ring on her finger, every muscle in her body tense. "I know what you're going to ask me."

"We don't know each other very well, but I'm a good listener. I'd hold anything you say to me in the strictest of confidence. You're rattled, and I hate to see anyone like that."

Did she trust him? Could she trust him? She stared at him, his long, wavy hair pulled back, a tiny scar above his light-colored eyebrow. Those very expressive brows. In the depths of his eyes, there was nothing but sincerity. Right? She couldn't always read people very well. "I told you I came here with my parents when I was five years old."

"I remember. You were even younger than Elias."

She drew in a deep breath. "Once we crossed the border, we used the last of our money to pay a smuggler to take us away, somewhere my parents could get work and where the border patrol wasn't."

"So that's how you got to Minnesota?"

She shook her head. "The smuggler put us with the luggage on the bus he drove. When my parents saw how hot it would be in the small compartment, they persuaded him to allow me to ride inside. That request saved my life." She choked on her tears. "My parents died in that cargo hold."

He pulled her into a side hug and allowed her to cry as she nestled in the crook of his arm. How long would she continue to mourn them?

After a good five minutes, her sobs ebbed, and she wiped away her tears and sat up. "Thank you for literally allowing me to cry on your shoulder."

"Anytime." To his credit, he didn't attempt to dry his now-damp red polo shirt. "But you talk to your mom all the time."

"I do. The authorities were unable to locate any family, so Mom and Dad adopted me, and I moved to Minnesota."

"At least you found a family to love you."

"I did. But I still can't help but wonder about the one that gave me life."

CHAPTER SIXTEEN

$\mathscr{B}$randon sat back and stared into the blue sky filled with puffy clouds. All around them, throughout the park, rang children's laughter. How Kayleigh prayed each of those little ones had a happy childhood. Hers had been wonderful, but there was always the lingering undercurrent of losing her birth parents.

Mom and Dad did whatever they could to keep them alive for her, but they had never met them, so they didn't truly know much to pass on to her. They loved her so much, and for everything they gave her, especially the gift of the Gospel, she would be forever grateful.

Once again, she spun the ring on her finger.

"Does that somehow play into the story?" Brandon eyed her ring.

"If it's the same ring, Mama always wore this. It was her most prized possession, and Papi understood that. It had been in her family for several generations. Even when there was very little to eat in the house, he never allowed her to sell it. He told her to always keep it. But by the time we crossed the border, we had run out of money. It had been days since we had eaten, and I was tired. Mama gave the ring to the smuggler in exchange for our bus ride."

She rubbed her hands together. "You can't imagine my disbelief when I saw it in the market. How many cat's-eye rings with chips can there be?"

"Not many. It's not one people usually think of as a fine piece of jewelry. My thought is that you're probably correct and it is the one that belonged to your mother."

"Now you know why I'm so driven to decode this engraving. If I can, I'll be able to connect with Mama again and have my past back. When they died, I lost everything. Mom and Dad and God gave me a future, but I feel like I can't step into it until I know who and what came before me."

"The future is what you make of the time and talent God has given you."

He was right. "I'll give you that point, but I'd still like that connection with Mama. I'd still like to be able to symbolically thank those who came before me for all they gave me and discover who took the ring from Mama before he gets away. Again."

"They never caught the smuggler?"

Kayleigh shook her head. "That's what still stings to this day. He made my parents get in that cargo hold, knowing how hot it was. Do they bear some responsibility? I suppose so. They should have known better, but they were tired, confused, and afraid. He took advantage of them."

He touched her hand, his fingers warm against her skin, soothing the hurt of her heart a tiny bit. "I'm so sorry about that. He should be brought to justice for what he did. Who knows how many others have died in his care? Or how many others will?"

"I don't like to think about it."

"It has to be tough."

She hadn't understood when she was young, but when Mom and Dad explained it to her when she was a teenager, it infuriated her. She stood. "I need to get back to work. If you'd like to come over for some spaghetti tonight, we can do a little sleuthing then." Where had those bold words come from?

He licked his lips, and she laughed. "I'm always up for spaghetti. What time?"

"I'll let you know when I finish at the office."

With so much to do, the day flew by, and before she knew it, she was on her way home after texting Brandon that she was leaving. He was waiting for her when she arrived.

"Sorry. It didn't take me as long as I thought it would to get here."

"No problem." She ushered him inside where she kicked off her sandals. Good thing she had worn them today, because she wouldn't have been able to make the hike back to the Cliftons' house in heels.

Once she had changed into a pair of leggings and put her hair in a pony-tail, she set about making supper. "I'm not great in the kitchen, so you'll have to excuse me for using jarred sauce."

"Jarred sauce?" He leaned forward on the kitchen island and shook his head. "That will never do. Where's your pantry?"

"Um. . ." She pointed to the left of the refrigerator.

"Sorry. I don't mean to be so bossy. My mom cooked every night and insisted that both of her boys learn, in case we ever had to live on our own, so I picked up a thing or two. I'm happy to do the cooking if you have the right ingredients."

"Go for it."

He rummaged for a while, exclaiming in triumph every now and again when he discovered an ingredient he needed or could use. At last he pulled himself from the pantry. "Got it. While I whip this up, why don't you tell me what you remember about this man?"

"Very little." She settled on a stool at the island. "I remember the bus was blue, which is my favorite color, and was very big to me as a five-year-old. He was hairy. That stood out to me. And very fair, which I had never seen much of before. That's about it."

He asked her a few more questions about her arrival in the States, and they chatted while he chopped an onion and some garlic and emptied cans of tomato sauce into the pot. Already way too comfortable in her kitchen, he found a spoon in her drawer and dipped it into the sauce, hemming and hawing, either from the taste of his dish or from trying to decide where to go from here.

Kayleigh's stomach picked that moment to growl. She tried to cover it, but that only made the sound more obvious. "Sorry."

He chuckled. "No problem. Dinner is ready whenever you are."

In a short time, Brandon had two plates, silverware, cups, and napkins set out while Kayleigh retrieved the Parmesan cheese and salt and pepper. Brandon prayed, and they helped themselves to the meal.

Only one bite was needed for Kayleigh to know she was in heaven. "This is delicious. Your mom taught you very well. My compliments to her."

"I'll be sure to pass them on."

"So tell me about your brother. Is he in the jewelry business too?"

"Jacob's a law student. Slacker."

She giggled. "I'm assuming you're kidding about that."

"It's an inside family joke. Anyone who doesn't work in the store is a slacker. We tease him about it constantly, but he's a good sport. He gives back as good as he gets."

"Sounds like a fun family to grow up in."

"It was. How about you? Any brothers or sisters?"

"Only child." Mama had had one other child, one who was nothing more than a fleeting image in Kayleigh's brain. That infant hadn't lived long, and soon afterward they departed for the States. Perhaps the loss of their child was what drove them to emigrate. "I often wished for a younger brother. Or older. Someone to protect me."

"Be careful what you wish for. Protective older brothers are the worst. At least that's what Jacob always told me. He got into scrapes. I got him out of them."

They finished dinner with plenty of nice chatter, and Brandon helped her load the dishwasher and clean the counters.

"I have a thought." Brandon hung the dish towel over the oven's handle. "Let's see if we can glean any information on the smuggler from news articles. This would've been a lead story, I would imagine."

"I have done a little bit of digging, but I haven't come up with much. For all my love of history, I'm not a very good researcher, and unfortunately, my story is all too common. Unless it's really a large number of people who die in the back of a semi, incidents like that don't garner much attention."

They sat at the table and Kayleigh opened her laptop. Brandon took over, searching for *death; bus; Laredo, Texas*; and the date they came.

The fourth result down sounded promising. With Kayleigh leaning over to see what he was doing, he clicked on that article.

> TWO DIE IN BUS INCIDENT
> *Two people, a husband and wife illegally entering the country from Mexico, died in the hot cargo hold of a Douglas Tours bus this afternoon. The bus was stopped by police after a tip that it might be transporting undocumented immigrants. The driver ran from police and has yet to be located. It's reported that the couple who died also had a child who survived the incident.*

Kayleigh leaned back for a moment while Brandon finished pursuing the article.

"Wow. You did make the news."

"I wish I hadn't. I truly wish I hadn't."

He rubbed her hand, relaxing her tense muscles and soothing her. His touch was sweet and comforting. At least she hadn't been alone when she'd read the article.

"What have the police said about the case?"

"As far as I know, from what Mom told me, they closed it years ago. They couldn't locate the smuggler, and that was the end of that."

"Sounds like they didn't try very hard." Brandon leaned back in his chair.

"Probably not. We're working to make life better and safer for those crossing the border, but people still die. People are going to cross. That's a given. As a Christian, I feel an obligation to help these people, at least ensure their safety until their status here is determined."

"I understand a little better about why you do what you do. It's because of how you got here."

"However I arrived, I did arrive. Thankfully, I was treated well and sent to live with a foster family who later adopted me. I'm one of the fortunate ones. But let's see what we can find out about this Douglas Tours bus company."

A good while later, her eyes gritty, Kayleigh shut the laptop's lid. "I'm afraid that was nothing but a waste of time. With the company shutting down soon after we arrived, there's not much information to be had." The article that mentioned her had appeared along with the search, but not much else. They had combed every source Brandon could think of to find out anything they could about the bus company both before and after they went out of business.

"And I would imagine that the police would have at least looked at the records of who was driving that day. They must have a name. That wouldn't have been that difficult to trace."

"Maybe my next step is to call the police and ask them what they know. I'm an adult now. Don't they have to tell me?"

"I don't know." Brandon mussed his hair. "We'll have to come at this from a different angle when we're fresher. With all the excitement over Elias earlier, it's been a long day. I'd better get going."

"Thanks for all your help, both when I was upset this morning and with the search just now. This isn't anything you have to do."

He glanced at his hands and yanked at a hangnail for a moment before returning his gaze to her. "Like I said, I'm a history nerd. This is interesting to me."

She walked him to the door, and then bolted and chained it behind him. Then she went around the living room and kitchen, switching off the lights and making sure the stove wasn't hot.

Just as she made her way down the hall to her bedroom, there came a crash from outside. Out back, to be precise.

The spaghetti in her stomach churned. She was tired and her brain was playing tricks on her. Had to be that cat she'd been feeding, that sometimes came by and wanted to spend the night inside. That was all. Or maybe Brandon had forgotten something and had come back to get it.

She was about to peek through the blinds on her patio door when her cell rang. Brandon. "I know, I know, you forgot something. I was just going to open the door and holler to you."

"No!"

At his shout, she almost dropped the phone.

"Sorry. But whatever you do, don't open the door. Don't turn on any lights. I think there's someone outside your place."

"Someone?" She gulped.

"A shadowy figure dressed in dark clothes. Let me put you on hold while I call the police. Don't worry. I'm in my car on the street right in front."

"Don't hang up."

"I won't. But I need to call. Unless you want to do it."

"No."

"Text me if you need anything right away. Okay?"

"Okay."

Her knees shook so much, she ended up sitting on the chilly tile floor, each breath, each heartbeat, far too loud.

And then her phone beeped.

She'd lost her connection with Brandon.

CHAPTER SEVENTEEN

*K*ayleigh sat in the dark hallway, staring at the phone in her hand. No bars. No signal. Another crash came from outside, this one closer to her bedroom, and she broke out in a cold sweat. She should move to try to get a signal, but she didn't dare. Whoever was out there wouldn't be able to see her here.

But she had to reestablish her connection with Brandon. She rose and, shaking her phone as she went, slunk up and down the hall. Nothing. Absolutely nothing. Once more she slid to the floor. She tried a text. It failed to send. She called and called, but it never connected.

She'd lived here for over a year and never had this happen. Not only was her Wi-Fi conking out, but so was her cell signal. She tried Brandon's number again. *Come on. Come on.*

Still no success.

They were in the middle of the city, for crying out loud. This shouldn't happen. At least he'd agreed to call the police. Hopefully he hadn't lost his signal too.

A tapping came from the patio doors. She stilled, holding her breath. Maybe Brandon hadn't been able to get through. Any moment now the glass would break. The intruder would gain access to the house. She spun the ring around and around on her finger.

Her hands shook so much, she dropped her phone on the tile floor with a loud clatter. She wiped the sweat from her hands and picked up the phone. *Lord, let me have a signal.* The screen was cracked. Apparently her sparkly case did little to protect her phone. But that wasn't important. When she glanced at the screen again, there was a bar. No Wi-Fi, but a bar. She dialed Brandon.

It didn't even ring before he picked up. "Thank God you're still there."

"I lost my signal."

"The police are on their way. Just be quiet and lay low. Other than *yes* or *no* to let me know you're okay, don't say a word."

"Yes."

"Good." He released a whoosh of air. In the background came the wail of sirens. "They're coming now."

Even though he couldn't see her, she nodded. *Thank You, Lord.*

Pounding footsteps came from outside as the sirens grew louder. A few moments later, someone knocked at the door. "Police. Miss Hewland, are you okay in there?"

Her legs trembled as she unlocked the door and opened it. "I'm fine."

"Do you mind if I come in?" He was young, no older than her. Maybe younger. She stepped aside, and not only did he enter, but so did Brandon.

He opened his arms, and she stepped into his embrace. "Thank you, thank you for not leaving me. I don't know what happened to my phone, why it cut out like that."

"Mine did too for a second, but I had already given the 911 operator all the information she needed. I was only worried that something had happened to you, that he had gotten in somehow."

The officer swept the beam of his flashlight around the open living room and kitchen. "Stay here while I check the rest of the place." Another swath of light shone through the kitchen window.

Kayleigh and Brandon stood huddled together, the top of her head resting underneath his chin. He whispered into her hair. "I was scared he had gotten in. This guy is stealthy."

"I was sure he was going to break a window any second."

The cop returned from his search. "I see no sign of him in here, no sign of a forced entry. What can you tell me about the incident? By the way, you can turn on the lights."

Kayleigh gave a shaky laugh and switched them on. She slumped into her oversized chair, her favorite, the most comfortable spot in the house, while the men took their places on the sofa. Then she related all that had happened that evening.

"Do you know who this might be?"

"A couple of years ago, I had an ex-boyfriend who stalked me. He left me hundreds of threatening voice mails and texts and sent multiple emails every day. He ended up doing some time, but I understand he was recently released." She couldn't even glance at Brandon. Would she see pity in his eyes?

"Do you have any information on him?"

She gave the officer his name. "I lived in a different apartment at the time. My landlord graciously let me out of my lease, and I moved here and changed my phone number."

"We'll check him out. Anything else?"

"That's it. I mean, I work in a job that some people don't like or don't understand, but as far as I know, no one has it out for me personally."

"And what kind of work is that?"

She told him what she did. "I've had dates that didn't want to continue seeing me because of it. When I go to friends' parties, sometimes there are people who ask me what I do, then avoid me for the rest of the evening. But those people, I've never met more than once."

He nodded and took a few more notes. "Sounds like this ex-boyfriend is our strongest suspect." He turned to Brandon. "And what about you?"

"I was in my car getting ready to leave when I saw movement outside Kayleigh's unit. I called her and then you."

"What size and brand of shoes are those you're wearing?"

"What?" A V formed in the middle of Brandon's forehead.

"Just the information, please."

Kayleigh slid to the edge of her seat. "You aren't seriously considering him a suspect, are you?"

"We can't rule out anyone at this point."

"He was on the phone with me the entire time I heard the noises outside except when I dropped the call."

The officer raised a dark eyebrow and noted that on his pad.

Brandon waved her off. "It's not a big deal. I'm happy to give them whatever information they need if it helps catch the guy."

A short while later, another officer entered, this one older and stouter than the other. "I'm sorry about your troubles, ma'am. It's hard to see much in the dark, but right now, there's no sign of him anywhere. He must have taken off. Do you have somewhere safe to go to stay the night? We'll be back in the morning to see if we can find anything else."

For the first time, exhaustion hit her. She must be relaxing, and it had been a long day. "My friend Paula doesn't live too far away. Let me see if I can get a hold of her."

"I'd be happy to drive you there." Brandon was already digging his keys from his pants pocket.

Kayleigh tried to smile, but fatigue weighed down the corners of her mouth. "Thanks for the offer, but I'll need my car to get to work in the morning."

"Then I'll follow you."

The older officer snapped his notebook shut. "We'll make sure that Miss Hewland gets to where she's going safely."

She couldn't allow Brandon to think she was ungrateful. "Thank you for the offer. I appreciate everything you did."

He stepped closer to her. "You sure you're going to be okay?"

"I'm a little shaken, but it's not like I haven't been through anything like this before. Though this is the first time I've had him show up at this place. I'll be fine, but thank you for your concern."

"If you need anything at all, let me know. I'll text you in the morning." He squeezed her arm and left.

She threw a few things into a bag and on still-shaking legs, made her way to her car. True to their word, the officers followed her all the way to Paula's apartment. This one, at least, had a locked lobby. Mom had told her not to buy that ranch condo because it wasn't secure. Kayleigh had laughed her off because Jason was behind bars.

Why was Mom always right?

She thanked the officers, bid them goodnight, then entered the building when Paula buzzed her in.

"Oh sweetie, I can't imagine what you've been through." Paula stood in her doorway and hugged her when she got there. "Here we thought Jason was a distant memory."

"Guess not." Kayleigh thumped to the soft blue couch in Paula's living room.

"Tell me exactly what happened."

Though she didn't give every detail, she sketched out the basic scenario. "That's about it."

"Hold on. Back up. So Brandon was at your house for dinner?"

"Yeah. And he's a pretty good cook." Kayleigh sat crisscrossed.

"How do you get so lucky?"

"Don't you remember Jason? The reason I'm here?"

Paula giggled. "Right. So that one wasn't so good."

"None of them have been."

"Except for Brandon."

Kayleigh couldn't help but nod.

"Did he kiss you good night?"

"What? No. We've only seen each other a handful of times. And tonight was business, trying to figure out who was driving the bus when Mama and Papi died." Though she wouldn't have stopped Brandon if he had tried to kiss her.

Her thoughts shouldn't even be meandering in this direction. Here she had a stalker after her, and all she could do was moon over some guy who was in it only to solve the ring's mystery. "It's getting late, and it's been a long day." She yawned, as if to convince Paula.

"Call in to work now and leave a message that you'll be a little late. You need some rest."

"Good idea."

Fifteen minutes later, Kayleigh had washed up and lay in the bed in Paula's spare bedroom, the one that doubled as her office. There was a single path leading from the door to the desk. Fortunately, it passed the bed along the way.

Though she couldn't stop yawning, she found herself staring at the dark-ened ceiling for the longest time. Nothing about this case made sense. Jason didn't have her new address.

The strangest part of it all was that the mystery man hadn't started showing up until she'd bought the ring. It could be nothing more than coincidence, but maybe it had something to do with it. She touched the cool cat's-eye stone. That decided it. On Saturday she'd take Brandon's suggestion, go to the Mexican market, and see if she could locate the vendor who had sold her the ring. Perhaps he knew more than he'd originally told her.

Still, sleep didn't come quickly. Every now and again she dozed but jerked awake the second her eyelids closed. She tossed and turned. This wasn't the best mattress, but it wasn't that uncomfortable. Paula's unit was on the building's third floor. There was no balcony, no door to the outside from this room.

She was as safe here as she was going to get, unless she went to Minnesota. Spring, though, was their busiest time at work, and she had too heavy of a caseload to take off. Besides, she couldn't question the man in the market if she was up north.

She pulled the sheet to her chin and stared at the ceiling, twisting the ring and rubbing the stone. Then, beneath her fingers, the stone moved. Wobbled, like it was loose. She'd have to take it to Brandon and have him look at it. Hopefully he could fix it or reset it or something.

She flicked on the light. Maybe she shouldn't take it off in case it got lost or stolen. But Paula wasn't going to swipe it, and Kayleigh would be sleeping right beside it. Tomorrow she'd put it in an envelope and take it to Brandon.

When she slid it off, she examined it. The stone was loose, but not in the way you'd think. Not like the prongs were worn or one was missing. This one didn't even have prongs, a fact she'd overlooked all these weeks.

It was almost as if the stone screwed into the setting.

What in the world?

CHAPTER EIGHTEEN

October 27, 1835

Fall's early dusk painted the sky with soft reds and oranges, almost like the colors of the tree's leaves that surrounded Josie and Chariot. Though nothing would be better than to stop and drink in the colorful bounty of the season, she kept moving forward. Not knowing when the Mexicans might attack the San Francisco mission, any delay on her part might be costly. Deadly.

She held Chariot's reins in one hand, fingering the smooth stone of her ring with her other. Did it wobble? Had it come loose from its setting? Creeping darkness and the urgency of her mission stopped her from examining it in the moment. She would have to study it later.

Could Father or John have done something to it? But what?

Another thought she couldn't contemplate now. Instead, she slipped her hands into heavy leather gloves and continued riding.

She carried Father's rifle with her, and the smooth butt, the hard metal, the weight of it on her back was small comfort. Over the years, she'd heard enough stories from the Indians about the spirits that occupied these woods. Some were good spirits. Some evil. Some that could keep you safe, others that would bring you harm.

Not that she believed any of the tales the Apache spun, but still. . .

She moved forward, making as little noise as possible. Even Chariot, despite his height and the fact that he could crush a human by lying on top of them, moved in silence. Though he was no small Indian pony, she had worked with him and trained him until he moved as if he were one.

As she made her way back to Mission San Francisco de la Espada, she stuck to the same path she had come with John not that long ago. The trampled grasses and crushed leaves made it easy enough for her to follow, even though she sat high astride her mount.

To even contemplate that the cottonwoods and pecans that formed soldier-like ranks around her might be out to do her harm sent a shudder through her. Never had she been frightened to move through these woods. Running Deer and Bright Star had never shied away from them.

She inhaled several deep breaths. No need to panic. That always brought trouble, or so Running Deer had taught her. Just as he taught her, she forced herself to control the speed at which her heart beat. *Lord, protect me.*

Soon, up ahead, the branches thinned, and the dim light brightened a bit. A short while later, she reined Chariot around the last of the trees and underbrush and stepped onto the prairie. The tall grasses waved in the light evening breeze. Now she could ride him as hard as she pleased until she reached the rest of their party.

Not too much farther, and she would be with Father and Charlotte again, surrounded by over a hundred better-trained infantrymen. Then nothing would be able to harm her. She'd been nothing but silly.

She allowed the pounding of Chariot's hooves to speak to her, to spin a poem in her brain.

> *The roaring lion attacks at dawn,*
> *The ravenous wolf at setting of sun,*
> *The trees conspire to drag me away,*
> *The rivers join forces to make me their prey,*
> *Ribbons of sunlight shall strike me at noon*
> *And slivers of moonlight slice through me at night,*
> *You are the swift arrow I set in my bow*
> *The straight shot to my enemy's heart*
> *To fell him like a mighty oak*
> *Once sturdy and strong*
> *Now nothing but soft green moss.*

She'd been so lost in the words that formed pictures in her head that she wasn't aware of a rider coming astride her until she caught sight of him from her periphery.

A spy's worst enemy was often herself. Her lack of attentiveness. Running Deer had told her she must always be on the alert. Never let her guard down. Never allow her mind to wander, as it was so wont to do.

Here it had happened twice on this trip. Had she been separated so long from her friends that she so easily forgot their most basic teaching?

And because of her lack of attention, this rider, one she'd seen before, approached her on his little black Mexican pony.

Manuel.

For several moments, she went cold all over before breaking into a sweat. How did he always manage to find her? To show up when she was alone?

He had no reason to be out this way. He must have been with the Mexican scouting party and followed her.

Thank goodness she didn't carry any incriminating messages on her person, though she knew a great deal about the Texans' troop movements. There was no way he was going to allow her to return to the rest of the party at San Francisco if he had any inkling that she knew about the troops at Concepción.

And he did. That was a certainty.

Before she even had a chance to grab Father's rifle from where she had slung it across her back, where it bounced with each of Chariot's hoofbeats, Manuel pulled Chariot to a halt. Though Josie kicked her stallion and urged him forward, pleaded with him to keep going, he couldn't fight the strong soldier slowing him.

Thank goodness she wore heavy leather gloves to protect her hands. He couldn't see the ring, though it did bulge.

"Ah, senorita, we meet once again." If possible, Manuel's bulbous nose had enlarged since their last encounter. His dark eyes glinted in the low light, and with the hand that didn't hold Chariot's reins, he pointed a pistol at her. "What good fortune I have in meeting you on the lonely prairie without anyone to defend you."

She spat into his face, the spittle dripping down his pockmarked cheek. "That's for taking an uncalled-for shot at one of the best men I know."

Manuel wiped the moisture from his face and sneered. "Ah, he must be your lover. I was correct in my assumption there was more going on between the two of you than you were telling me. Since that's the case, I can say that my firing on him was more than justified. You see, he possesses something that is rightfully mine. The day I took you sealed you to me forever." He raked his gaze from the tips of her moccasins to the top of her uncovered head.

Her throat burned. "I'm not an object that I belong to anyone but to God."

"That is where you are wrong." He hacked a cough. "In God's eyes, we are one flesh. Because of that, you can never belong to anyone else."

"It was without my consent."

"That matters little. You are sullied, stained beyond hope and beyond redemption. Who will have you, especially when they discover that you bore my child?"

Could it possibly be that her dreams were more real than she'd dared to believe? "My baby. What happened to him? He's alive, isn't he? Tell me where he is."

"Who are you to question me? Get down." Manuel growled the words. With his gun trained on her chest, she had no other choice but to obey. Her mind whirred, puzzling out how she could grab a few seconds when his attention wasn't so focused on her that she might be able to get a hold of Father's rifle.

She slid from Chariot's back, her moccasined feet making very little noise as she hit the ground. "What is it you want from me?"

"I want my ring. I saw you that day, running away from the munitions wagon where I dropped it and didn't have a chance to search for it. Now, which is more precious to you? Your virtue, which I've already stolen from you and will happily do so again, or that ring?" He was so close, the stench from the few rotten teeth that remained in his mouth almost overpowering. She held her hand behind her back.

Every nerve ending in her body sounded an alarm. Every muscle went on high alert. Like the rush of the wind, an idea blew through her.

She straightened, filled her lungs with as much air as possible, and screamed her loudest, most bloodcurdling Indian war whoop. "Snake! Snake! A rattler." She pointed to the dry, brown grasses behind Manuel.

With a puff of dust, he whirled. Her opportunity presented itself.

In a single, well-practiced motion, she flung herself onto Chariot's back, dug her heels into his hindquarters, and set off. She withdrew Father's rifle and clung to it.

Behind her, Manuel let out a string of curses. Not too much later, his pony's hooves pounded behind her. Still riding as hard as she could, trusting Chariot to keep her steady, she hugged him with her thighs, leveled the rifle at Manuel, and aimed just in front of his horse.

Then she pulled the trigger.

CHAPTER NINETEEN

Present day

$\mathscr{K}$ ayleigh sat in her office, which was hardly bigger than a closet. Her desk took up much of the space. With permission from her supervisor, she'd decorated the walls with photographs of roses, peonies, and tulips. Scattered across her desk were pictures of her family. Trips out west, Christmases, graduations.

Dad was in all of them. An ache filled her chest. At least he wasn't here to know she was being stalked again. He'd loved her with a fierce protectiveness, and he would have either ensconced himself in his favorite recliner in her living room with a shotgun or demanded that she move back into her pink bedroom in Minnesota.

If she got no last-minute emergencies, today was a day for paperwork. Oh, the joys of working for the government. A ceaseless stream of paperwork. Paula had encouraged her to call in sick today, but if she did, the mountain of forms she had to fill out would grow exponentially.

But no matter how hard she tried, she couldn't concentrate. She yawned and sipped her Diet Coke, a very welcome shot of caffeine entering her system. Even that didn't help.

She had shut the door to her tiny space to dim the noise coming from the rest of the office, not that there ever was much. That was nothing more than another futile attempt to focus.

The ring lay in an envelope in her purse in her bottom desk drawer. Like a siren song, it called to her. Last night she hadn't wanted to fool with it in the dark in case she broke it so it couldn't be fixed. This morning she was in such a hurry to get to work, she had scooped it up and dropped it into the envelope without so much as glancing at it.

Now she could no longer resist its pull. She opened her drawer and withdrew the envelope from her purse. The stone still jiggled, maybe more so than ever. She should have left it alone when she wore it. Maybe because of its age she shouldn't be wearing it at all. In any case, all of her turning of it must have loosened the stone.

She sighed. Lila would just have to understand. Kayleigh slipped the ring back into her purse and went to Lila's office. "I'm going to take a couple of personal hours. I heard a noise outside my place last night and called the cops, so it was late before I got to bed. Now I have a pounding headache." That much wasn't a lie.

Lila clucked her tongue. "I heard the message you left last night. Was it Jason again?"

"I don't know. The police are still investigating. I just need a break."

"Go ahead. You do look beat. Take the rest of the day. The work isn't going anywhere. If something comes up, I'll try to let one of the other case managers handle it."

"Thanks so much. I'll make this up to you."

Lila waved Kayleigh away. She darted from the building and, thanks to the lightness of the traffic at this time of day, was soon at Brandon's store.

When she reached the counter, she dinged the bell, and Brandon appeared from the back. "Good morning. I would have thought you'd sleep in today."

"A little too wound up from last night still, I guess, though I am taking some personal time from work."

"That's good. Hope you can fit in a nap."

"Do I look that bad?" There were bags under her eyes when she'd put on her makeup this morning.

"Not at all. In fact, you look as lovely as ever."

Heat bloomed in her face. "I wasn't fishing for a compliment."

"I know."

The door opened again, and another customer—or a true customer—entered. Brandon shrugged. "Did you need something, or can I go help this man? I don't know how long it will take."

"Go. I know you have work to do. I can wait."

He allowed the man to browse for a minute or two before approaching him. "How can I help you?"

The guy, probably younger than Kayleigh herself, wiped his hands on his jeans. "I'm looking for an engagement ring for my girlfriend."

"Congratulations. We have a wide selection. Has she given you any clue as to what she wants?"

"Not really. She's not that flashy. More athletic than girly-girl, if you know what I mean, though she does want white gold, whatever that is. Isn't gold gold?"

Brandon chuckled. "Why don't we take a look over here." He led the young man down the case to where the engagements rings and bridal sets were. For quite some time, he explained the different types of bands and diamonds and settings.

"Oh, I don't know." The customer turned to Kayleigh. "What do you think, ma'am?"

This could be kind of fun. Rings were her thing, after all. She wandered their way and peered through the glass, now covered in fingerprints. "If she's not flashy, maybe a solitaire? Or something like this three-stone one that doesn't have any prongs to get caught on anything."

"That's called bezel set." Brandon pulled it from the case and passed it to the customer.

"I do like it." The man examined it. "Would you try it on?" He handed it to Kayleigh.

She slipped it on her finger. While it wasn't her style, it was very pretty.

A grin spread across the man's face. "I'll take it."

While the soon-to-be groom paid for the purchase, Kayleigh wandered the store, studying the different styles of cross necklaces, the men's watches, and the rows of glittering diamond earrings.

And then she spied a small section of cat's-eye rings. She gasped. They hadn't been here when she'd brought her ring in. So why did Brandon have them now?

Once the customer exited and the store was quiet again, he met her by the rings. "Thanks for being a good sport."

"Anytime. I hope they're happy."

"That's an elusive quality in a marriage these days."

"You sound cynical."

He waved her away. "Just realistic. My parents have been very happy, but I know so many others aren't. Sorry for the soliloquy. I see you discovered my newest collection."

"I didn't think I'd find these in a fine jewelry store. It's not like it's a precious stone or anything."

"Yours piqued my interest, so I ordered a few. Not everyone wants or is able to spend thousands of dollars, though that would be great. These rings aren't easy to find. You never got a chance to tell me what brings you in today."

"You know how I have this bad habit of spinning my ring?"

He nodded.

"Well, I think I fooled with it a little too much last night. The stone is loose." She withdrew the envelope from her purse, opened it, and handed the ring to him.

After a minute of studying it, he turned the stone, and it popped out altogether.

"Oh no. I did break it. Can you fix it?"

"Well, it's going to be very tricky, especially with its age."

Her stomach dropped. "I can't believe I was so stupid and careless with a ring that old."

A twinkle lit in his green eyes.

"Wait a minute. You're teasing me."

"I am. But this is intriguing. The ring isn't broken at all. It was meant to come loose. It was a while ago, but I read a book about spying during the Revolutionary War."

"You are a history nerd."

"Anyway, it talked about how rings were used to pass messages, not only during the Revolutionary period and not only in America, but in various other times and places. The stone could be screwed in and out." He set the piece of quartz to the side and peered into the hole now left by the missing setting. "Oh yeah. I never thought I'd see one in person, let alone hold it in my hand, but it seems this one was used for spying. There's a piece of paper inside."

She leaned over the counter to get a good look. "There is. It's small, but it's in there. How are you going to get it out?"

"Very carefully. Hang on, and let me see what I can do." He disappeared into the back room.

During the time he was gone, she made several circuits of the small shop. It was all kinds of exciting that her ring was used for spying, but it only raised more questions. Why was the message in there after all these years? Apparently it was never delivered to its intended recipient. Had the messenger been discovered? Shot?

And how did it end up as the treasured possession of a poor Mexican family?

Brandon returned, raising some tweezers in his hand. "I come triumphant."

"You got the paper?" Kayleigh worked to keep the squeal from her voice, but some still seeped out.

"Yes. All folded up. Because there's the possibility of it being as much as two hundred years old, I'd rather not unfold it myself for fear of it disintegrating. Let's contact the museum and see if they have a conservator or someone like that who might be willing to unfold it for us. Is that okay with you?"

"Of course. I don't want anything to happen to it even though I'm dying to know what it says. Maybe it'll solve the mystery of where the ring came from."

"Could be." He leaned against the case. "Listen, I have something to tell you about my interest in the ring."

The way he said it sent her heart thumping around in her chest. Like he was about to break some really bad news to her. "What?" She drew out the word, buying some time to brace herself.

"We have a legend in our family." He rubbed his forearms, drawing attention to the cross tattoo. "It's about a cat's-eye ring that was apparently used for spying purposes. The legend has grown to include tales about Stephen Austin and Sam Houston. I don't know how many—if any—of them are true."

"You're kidding me."

"Nope. It belonged to an I-don't-know-how-many times great-grandparent of mine. According to the legend, it was stolen somewhere along the way."

The world around her buzzed for a few moments. Could it be that the ring had never truly belonged to her family? That they had come about it in some nefarious fashion? Her stomach went cold. Then again, what were the chances that she would buy the ring and, unbeknownst to her, walk into the very jewelry shop owned by a descendant of the ring's true owner?

Infinitesimal. She had better odds of getting struck by lightning while being hit by a hijacked bus at the same time. "Let's not get ahead of ourselves. As of right now, we have no idea what that paper says. It could be nothing more than the receipt for the price of the ring."

He stared at her and bit the inside of his check. "Sure. Of course, you're right. This could be nothing more than a coincidence. There had to have been more than one ring in circulation at the time. We don't know how many of them were cat's eye. This is where I think it's best to bring in an expert to help us solve the mystery."

Maybe it would be wise to not go along with the agreement. After all, she possessed the ring. She'd bought it fair and square, and he had no right to it. If she went along with the plan to call in an expert, she might lose it. The best way to hang on to it would be to turn and walk out of this store and never come back.

Then again, if she were in Brandon's place—and technically, she was, because she was seeking the truth to her family's legend—then she would hope the other party would do the right thing and bring the ring home where it belonged.

"Fine. Let's contact someone who knows more about this than we do."

CHAPTER TWENTY

October 28, 1835

Somewhere in the distance, a baby cried. Screamed at the top of his lungs, wanting his mother. Inconsolable.

The screams tore at Josie's very soul and knifed right through her because the infant was crying for her. The infant was right in front of her, reaching for her, flailing, face red and streaked with tears.

When she reached out to pick him up and comfort him, she couldn't grasp him. He wasn't there at all. She grabbed nothing but air. Where had he gone?

Now the crying came from behind her, a lusty wail, higher in pitch than before. She spun around. There the child was, her little love. Distraught and distressed. Again she went to the baby and attempted to pick him up. Again, she touched nothing but air.

Her child was gone.

The screeching now came from one side, then from the other. How could she console the little one when he kept moving, this tiny baby who shouldn't even be able to get around?

Wait. There the infant was, in a woven basket in the distance. Josie ran in the crying's direction, the hem of her buckskin dress slapping against her thighs. By the time she reached the child, she couldn't draw a deep breath. This time she would get him. This time he wouldn't disappear.

With a start, Josie woke from the dream, her entire body pounding, her chest heaving, sweat trickling down her back.

She lay on a pallet in a small, dark stone room. No moonlight shone in, so it must be the deepest part of the night. She took several deep breaths of chilly, damp air. Where was she? A light snore, a slight whistling, came from beside her. Charlotte.

It had all been a dream. A nightmare. One she'd had before.

Her child had gone missing. She couldn't find the baby, except that he cried for her. Every time she reached for her infant, he disappeared.

Was God punishing her for something, perhaps something she did when she was very young? Life had been cruel to her and had torn away from her those she had cherished the most.

Especially her child.

Now the child was dead, or so Manuel had said. Or had he? She replayed the conversation they'd had yesterday, before she shot in front of him and caused his horse to throw him. He hadn't answered her question about the baby. Josie sat up.

Did that mean that the child had lived? That her dreams held a kernel of reality? She couldn't give up, wouldn't give up. She stroked the smooth stone of Mama's ring and allowed it to comfort her. She'd let Mama down. Allowed Manuel to kill her.

But she wouldn't allow him to steal her child. If it took moving heaven and earth to do it, she would find her little one.

The stone on the ring wobbled. She slipped it from her finger. The stone was quite loose. She fiddled with it a moment more.

Within a few seconds, she had unscrewed the stone. She scooted closer to the door and cracked it to bring in a sliver of light so she could peer inside the resulting hole.

A piece of paper. Yes, Father had once told her that the ring had been used to pass messages during the Revolutionary War. That's why John wanted her to tell Mr. Austin about its past—so that he would know there was a hidden message in it.

She retrieved the cloth pouch that held a variety of small medical instruments and withdrew the pincers. Once back in the sliver of light from the doorway, she pulled the paper out.

As she read it, she sucked in her breath. This wasn't Mr. Austin's reply. This was John's note. Or at least part of it. Maybe there was a note about the Mexicans and their troop positions that Mr. Austin had kept.

What was written there brought tears to her eyes and warmed her from the inside out. Surely her face must be flushing. Good thing there was no one around watching her.

Dear, dear John. She clasped the small paper to her chest. He'd taken out Mr. Austin's reply but left this in here. Perhaps he intended for her to find it. With these words, the ring took on even more importance to her. She would cherish it all her days.

While part of her begged to run after John and discuss his words, she couldn't do so. Not right now when a battle loomed on the horizon, a storm coming with the morning.

But soon.

Charlotte stirred in her sleep, the pattern of her snoring changing for a moment before falling back into an even rhythm.

Once she had arrived at San Francisco last night, she and Charlotte had been assigned one of the small apartments that lined the mission's outer wall, each no more than a single room. All of the apartments on one side of the wall shared an adobe oven and a well.

What would today bring for John and the others at Concepción? When she had arrived here last evening, Mr. Austin told her it was too dangerous to ride at night but that they would leave at first light.

She could only pray the reinforcements would arrive before the Mexicans decided to attack. First light might be too late. But what could they do? Darkness had descended by then, draping itself around them. With no moon to guide them, they would get lost and be open to attack by Indians, by Mexicans, by prey.

How she had managed to get away from Manuel yesterday was nothing but God's pure grace. Somehow he hadn't managed to get a shot off in time for it to be in range to hit her. Thank goodness for her swift horse. Chariot had put a great deal of distance between them and Manuel in no time.

This was one encounter no one would ever know about except her and God.

Like a crescendo in a piece of music, the din of voices, clanking of gear, and neighing of horses in the square in the middle of the mission rose until it woke even Charlotte.

She sat up and rubbed her eyes. "Is it morning already?"

Josie nodded. The darkness had thinned by now, and soon the soldiers would ride for Concepción. All Josie could do was pray they would make it in time to help the small force that was there.

Pray that John would be safe.

Pray that they would win the battle as they marched toward San Antonio de Béxar.

"I'm going to see what the troops are doing and watch them leave." Josie stooped over to slip on her moccasins.

"You aren't going to go with them, are you?" Deep hallows marked Charlotte's pale blue eyes.

"I doubt they'll allow me to." This promised to be more than the small confrontation at Gonzales. This was likely to be a full-scale battle.

And today she had no will to spy. The dream had sapped every ounce of energy and spirit from her. It always did. If she could hold her child, even if only for a moment, cuddle and rock her baby, tell him of the depth of love in her heart. Pray for a beautiful life for her little one.

The ache in the center of her chest, the longing that brought her physical pain, never went away. As long as she drew breath, it never would.

Only John's note brought a bit of brightness to her day.

She slipped from the tiny apartment to the hazy dawn. At least four hundred men, all dressed differently, each astride their own horses, filled the green, Father among them. He hadn't slept in the room with them but had billeted with the rest of the company.

Mr. Austin must have spied her because, astride his mount, he disentangled himself from the rest of the soldiers and steered his mount to where she stood at the edge of the group. "Good morning. I trust you slept well."

"Yes, thank you." No need to go into details. She rubbed the ring that was back on her finger where it belonged.

"When we were on our way here, John told me you're the one who spied the dragoons on the opposite side of the river at Gonzales and that you're the best scout and spy Texas has. I think we can use you, especially since the rest of us will be busy fending off the Mexicans. How about riding with us to Concepción? I won't allow you near the battle, but I want you to keep your eyes and ears open."

John had said that about her? To Stephen Austin, no less. Her stomach fluttered, and she pressed her midsection to still it. "Of course, I'd be happy to do it."

"We ride out in five minutes, so you'd best get that beautiful horse of yours and be ready to go. We wait for no one." Mr. Austin clicked his tongue, pulled on his reins, and whirled toward the rest of the troops.

After informing Charlotte of her plans, which earned her a scowl, and asking a Tejano woman named Mrs. Navarro to watch after Charlotte, Josie raced to the stables, climbed aboard Chariot, and joined the group.

This time the ride to Concepción didn't seem as long. In no time, the twin steeples of Concepción's church rose above the prairie.

Mr. Austin sent her ahead with two other scouts, including Almaron Dickinson. A short distance from the mission, they hobbled their horses and continued on foot through a small stand of trees. Silently, swiftly, Josie moved through the woods and soon was at the outer edge overlooking the prairie between the mission and the river.

The Texan troops milled around, and the music of laughter floated on the slight morning breeze. She gazed at the men with her, furrowing her forehead. "Am I seeing things, or does it appear to you that the battle is over?"

The other two gaped, their mouths wide open. "I don't know." Almaron Dickinson shook his head. "It sure seems to be that way."

They stepped farther onto the open, grassy area between the mission and the river. At that point, she spotted the brightly clad bodies of several Mexican soldiers lying scattered about the field.

Holding her breath, she intensified her search. No Texan bodies that she could pick out, only those dressed in bright blue.

When she peered up, there was John, riding toward her. The air whooshed from her lungs. He didn't have a scratch on him, from what she could tell. "What happened?"

"We whooped them, that's what happened." A slow grin that produced twin dimples spread across John's face. "Some very wise scout told us to use the lowness of the river as a defense if we needed it. And we did. We were surrounded by far more troops, but from below the bank, we were able to get off good shots. I'm sure we had less ammunition than they did, but we used ours wisely. And ours is good, not that cheap Mexican stuff. One of their bullets bounced right off the knife in Pen Jarvis's belt and another off the Bible in my coat pocket."

Josie gasped. "You could have been killed."

"I was in no danger, I assure you, even without my Bible, which survived without a scratch."

Almaron gave a hearty laugh. "They couldn't shoot an elephant from ten paces."

The group joined him in his mirth for a moment before John sobered. "The gully saved our lives. For the most part, the bullets and cannonballs went right over our heads. Sure, we got a good shower of pecans they shot from the trees, but that was it. Except for Richard Andrews. He's been shot pretty badly, I'm afraid."

What could they say to that? To have only one seriously injured man in battle was almost a miracle.

John brightened a bit. "The Mexicans left their cannon behind, so we have another to add to our arsenal. They're on the run, though, headed toward San Antonio de Béxar. I sent a contingent to hunt them down. We'll send the rest when they arrive."

Josie dismounted and wandered around the field among the dozens of bodies twisted and contorted in death, still in the damp grass.

She examined each face, each body type. Would it be, could it be that Manuel would be among the dead, that his reign of terror over her was finished for good, that she could live the rest of her days in peace, free from worry that he would find her?

Then again, if he had been mortally wounded, she may never discover what had happened to her child. Manuel held all the answers. He had to be alive. They couldn't kill him.

"Are you looking for someone in particular?"

John's voice behind her had her clutching her heart.

"I didn't mean to startle you."

She shouldn't have been startled, but she was so focused on her task, so busy praying she wouldn't discover what she was seeking, that she had let her guard down. "It's fine. I should have been paying better attention."

"Can I help you search?"

"No." The word shot from her lips more forcefully than she had intended. She softened it. "No."

"Come on, it's me. Us. You know you can tell me anything."

Almost anything, but not this. Despite the words he'd penned on that paper scrap, she couldn't share this with him.

The blazing shame of it all raced through her. If that's how she felt about herself, how much more would he shun her for what she'd done. "It's nothing. I just wanted to pray for their families. As much as they are enemies to us, they have mothers, wives, sisters, and daughters waiting at home for them, hoping they'll return."

"That's very kind of you. I'm ashamed to say I never thought about it, and here I'm supposed to be a spiritual adviser."

She forced herself to turn away from him. Because if he found out who she sought and why she sought him on the battlefield, if he knew how she'd allowed Manuel to steal her innocence and give her a child, he would advise her of the destiny of her eternal soul.

CHAPTER TWENTY-ONE

March 3, 1836

MISSION SAN ANTONIO DE VALERO

A damp, chilly rain fell yet again, as if the earth were crying, weeping over the miserable condition of the people that roamed it. Curls of white smoke rose into the bleak sky from a few weak fires on the mission's main plaza, and the woodsy odor of them perfumed the air.

The dampness permeated the ground, the hundred-year-old stones, even down to Josie's very own bones. Clothes never fully dried because there was no sunshine or gentle breeze to hang them in.

Muddy puddles dotted the Alamo's western plaza, the one nearest the gentle river, though with the almost-constant rain, it must be swollen beyond its usual three feet of depth. As Josie dodged the puddles, she pulled her shawl tighter around her shoulders and wrapped her hands in it. She may never be warm again. Never had there been such a cold, wet winter.

Today was the coldest, dreariest day of all.

Two years ago today, she had delivered a child. Was that child alive or dead? If only she knew, perhaps this perpetual aching in her heart would cease.

Just to hold her child in her arms for a few minutes would be heaven.

She splashed through another puddle.

As soon as San Antonio de Béxar had fallen to the Texans in December, Father had brought her and Charlotte to the town. Only a very few of the fighters who had battled with such valor at Gonzales and Concepción and the other skirmishes throughout the fall remained. The rest had scattered like dandelion seeds on a puff of wind. Now, with the dwindling number of soldiers here and the arrival of Mexican troops from the south, Father decided it was safest if they retreat within the walls of the crumbling mission. John used the spacious church every Sunday for services and every Wednesday for prayer meetings.

Several times John had asked for her ring and then sent her east on missions to Sam Houston in San Felipe. With Mr. Austin's frail health, Mr. Houston had replaced him as commander of the Texas forces. Always Mr. Houston took the ring for a few minutes, then returned it to her. As tempted as she was to read their messages to each other, she never did.

Now she scurried to the small home William Travis occupied. He had taken over command of the fortress after Mr. Bowie had fallen quite ill. Hopefully this meeting he had summoned her to wouldn't take too long. As Charlotte neared the time of childbirth, she was able to do less and less. She would soon be hungry and ready for breakfast.

Josie knocked and ducked inside the small, smoky residence. The owner of the house, a man with the deepest, most piercing and discerning brown eyes, rose from the small table beside the fire. "Miss Wilkins. So glad you could join us."

Chairs scraped back on the rough stone floors as other men rose from the table. William Travis, with his pointy, angular features. Davy Crockett, his cheeks ruddy, a coonskin cap on his head. And of course, Father. In the corner stood John, a head taller than the rest, his blue gaze ever on her. She bobbed in greeting.

In the months since the battle of Concepción, when John had pressed her to reveal her secret, she had done all in her power to avoid him, which was not an easy task given the small number of residents now dwelling in the mission's walls.

Or given what the note had said.

She ripped her attention from him to those gathered around the table. The number of important men in the room set Josie's knees to trembling. They must have a critical mission for all of them to be around the rough wood table littered with papers and quills and pots of nighttime-black ink.

Father came to her side. "Gentlemen, if you haven't already met her, this is my daughter, Josephine. Not to boast, but she's the best scout and spy you have within these walls. If we need to send a sensitive message, she's the one to deliver it."

Josie worked to keep her chest from swelling at Father's words. He could have done everything in his power to keep her home and under his protection. In fact, he had every right to do so. And it wasn't because he didn't care about her that he allowed her to complete these missions.

Just the opposite. He loved her enough to allow her to use the talents and experiences God had given her to help others.

William Travis shook his head. "Seems risky to me." He strode across the room until he stood almost nose to nose with Josie. Well, not quite nose to nose since he was a head taller than her. Still, she didn't back down but stared at his chest.

"I can do it. I've been delivering messages to Sam Houston for months." Josie straightened her spine and bore her stare into Mr. Travis's face.

"Are you sure? Your Father tells me that you have something of a history with the Mexicans."

Any mention of her past sent her stomach roiling. She tamped down the bile that rose in her throat and pushed away the memories that exploded in her brain. So Mr. Travis needed to send some kind of communication to those who now surrounded the mission.

Still, she managed to keep her hands from shaking and her knees from buckling. "I do, but I can assure you that it won't affect whatever task you have in mind for me."

Mr. Travis shook his head. "I'm not sure sending an unchaperoned woman alone to the Mexicans is the wisest course."

Father scratched his chin. "I agree with you on that point. Perhaps we should send John Gilbert with her."

Though her gut had rebelled at the idea of going to the Mexicans alone, it did provide her the opportunity to perhaps get more information about the birth of her child. With John along, though, he would not only question her on the way, but he would also hinder her efforts at searching for more clues. "Begging your pardon, but Pastor Gilbert would be a target for the Mexicans, one man they can eliminate quite easily."

John leaned away from the wall and stepped into the small circle of candlelight. "This is my decision, Miss Wilkins. The message that needs to be delivered is of a sensitive nature and will require negotiation. I request that you go, as you may be able to aid me with my Spanish skills."

"As a man of the cloth, I believe you are required to tell the truth." No matter that her words came off as haughty. John had only requested her so that he could corner her at last and shake her secret from her.

"Mr. Travis will also accompany us."

At John's words, she clutched the top of the ladder-back chair. So he didn't want to be alone with her? Why, then, did she wither like a flower in the frost? This was what she had wanted. This was why she had avoided him all these months. He muddled her so that she didn't know her right hand from her left anymore.

Mr. Travis paced the small room, rubbing his arms as if to warm himself. "Very well. Even though I don't like it, even though it will require us to watch her as well as the Mexicans, you're her father, so if you don't have any qualms about sending her out, neither do I. She and John and I will leave as soon as possible."

If they were sending Mr. Travis and John, why send her along too? John must have made a persuasive argument for her to accompany them. Not that she was going to miss this chance to do more sleuthing. Maybe they believed no one would harm them if a woman was nearby.

After they went over what she was to say and gave her a few responses depending on how Santa Anna reacted, the meeting adjourned, the men dispersing to their various duties.

As she made her way to the door, John grabbed her by the shoulder and held her from moving forward. "Why have you been avoiding me?"

She kept her back to him so he wouldn't find the tears pooling in her eyes. "You are mistaken."

"I am no such thing. Each time I see you coming along one of the paths, you turn and hurry in the opposite direction. At the end of Sunday services, you make sure to have Charlotte's elbow and do nothing more than nod at me. What have I done to deserve such treatment?" The anguish in his voice was almost her undoing.

"Please, not now. We have a mission to fulfill."

"Mr. Travis is making the final preparations. We have some time to speak."

"The truth is too horrible to bear. You would hate me forever." At least this way, she was the one shunning him. How much more would it sting if he and the entire mission shunned her? She had made friends with the Tejano women. When they learned her secret and refused to speak to her and kept their children from her, life would be unbearable here, with no escape. Even Susanna Dickinson would turn her back on Josie.

And to lose all hope of a future with the man she'd loved from the moment she first met him on her return to Gonzales, that was a fate worse than death.

"Don't you know, Josie, that I could never hate you? Come. It's quieter on the far side of the mission, under the tree by the acequia."

He had used her first name. "Pastor Gilbert." She choked on her next words.

"I see the pain in your face daily. I promise not to tell anyone. I can be your friend, or I can be your pastor, but I want to help. The choice is up to you."

She studied the tips of her moccasins sticking out from underneath her dark blue gown. If she could but flee and never look back. Start over where no one knew her or that she'd been kidnapped. Yet the biting pain would always be there. She could never fly far enough away to leave it behind, even if she sailed to the moon.

Sooner or later, someone would discover who she was and what she had done. As a minister of the Word, John had an obligation not to disclose her secret, didn't he? "You must promise never to tell a soul."

"If that is what you wish."

"It is." Straightening her spine, she followed John to the spot beside the acequia.

This place had been her escape since they had arrived here. It would no longer be so but would become the place that she lost John forever. The place that she exposed who she was to the world.

What would he think? How hard would her condemnation be?

She paced in a small circle underneath the tree, her knees and stomach and heart all trembling. "That man from the river in the fall, the one you rescued me from, killed my mother and sister and kidnapped me. His name is Manuel Garcia."

"That was him? You should have told me. I could have taken him prisoner."

"I was so scared and so thankful that you had arrived, the thought never crossed my mind. Besides, I couldn't bear the thought of a fight between the two of you."

"Perhaps I could have spared you some pain. I remember how hollow and haunted you appeared when you returned. It's good to see you hale and hearty now, though still troubled in spirit, if I don't miss my guess."

"Yes." She swallowed hard. "Manuel not only took my mother's ring. . ." How did she tell a man of such a thing? "He stole something more precious."

"Her life and that of your sister."

"Yes that, but. . .something more." She toed the grass, her focus on its pale greenness instead of John's face. "Oh please, I cannot say it. It was horrible, the way he hurt me."

"Your innocence. That man took your innocence."

Tears fell one after the other, a waterfall down her cheeks. "I am a stained woman, and I will never be pure again. What I did was shameful."

"You did no such thing."

His voice carried such a stern note, it drew her attention away from the grass. His face was soft, his eyes were watery.

"I should have stopped him."

"You were a young girl, hardly more than a child. He was a strong man who had already proven himself capable of killing."

"Sometimes I wish he would have killed me."

"No." The word was sharp, and he grabbed her by her upper arms, his touch more than pastoral. "Listen to me. None of this changes how I view you. You did not give yourself willingly but under force and duress. To me, to God, you remain unsullied. What he did was horrific. You weren't complicit in the least."

Could his words ring of truth? But he didn't know the entirety of the matter. "There is more."

He raised one fair-colored eyebrow.

"A child was born of that union. Two years ago to the day."

John sucked in his cheeks. "Oh Miss Wilkins, you were so young and alone. You must have been terrified. Where is the child now?"

"That, I don't know. I am sure I heard him cry, but the midwife later told me my baby died. Every night, though, I dream of my child and hear him weeping and wailing for me. I think the little one lived and Manuel took him from me."

"So it was a boy?"

"I don't know." She worried the hem of her apron, balling it up in her hands.

"That still doesn't affect the way I see you. I only pity you more."

Pity was not what she longed for from John. The thing she desired most, though, was now surely out of her reach.

"That is why I went to the Mexican camp on the day of the battle of Gonzales. I wasn't searching for the ring, although that was a happy coincidence. What I was searching for was evidence that my child is alive."

"What did you find?"

"Other than the ring, nothing. Not a single thing. And that is what's most heartbreaking of all." She clutched her hands together. "I need to know."

"I will help you. Whatever you need from me, I'll give it to you. Support, prayers, confronting Manuel."

"No, no, please don't contemplate such an action. Doing so will only put your life and mine in danger. I just don't know where to go from here, that's all."

"I want you to be happy. That is all I have ever wanted."

"I'm trying, trust me. I find joy racing across the prairie on Chariot's back. That's my most joyful spot."

"So I see. But remember that true joy is only found in the Lord. I thought coming to Texas would satisfy the deepest desires of my heart, that it would erase the pain the manner of my father's death caused."

"You are one of the most content people I know."

"Only because I discovered the secret."

Josie leaned in. "What is it?"

"Give everything over to God. All your sins, all your hurts, all your trials and pains. He will heal and restore and bring you everlasting peace that surpasses all understanding. Place your trust and faith in Him. He will carry you through."

"There can be no peace for me until I have the truth about my child."

He drew her close to him, his rough homespun shirt scratching her cheek as he pressed her close, the top of her head not even reaching to his chin, her heart pounding out of her chest. He smelled of woodsmoke and dampness, but his embrace was tight. Firm. Sure. Secure.

She allowed herself to relax into his chest. For the first time in months, she was truly warm, both inside and out. His heart beat in her ear, its tempo a strong allegro.

She could spend eternity here. His breath brushed the top of her head and sent tremors to the tips of her toes. Was he as affected by their closeness as she was?

Judging by the rapid thudding of his heart, he was.

"You truly don't blame me?" She didn't move in his hold.

"No. It is unspeakable, yet I wish you had told me sooner. I could have helped you."

"And what if you hadn't believed me? I would have shamed myself for nothing."

"Never. Never." When footsteps approached, he released her, and she stepped backward.

Father appeared around the corner. "There you are. I've been searching for you. Please, be careful when you go. Even though there are three of you and this is a peace mission, I worry. Santa Anna has come prepared to fight. He may not take kindly to an overture being made to him."

"So the situation is that dire?" Josie leaned against the tree, the dampness of the rough bark seeping through her wool gown and into her very muscles. Where a moment before there had been a warmth that had been difficult to explain or comprehend, now there was only bone-chilling cold.

"We are surrounded, under siege with far fewer men than Santa Anna has with him. If we can hold out until Sam Houston arrives with reinforcements, we'll be fine. That is why we need to hold Santa Anna at bay for as long as possible."

She nodded. It was impossible to miss the fact that Mexican troops, still dressed in their finery, surrounded the old, crumbling mission. They shot cannonballs toward the mission every day. Her assignment today took on an added importance.

A few hours later, Josie and John set out on foot to cover the short distance from the mission to Santa Anna's position in Béxar, John carrying a white flag, the town now under Mexican control. At the last minute, the leaders decided it would be too dangerous to send Mr. Travis on this mission. He was too high ranking. The Mexicans wouldn't have hesitated to shoot him on sight, white flag or no white flag.

John adjusted the banner in his grip and walked closer to Josie. "Allow me to do the speaking."

"They sent me along in case anything went amiss, so that I could charm the general." She flashed him a saucy smile.

But that smile disappeared as all too soon they approached the Mexican encampment, triangular tents along the river's edge lined up in perfect rows like good soldiers should be. Camp chairs sat in front of the tents, along with foldable tables holding tin cups and pottery pitchers.

Josie wiped her damp hands on her gown, drawing in a deep breath.

As they closed in on the camp, the sentry stopped them, his rifle pointed at John's stomach. *"Alto!"*

John pointed to the white flag. Before the confrontation grew, Josie pulled her shoulders back and stepped between the two men, one tall and lean and fair, the other his complete opposite.

She shuddered, the world spinning in front of her, her breathing light and rapid.

No. She shook her head and forced herself to focus on the blue coat in front of her. This wasn't Manuel. Not all Mexicans were like him, though the way this one scowled at her from underneath thick eyebrows, he didn't care much for either her or John.

John gripped the white flag, and it fluttered in the slight breeze. "We have come from Captain William Travis with a missive for General Santa Anna."

The man snorted even as he eyed Josie up and down. She fought back the stomach acid that burned in her throat and struggled to keep her breathing even. "You are nothing but a bunch of ragtags. If your great commander wishes to speak to our leader, he shouldn't be a coward hiding behind a woman's skirts. He should come to us face-to-face like a man."

John came aside Josie. "And have you shoot him like a rabid dog? No, *gracias*. We will arrange a neutral meeting without weapons so that we can sit together like reasonable men and talk about our disagreements. Solve this before any more blood is shed."

John and the Mexican soldier continued to negotiate for a meeting for several more minutes. He didn't need her to translate. His Spanish was as good as hers.

Meanwhile she scoured the area for any sign of Manuel but didn't see him. There was no sign of any of the soldiers, for that matter. Turning her attention from John and the sentry, she listened for a moment. There it came. The sound of drilling, the bark of the commands sharp but with an even cadence, like the cawing of a crow.

John and the sentry's exchange faded to a buzz. The drill could end at any time, and the men would be dismissed. Time was of the essence, her chance to spy a little more. She might have mere minutes, so she had to act fast.

She returned her attention to the exchange between John and the Mexican. When they paused, she tapped on John's arm and whispered to him. "I have to use the privy."

One of his eyebrows shot up. "Now?"
She nodded and kept her focus on the ground.
"It can't wait?"
She shook her head.
"Very well. But hurry. And don't go far."
"I won't." She raced away as if the matter was urgent.
Because in truth, it was.

CHAPTER TWENTY-TWO

*H*eedless of the hem of her white gown dragging through the mud, even though she would have a devil of a time getting it clean, Josie raced through the trees near the riverbank, around the bend, and into the open and the Mexican encampment. The straight rows of tents mimicked the neat and orderly way the army moved.

Here and there, swirls of smoke rose from cooking fires, the fragrance of spiced meat like incense curling into the air, the wisps of sweetness an offering. Mud squished under her moccasins, sucking at them, and she slowed her pace to avoid slipping and falling on her backside.

All the tents were of identical white canvas, perfect little triangles, three ropes connecting them to stakes sunk into the soft ground. Boot prints led every which way throughout the camp, around and on top of each other, such a kaleidoscope of marks that it sent a headache pounding in Josie's temples.

How was she supposed to pick out Manuel's tent among all the others? She didn't have time to search all of them. John would come after her if she was gone too long. The men would return from their drill. If only she had thought this through better. She smoothed her dirty gown, ironing it with her fingers as if she could erase the wrinkles.

She opened the flap of the nearest tent and ducked inside. Two cots, the beds made with small pillows and rough, gray woolen blankets, took up most of the space. Rolled-up packs sat like little cats curled at the end of each bed.

Everything inside was uniform. There was no way of telling who anything belonged to, and she didn't have the time to go through each pack to try to determine its owner. There had to be some way to distinguish Manuel's dwelling and his belongings. But what could it be?

She exited the tent and surveyed the scene. Thank goodness the rhythm of the drill continued, but precious moments ticked by. Before long, John and probably the sentry would initiate a search for her. She had no choice but to hurry.

Just then a Mexican girl no older than Josie herself, her black, shiny hair loose and reaching almost to her waist, emerged from one of the tents down the row. Dressed all in black, she drew a black shawl embroidered in bright red and blue and yellow thread around her shoulders.

Josie hurried toward her. *"Perdóneme, señorita."*

The girl turned, her dark eyes large in her thin face. The wife of one of the soldiers? His captive? Josie bit the inside of her cheek until the metallic flavor of blood filled her mouth, and she buried the memories as deep as the soil of her mind would allow.

The young woman's face relaxed, as if she was glad to discover another woman among the troops. "I haven't seen you here before."

"I've just arrived, and I'm searching for Manuel Garcia's quarters. Silly me, I believed I would be able to find him without any problem, but everything looks the same, and I just can't discover which tent is his."

"Next row, third one over." The girl pointed in that direction. Strange that she would know just where it was without the slightest hesitation.

Josie had no time to ponder what that meant. *"Gracias."*

"I'm Teresa."

"Nice to meet you. I must go." Although it was quite rude, Josie scurried away in the direction Teresa had indicated.

After darting her gaze in both directions to be sure she wasn't followed and that no one was watching, she scrambled into the tent. This one was identical in almost every way to the one she'd been in before with cots, wool blankets, rolled-up packs. Which one, if either, was Manuel's?

She went to the left, and as she approached, the odor of cigar smoke wafted from the stained blanket. This was Manuel's.

Without thinking, she smoothed it out, the scratchy fibers rough underneath her fingers. Her skin, worn from years of hard work and scrubbing, caught on the bed covering as she lifted it. Nothing. No papers. Absolutely nothing. Not a single clue as to what happened to her child.

She knelt on the muddy ground to peer underneath the bed, dampness soaking through her gown to her knees. Because the light was dim, she lifted the heavy canvas tent flap at the head of the bed. Nothing underneath there but more swampy-smelling muck. With a sigh, she dropped the flap.

That left only the bedroll. Pulse pounding in her neck, her hands shaking, she picked it up. Too much time had gone by. John would be worried about her and might even come searching for her. She had to be swift.

Manuel had tied the roll with a knot, and she struggled, her hands trembling, to loosen it. At last it fell open, exposing a medical kit, some hard tack, a sewing kit, and a few other items.

Folded inside was an envelope. Without bothering to examine it, she tucked it into her skirt's pocket, put the roll back together, cinched it tight, and exited the tent.

"Dismissed." The drill sergeant's command floated on the chilly breeze. The men would be drifting this way any minute. The sands had finished running through the hourglass. Lifting her skirts, Josie dashed across the grounds, slipping and sliding as she went.

Teresa called to her, but Josie paid her no heed. She raced into the stand of trees and through them, brambles catching on her dress, ripping it in places. None of that mattered now.

A few moments later, she emerged from the trees, breathless, her hair sliding from its pins, strands of it caught in her mouth. Both John and the sentry turned her way, their mouths dropping open at what surely must be her disheveled state.

John was by her side in a flash. "What happened? Are you hurt?"

She waved off his questions. "No. I saw a snake, that's all, and it spooked me. Then I had a rather unfortunate run-in with a thornbush on the way out. Nothing that a little thread won't remedy." She smoothed back her hair the best she could, her hands shaking. Her parents had taught her better than to lie, and here she was, telling a falsehood to a preacher no less.

"Then it's time we were off." He turned toward his Mexican counterpart. "Mr. Travis will meet with Santa Anna tomorrow morning at ten to discuss terms. Unarmed. That is key. No weapons are to be brought to this meeting."

"The same goes for your Mr. Travis and any who accompany him. If we see so much as a flash of that famous knife Mr. Bowie has created, you will all pay with your lives for such treachery. Make no mistake about it, Santa Anna does not offer empty threats."

John steered Josie away with a gentle hold of her upper arm, both of them walking backward, him steadying her, until they were out of range of Mexican gunfire. Only then did they turn their faces toward the mission.

"Now, do you care to tell me what your little disappearing act was about?" John's voice was firm.

"I told you why I needed to leave."

"I am not buying the goods you're selling."

"But it's the truth."

"Above all, don't lie to me. I can't stand it, and neither can God."

She sighed. "I'm sorry." Right now, nothing pulled her like the need to get to her own dark, damp quarters, light a candle, and read whatever this envelope contained. In private. She prayed it was the information she'd been seeking for years now.

"This has something to do with Manuel and your child, doesn't it? You discovered information."

"I have no idea. I found an envelope in his belongings. It is likely nothing more than a missive home." She dragged in a long, deep breath.

John held her by the elbow as he guided her over a puddle, as if mud didn't already cake her boots and her gown.

"Thank you. I appreciate your kindness to me."

"Oh Josie." His voice was thick.

Before they could say more, they reached the wood picket fence that made up this section of the Alamo's crumbling walls.

"Welcome back." Mr. Travis called to them from just outside the gates, which he, Davy Crockett, and Father swung open for them. No sooner had they stepped inside than the men shut and locked them. They moved toward the long central yard where the leaders peppered them with questions.

"One at a time." John's voice carried over the din. "Actually, just let me tell you what happened."

This was Josie's chance to escape unnoticed, which she took advantage of. While John passed along the information about tomorrow's meeting, she slipped away to her family's quarters. Charlotte sat in the rocking chair that Father had brought with them, knitting something for the coming child.

"Gracious, Josie, what on earth have you gotten into? And where have you been?"

"I'll answer your questions in just a moment. I wanted to peek in on you to make sure you were okay, but I have one more item I must take care of. I will return in a few minutes."

Charlotte clucked. "Well, you're gone more than you're home, so what more should I expect? Surely not that you would be my companion." She frowned, and soon her needles clacked a steady beat as she wound the pale yellow yarn around them and pulled it through the loops.

As soon as she had her answers, she would make it up to Charlotte.

Josie retreated to a quieter corner of the mission where the acequia ran under the thick walls of the convent yard, a viaduct bringing life-sustaining water to those sheltered here, a spot where cottonwoods would shade the nuns on hot summer days one hundred years ago. On a large rock beside the water, she sat and drew out the piece of paper.

The writing was scrawling, uneven, and difficult to read. While she spoke Spanish, reading it was different. After a few minutes struggling to decipher the script and string the words together, she figured it out.

And what she read there stopped her heart from beating and her lungs from drawing in air.

CHAPTER TWENTY-THREE

*S*o you still haven't heard anything back about that scrap of paper found inside the ring?" Paula sipped her water and swiped another chip from the basket between her and Kayleigh, dipping it far into the bowl of hot salsa. This restaurant in the Mexican market made the best.

Kayleigh dipped in her own chip. "It's going to take a while. Brandon found this group at MIT that uses scanning technology or something like that to see the contents of old letters without having to open them. They've used them on letters that were folded in fancy ways before envelopes were invented, but it has its uses in delicate papers like this too."

"So that scrap of paper is in Massachusetts?"

"Sure is."

"That's kind of cool."

The waitress arrived with Paula's chimichangas and Kayleigh's taco salad. She took several bites, savoring the spiciness of the meat and peppers with the cooling of the sour cream and guac. "I'm just bummed that the ring seller hasn't returned to the market. We've been here every Saturday for weeks. On top of that, I'm worried that any information I discover, including what's written on that paper, might prove a connection between Brandon's family and the ring. That I might end up losing ownership of it because of this."

"Oh sweetie, that would be so sad. Whatever you need me to do, I'll do for you. I can testify to all the times you told me about the ring."

"Let's hope it doesn't come down to a lawsuit."

"So have you seen him since he found the paper?" Paula wiggled her eyebrows, which elicited a fit of laughter from Kayleigh.

"You are the craziest person I know. You'll do anything to get someone else married off but won't lift a finger when it comes to your own love life."

"That's my calling. What can I say? I also noticed that you never answered my question."

Kayleigh huffed. "Fine. Yes, I have seen him. We've had lunch a couple of times, that's all. He's nice, but now with this ring thing, I'm not sure I can trust him. What if I lose all I have left of my mother?"

"Has he said anything to you that might make you think this? Has he threatened to take the ring? Mentioned even wanting it?"

"Well, no. All he's said is that his family has a legend about a ring."

"You're being paranoid. I get that you're scared of losing it so soon after you discovered it, but your memories are what's most precious."

"Cloudy memories. I was so small when Mama and Papi died that I hardly remember them. Mom and Dad always did a good job of connecting me with my culture, but they couldn't tell me much about my birth parents. There are so many things I'd like to know but probably never will. If only I could find that ring seller."

"I can't imagine what it must be like to be in your place. I really can't. All I can say is that God put you in the family He wanted you in. Does that sound trite? Too much like a platitude?"

"A little, but you're right. Still, I can't help but wonder. Now I have what I believe is my mother's ring and I could possibly lose even that."

"You don't know that for sure." Paula wiped her hands on her napkin. "Don't think the worst until it happens. Have faith."

Kayleigh's phone picked that moment to ring. Brandon. More fodder for Paula. She answered it. "Hey there."

"Hey there yourself. I just got an email from MIT. I haven't opened it yet, thinking you might want to be here when we find out what the paper said."

"Yes, of course I would. Don't do anything until I get there. Give me about thirty minutes."

"Okay. You're torturing me, you know."

"Ha! I don't feel one bit sorry for you. Patience is a virtue." One she was having difficulty practicing herself right now. She wouldn't be able to get to Brandon's house fast enough.

She ended the call and turned to Paula. "I have to go."

"That didn't sound like work." Paula played coy.

"No, it was Brandon. He has information from MIT. I'm headed over there now. Want to come?" Maybe if she did, she'd leave Kayleigh alone about Brandon. Or any other man, for that matter.

"Wish I could, but I have to get over to church. It's Friend's Sunday tomorrow—you know, bring your friend to church day—and I promised I'd help set up."

"Okay."

"But text me as soon as you find out. I'm dying."

"Me too." Kayleigh settled her part of the bill and scurried to the lot where she'd parked.

As soon as she spied her little gray SUV, tremors overtook her. The driver's side window had been smashed in. She walked around. All four tires were slashed. When she peered inside, there was a note on the seat.

I'LL GET THAT RING.

She leaned against the car and took several deep breaths before dialing the police. Once they were on their way, she texted Brandon to let him know what happened and that she'd be late. Thank goodness for auto correct, because her message wouldn't have made sense otherwise, not with the way her hands were shaking.

All the while she waited for the cops to show up, she kept her phone in her hand. At least there was a steady stream of people coming and going from the lot so she wasn't totally alone, but who knew which one of them might be the man stalking her?

Brandon pulled up about the same time as the black-and-white police car. Not just one, but multiple ones. The San Antonio cops were getting to be very familiar with her, which was not necessarily a good thing.

Brandon made it to her first. He walked a circuit of the car, then returned to her. "I can't believe someone would do this to you. Whoever it is really has it out for you."

All she could do was nod. He hugged her. It turned out to be awkward as she stood with her arms at her sides. When the police approached, he released her.

One of the officers was one who had been at her house a few weeks before. Though he was middle-aged, his sandy hair and mustache peppered with gray, she was tiny beside him. Even Brandon was small in comparison. He looked to be close to seven feet tall. "Sorry to have to meet you like this again, Miss Hewland."

"Me too." While the other officers searched the scene and took pictures, she relayed to him all that had happened.

"So you didn't see anyone suspicious at any time throughout the morning?"

"No one. Then again, I can't say I was looking for anyone. I was just enjoying my morning off. When Brandon called me about something, I came here to get in my car, and this is what I found."

He pulled a pen from behind his ear and jotted a few notes on his pad. "Strange that on a busy Saturday morning, no one saw who did this."

"I have to concur." Brandon motioned in a wide arc across the lot. "Someone must have seen something."

"I did arrive pretty early. If they did it right after I got here, it's possible they were able to get in and get out without being seen."

"And what time was that?" When she answered, the officer made a few more notes. "The good thing is that this is a public area with plenty of surveillance cameras around. One of them must have picked up something. You need to be very careful. This may or may not be related to the noises at your residence. We'll check into it. In the meantime, contact your insurance company."

"And a tow truck." Kayleigh sighed and leaned against the SUV.

While the officers completed their investigation, she called in the insurance and once again got the information for which towing company they wanted her to use. At last the authorities left, and only she and Brandon remained along with those who were using the public lot.

"You didn't have to come all the way down here."

He shrugged. "What else was I supposed to do on a Saturday? The only things I had on my docket were doing laundry and cleaning out my sock drawer. Nothing that can't wait a few hours. Or days. Or weeks."

She couldn't help but grin. "You can go weeks without doing laundry?"

"You'd be surprised how rarely men wash their clothes. We just make sure they don't smell like sweat, and we're good to go."

Now full-blown laughter burst from her lips. "You're crazy."

"Maybe, maybe not."

The towing company had asked if she was in a safe location, meaning it would take them a while to get there. Since they said they would call when they were getting close, she and Brandon went to the market, got some water, and sat in the shade to wait.

"So, do you have that email about the note on your phone? Can we open it here?"

"Yeah, of course. I almost forgot about it with all the other stuff going on." He pulled his phone from his pocket and started tapping.

Here it came. Either it would be disappointment because it wouldn't shed light on anything, or it would give her a glimpse into the past, or it would favor Brandon and she'd lose the ring forever.

She forced herself to breathe.

He scanned the email, and she leaned over his shoulder to peek at it. She skimmed the formalities and got to the heart of the matter.

> *The paper, being so small, was difficult to read. It appears to have been written in haste. However, I believe I've been able to decipher it. The note reads, "SA, care for the woman I love. JG." And then there's an apparent answer. "I will. SA."*

"Great." Kayleigh's shoulders slumped. "All we've ended up with is more initials."

"But wait. Let's think this through. JG matches the initials on the ring."

She brightened a little. Maybe with a little detective work, there was more to this note than first met the eye. "So JG must be the key to solving this entire mystery. If we can figure out who JG was, maybe we'll figure out everything else."

"That's a possibility."

Kayleigh groaned. "You told me that cat's-eye rings were supposed to bring good luck. But so far, it's brought me nothing but headaches and troubles."

"Hey." He bumped her shoulder. "We got to be friends."

"How do you suggest we figure out who JG is? To me, this is beginning to feel like sticking your finger into a haystack and expecting to touch a needle."

"We're not too far from the Béxar Heritage Center in the courthouse. If you're up for a little walk, we could check that out. Maybe they would have some idea of who JG is."

She shrugged. Was the information she gleaned from this searching going to change her life? It wouldn't change the fact that her birth parents were dead. It wouldn't change the fact that she had grown up with the family she did and belonged more to their world than the one she'd been born into. "I don't know. Maybe we're on a wild goose chase. Maybe none of this means anything. These are people long dead."

"I thought you were a history geek like me. There's always an important story to learn at the end. Along the way, we might discover something about ourselves. That's why I love this kind of stuff."

"The best thing, the safest thing, would be for me to get rid of the ring. Then whoever is stalking me will leave me in peace."

For a minute or two, Brandon stared at the crowd in the market. Spanish mixed with English in a unique music of its own. The fragrances of spicy meat and frying oil mixed into one delicious smell. Bright colors from the *papel picados* swirled along with the colors of the patrons' clothing.

He took a chug from his water bottle. "I get what you're saying, but don't give up yet. What if you have some kind of connection to either JG or JW?"

She sipped her water to keep from losing her composure. The thought hadn't crossed her mind. Could she be related to the mysterious JG or maybe to JW? To know a piece of her past would be amazing.

Brandon had a point. Getting rid of the ring might not solve any of her problems. If she did, she might, just might, be throwing away her own heritage along with it.

CHAPTER TWENTY-FOUR

A slight breeze chilled Josie as she stood among the pecan trees, their bare branches rattling in the wind. She drew her shawl tighter around her shoulders. As she did so, the letter in her hand fluttered toward the leaf-littered ground. Much as she tried to capture it before it hit the damp leaves, she missed, but as soon as it landed, she scooped it up, lest the ink that formed the precious words blur and obliterate them forever.

She had to reread it to be sure she hadn't misinterpreted it the first time around. Once she had scanned the page again, air returned to her lungs with a whoosh.

> *March 3, 1836*
> *San Antonio de Béxar, Texas y Cohila*
>
> *My darling,*
>
> *These horrid Texans are delaying my return to you. We have them on the run now and should annihilate them soon. Santa Anna has vowed to take no prisoners. Today is Luisa's birthday, and I'm sorry that I'm not there for the celebration. But she is yours, to keep you from being lonely while I am gone. You will have a fine fiesta without me. Though you will cry because this letter isn't longer, I must sign off and go drill. Soon the blood of these Texans will stain the mud red.*
>
> *Be faithful to me,*
> *Manuel*

Luisa. That's what Manuel called the little girl, apparently his daughter.

Her daughter.

Two years ago, on March 3, was when Josie had given birth to her child. Her dead child, according to Manuel and the women who had attended her.

Her hands shook, and she couldn't draw in a deep breath. Her lungs burned and her head spun.

This was it.

Proof that she had delivered a little girl. Oh, how wonderful to know the gender of her child.

A daughter.

A daughter Manuel stole from her and brought to his wife. Was his wife barren? Was that the reason Manuel took Josie, got her pregnant, and then told her that her child hadn't survived the delivery?

Was that why, in her dreams, her child cried?

That had to be the answer. She heard the lusty wails every night because she had heard them that day two years ago. Her daughter had lived and was still living, someplace far away from here.

There was nothing on the outside of the envelope, nothing to indicate where Luisa might be. Likely Manuel hadn't had time to address it before the sergeant called him away to the drill.

Naomi. That's the name she had chosen on those long nights sleeping alone, Manuel snoring in his room across the hall after he had paid her a visit. She'd been far away from her own people, not by her choice. Mara would have fit better because she was bitter, but Naomi meant sweet. Naomi would have been a bit of sweetness during bitterness.

Once, in the deep shadows of the night, when Manuel came to her and before he could violate her once again, she had told him what she planned to name their child. He had scoffed at her and told her she was nothing more than a silly child. And then he took her by force as he did almost every night.

When he had left her, ashamed, humiliated, and unclothed, she'd wrapped herself in the quilt, shaking until its warmth, like a motherly embrace, had calmed her. Then she dressed, the cotton fabric slipping over the slight swell of her belly, and lay on her side, cradling her unborn child.

That was what happened every night. Her Naomi, calming and comforting her. No matter how she was conceived, Josie had loved her.

Loved her still.

She wiped those images away. What did Naomi look like? She must have dark hair and dark eyes, that much was for sure. Did the little girl inherit her grandmother's dimples? Her grandfather's height? Her mother's sense of adventure?

Mother had always told Josie she'd been a handful as a child. That was why there were so many years between Josie and Laura. But Mother had told the story with a smile on her lips and a light in her deep green eyes. Never, not for a single minute, had Josie ever doubted Mother's love for her, no matter what antics Josie had been up to.

Would she have been able to forgive Josie for allowing Manuel liberties with her? For giving birth to a child out of wedlock? Though John had assured her of his forgiveness and of God's, the reality of it was as elusive as a morning mist.

"Oh, my sweet, sweet Naomi." A well of tears that Josie had dammed for years sprang forth and soon wet her entire face and dripped from her chin. "How I love you. How I long for you."

She gazed through the tree branches to the gunmetal skies above. "Lord, do you hear me? Take care of my beloved daughter and bring her back to me. I need her. She needs me. A mother shouldn't be separated from her child. You have the power to return her to the place she belongs. I beg You to do that for me. Please, Lord, after all I've been through, at least I should have my daughter."

The thought of how she would explain her child to her curious family and neighbors flitted through her mind, but she dismissed it as fast as it came. First, the reunion. She would worry about the rest when that happened.

She leaned against the strong trunk of the pecan tree, needing it to keep her upright, no longer trusting her knees. And there, in the peace of this quiet sanctuary, she poured out every ounce of grief she had never been allowed to experience. Manuel had beat it from her. Then Running Deer had rescued her from him and she had returned home where she'd had to bury her child in an untouchable, unreachable part of her heart.

Once spent, she lingered for a while longer, washing her face with icy cold water from the acequia until she was sure no remnants of her weeping remained.

In addition to the information about Naomi, the letter would be of importance to Mr. Travis and the other leaders of their small band of soldiers. She needed to share it with them, though she wouldn't allow them to keep it. She couldn't lose this one connection with the daughter she had once believed dead but who now lived again.

Naomi was out there.

Josie would find her.

❧

John stood over Mr. Travis as he read the letter Josie had found. Then he gazed at Josie, his stare so intense it threatened to set her midsection on fire. He must be fitting the puzzle pieces together. "So that's where you went off to. Why didn't you tell me when we were headed back to the mission?"

She should have never shown him, or anyone for that matter, the letter. Josie swept a mud-laden strand of hair back from her face. "I didn't know at that point what it contained. There was no need in getting your hopes up if it was nothing more than a love letter back home. As it is, I'm not sure it contains anything useful. When Santa Anna raised the red flag over the San Fernando church, we already knew he had no intention of taking anyone prisoner."

At some point, the battle would have to be fought. Either that, or the Alamo's occupants would starve to death. Many men, including John and Father, stood to lose their lives.

Perhaps the women too.

Mr. Crockett nodded, his light blue eyes intense, even in the room's low light. "That's true, but now we know the red flag isn't an empty threat or an intimidation tactic. We need to be prepared for what is coming. We aren't in the best tactical position, only some crumbling stone walls and a few wood stockades separating us from them. We need reinforcements, and we need them now."

William Travis took the letter from the table where he had placed it and held it closer to his face, then peered at Josie. "Who is this Manuel? How did you know to go to his tent out of all of them?"

That was a question she would have to dance around.

Father, however, didn't feel the need to do so. "The story is long, but suffice it to say that he invaded my home and murdered my wife and my youngest daughter and took Josie captive. Without Running Deer, an Indian friend Josie had, she might still be on the other side of the battle lines."

Mr. Travis eyed her. "I don't know whether to call you brave or foolhardy. If you had been caught—"

"I know what the consequences would have been, and I was willing to take the risk. Just because I'm a woman doesn't mean I am unable to do my part for this cause. If I go back during your meeting with Santa Anna tomorrow, I might be able to find more information."

"Out of the question." Each of the four men in the room chimed in at the same time with the same answer.

John softened and touched her sleeve. "First of all, Manuel will know his letter is missing and might even deduce that you are the one who swiped it. Second, the sentry was suspicious enough of you today. If you go back, they'll all have their hackles up."

"And I suppose there's a 'third of all'?" She eyed each of the men. Mr. Travis continued to peruse the letter, as if he could glean more information from it. Mr. Crockett stood in his buckskin, arms crossed, studying her. Father scowled, never a good thing. She would hear it from him tonight.

Mr. Travis stepped closer to her. "Yes, there is a third of all. If they believe you are up to something, you could well endanger the meeting and bring this battle to a head far sooner than we're ready for. We have to hold them off until our reinforcements arrive."

From the appearance of the organization and precision of the Mexican camp, that couldn't happen soon enough. They were much better prepared for battle this time than at either Gonzales or Concepción.

The meeting broke up soon thereafter, and Josie hurried back toward her family's lodging. She hadn't gone very far before John caught up to her. "Wait for me. You're in a big hurry."

"I'm just trying to walk off a little bit of frustration."

He stepped in front of her, blocking her path. She blew out a breath. A confrontation with him was not what she needed right now.

"There's more to it than that, isn't there? Manuel mentioned a child in the letter. Do you think that child could be yours?"

"That is my child's birthday."

"Then you can be sure."

Those words said it all. It burst the band she'd tightened around her heart so she wouldn't get her dreams dashed. Certainty expanded in her chest until her ribs about broke open.

"I have a daughter, John. A living, breathing daughter."

"How providential that you discovered her existence on the very day she entered this world."

"Two years." She crushed the letter in her hand, then relaxed her grip so that she didn't ruin it. "For two years, I have believed her to be dead. Knowing the truth is almost more torturous than not knowing."

"Why is that? I would think you would be relieved."

"Because now that I know she is alive, I need to find her. I have to get my daughter back."

CHAPTER TWENTY-FIVE

March 4, 1836

Josie stood in front of the mission's church, the cool wind whipping at her skirts and sending dead leaves skittering along the still-damp ground. Just over the wall, in plain sight of the Alamo and all within her, a red flag flapped in the breeze.

The red flag that Santa Anna himself had raised—the call for his army to make the rivers run red with Texan blood.

Her veins turned to ice. That red flag spoke more than any words, any promise, or any threat.

They were ready to slaughter all of the Alamo's inhabitants. John. Father. *Lord, may it not be so.* She stood frozen to the spot. If only Sam Houston's contingent would hurry up and arrive. They needed every man they could get. A small group, maybe thirty volunteers or so, had arrived from Gonzales, but it wasn't enough, not with Santa Anna's bloodthirstiness. He was vicious, cruel, and vengeful.

Every day, the Mexican cannons chipped away at the unstable wall. Not much longer, and it would fall. She turned her attention to the packed earth beneath her feet. Would it soon be stained red with the blood of some of the men she curtsied to daily?

She rubbed the chill from her arms and turned inside the church.

Or what was left of it. All the pews had been removed. The frescos on the walls were fading. The building was almost one hundred years old, and it showed its age. It was more of a shell than anything. Yet this was where John preached. It was a place where the Alamo's inhabitants congregated each Sunday morning for worship, a place where they met God.

A God she needed more than the air she breathed.

She entered, her eyes adjusting to the dim light. Because the thick stone walls kept out the wind, it was a little warmer in here. At the front had been a stained-glass window. The men had broken it out, built a dirt ramp up to it, and poised a cannon on it, pointing toward the Mexicans' position.

Yet a calm sacredness settled over Josie, one she couldn't explain. God was here, no doubt about it. His presence was as strong and as real as the brown fabric skimming her arms.

She dropped to her knees at the ramp's base and gazed heavenward. A shaft of sunlight slipped through the opening where the cannon was and lit the earth in front of Josie.

"Oh Lord, what am I supposed to do?" She crumpled, covering her face. "I have a daughter, one conceived with a man I despise. Forgive me for my role in it and assuage my guilt. Cleanse me, Lord, cleanse me. Forgive my trespasses as I forgive those who trespass against me. How am I to forgive the one who stole my innocence and my daughter?"

Her daughter. Flesh of her flesh and bone of her bone. The same blood flowed through their veins. Maybe her little girl had Father's pointed nose. Perhaps she had Josie's own round cheeks. It would be wonderful if she had Mother's kind eyes.

According to the letter, Manuel's wife was caring for Josie's daughter. Did she sing to her at night? Did she kiss away all her scrapes? Did she tell her she had a mother who loved her more than life?

While she had never seen her in the flesh, she had carried Naomi for nine months. For all that time, Josie had nurtured that child. The thought of having a little one to love had made the time she'd spent in captivity bearable. At least Josie hadn't gone insane. She'd had a job—to give her child life.

She had done that job to the best of her ability. Manuel had snatched the result from her. What kind of despicable man stole a child from her mother?

Josie's stomach lurched, but she forced herself to swallow to keep from being sick in this holy place. She returned her gaze upward. "Tell me, Father, how I am supposed to go about finding my daughter. I have no idea where she is, who she's with, or what she looks like. I need Your help, Lord. I need You to point the way and show me."

She bent forward until her forehead touched the cool ground and her tears wet the dirt beneath her. "I beg of You, return my daughter to me, my precious little one. I need her. She needs me." Her voice broke on the last few words.

She could say no more. What she felt in her heart couldn't be articulated because it was deep and primal. God knew. God understood. "Please, please, please." She dug her fingers into the dirt, the sand covering her nails. Even her whisper echoed in the almost empty church.

Though she lay there until the shaft of sunlight moved on and she shivered, no answer was forthcoming. In heaven above, God remained silent. She had no plan of action. She was as much Manuel's captive now as she had been when she'd been under guard in his house.

Until she located her daughter, she would never rest. She would never know peace.

As the chill deepened and the light lessened, a soft touch to her back sent a wave of warmth through her. Moments later, she was in John's arms as they both knelt in the hollow church. She rested on his shoulder as she allowed the well of pent-up tears to release once more.

All the pain and hurt Manuel caused when he violated her.

All the sorrow for the mother and sister she lost.

All the anger at being separated from her daughter.

All of this spewed from her as John caressed her back and she wet his homespun shirt with her tears. At last her store of tears ran out. There would be more along the way, no doubt. For now she was spent.

She rocked back on her heels, gulped air, and hiccupped a few times.

John wiped away the last traces of her weeping and kissed her cheek. "Tell me."

"I fear never getting my daughter back. She's lost to me forever, John. Forever. I'll never hear her voice or see her smile. I'll never know if she's happy, if she marries, if she has children of her own. For one brief, beautiful moment, I had her. Then she was ripped away from me. I will never get her back."

"Never is a very long time."

She scooted farther from him. "You don't understand. She's part of me. It's like I am missing a leg. Those phantom pains are very real."

"I never said they weren't. I can't imagine the heartbreak you have suffered, all you have been through, all you have come through. But what are you going to do?"

She came to her feet. "Nothing." Her shout rang throughout the church. "Nothing. What can I do?"

He came to her and took her hands in his, but she backed away.

"Lord willing, there will be other children."

"None of them will replace the one I lost. None of them will ever be her."

"I know. I know." He took off his hat and finger-combed his hair. "I wish I could give you the answers you seek. All I can tell you is to have faith, but that seems so trite in these times when we may never know or understand the reasons He allows events to happen."

She forced herself to relax her shoulders. John was trying to help her. He just didn't know how. No one did. She didn't know how to tell them to help her. "If I could confront Manuel. . ."

"That isn't a wise decision. He will only feed you falsehoods. Do you expect him to disclose your daughter's location and allow you to go to her when all he's done is lie?"

Why did John always make such strong arguments? He was right, of course. But she would never admit it to him. "There has to be a way. I have no right to ask this of you, but I need your help."

"If I find out anything or have the opportunity to inquire, I will, but don't get your hopes up. And please, don't do anything rash. What if something happens to you and then your daughter manages to find you? You wouldn't be able to be there for her. You will have missed your chance."

She tightened her muscles to keep from running headlong into the Mexican camp and demanding answers from Manuel. John knew her too well, knew what her tendencies were, what her instincts were. She gave a slow, single nod.

He returned his hat to his head, the brim of it casting a shadow over his sloping nose and high cheekbones. "Right now, our focus, my focus, needs to be on the battle that will take place any day. If we take our sights from that for even a moment, if none of us survives, then what will become of your search?"

"You think it will happen soon?"

"Santa Anna has made his ultimatum and declared his intent. He is not a patient man, and he is not stupid. He will not sit idle and wait for our reinforcements to arrive. He'll attack while our backs are against the wall, when he has the greatest chance of success."

Her heart catapulted around her chest. "Do you believe he'll succeed?"

Underneath his hat's brim, John's eyes were unreadable, but he drew his mouth into a thin line. "They have the upper hand. We're trapped inside this mission. There's no escape for us. We're outnumbered."

"None of that sounds good. Why, then, did we enter?"

"Many of the men believed it afforded us the best protection. None of them foresaw Santa Anna coming and besieging us for eleven days now. It will be a miracle if any of us makes it out alive. While you're praying, offer up a few that Houston arrives with plenty of men. Soon."

"Oh John." She couldn't stand to lose him too. He was her rock, the only one who knew her secret. And Father? She'd be an orphan. If she even survived.

Once again, he drew her into an embrace. She relished his strong arms around her, his breath on her cheek as he bowed low to whisper into her ear. "I didn't mean to frighten you."

"It's better that I know the truth, know what to anticipate. Perhaps I can think of a way of escape." She gasped and leaned backward. "That's it. Why didn't this idea come to me sooner? We're waiting for other Texans and Americans to come to our defense, but we have Indian friends."

"Friends who won't want to get caught in a conflict between us. If the Mexicans win, they will have to live among them. No."

"Please, John, let me go and talk to Bright Star and Running Deer. Allow me to explain the situation to their father and the elders. If they decline, I won't push them any further. We can't wait here and allow the Mexicans to slaughter all of us without at least trying."

John heaved a sigh and turned in several circles, rubbing his chin and his shoulders. This wasn't the first time she had observed this behavior in him. It signaled that he knew what needed to be done but wasn't happy about the way he had to go about it.

"There is one condition."

"You want to come with me."

"Yes. Either we go together, or we don't go at all."

She couldn't turn down the opportunity to spend what would probably turn out to be an entire day with him or to introduce him to Bright Star and hear her opinion on the man Josie had loved for a long time.

"Very well. I agree to your terms."

In reality, it was a long shot. The Mexicans wanted a bloodbath. One way or another, they would get it.

CHAPTER TWENTY-SIX

March 5, 1836

The early morning mist had yet to lift, and the sun had not yet painted the eastern horizon with its pink brush when William Travis opened the wood gate for Josie and John to ride through. As Chariot's hooves pounded on the dewy ground, Josie's heart pounded in her ears.

This was one of the last remaining hopes they had to save everyone inside the Alamo.

She would have to remind Bright Star and Running Deer of their long relationship and how many times Father had helped them with food or blankets when the winters were long and cold. Of course, because Running Deer was the one who had rescued her from Manuel, the Wilkins family owed him a great debt, one they would never be able to repay.

The moment he had discovered her at Manuel's house in Béxar de San Antonio was one that would remain in her vault of memories forever. He had plied Manuel with several pieces of gold jewelry. Every woman in the tribe must have contributed a bracelet just to free her.

She owed Running Deer more than monetary repayment. She owed every person in that tribe her very life.

And here she was, about to ask them to save lives once more.

John rode tall and straight on his horse, the mare's hair as shiny black as Bright Star's. The tail of John's greatcoat flapped behind them as they galloped over the open prairie on their way to the Indian encampment. His gaze didn't veer from the course in front of them. He jumped a small creek, and she followed, the water in it gurgling below them.

Now he did peer over his shoulder. "Are you keeping up?"

"Don't worry about me." A gust of wind carried her words away.

"What?"

She spurred Chariot on until they drew even with John. "I'm right with you."

"Good. I don't want anything to happen to you."

Did she detect a slight bit of huskiness in his voice?

"Don't fret about me."

They continued alternating through stands of trees and open fields until they came to a larger river. In the distance, smoke curled into the now-blue sky, several wisps rising above the trees and into the azure expanse.

"Well done, Josie."

"I told you I knew just where they would be. I have been here so many times, I could find it blindfolded." If not led by the rising smoke, she would be led by the odors of venison and corn cakes cooking over the open fires.

After another few miles, their teepees came into view, a large circle of them gathered around a large grassy area where women with papooses on their backs squatted to cook the morning meal and warriors prepared their arrows for the day's hunting expedition. Here and there, hides hung on ropes strung between the living quarters, being dried and readied to be turned into dresses or trousers or moccasins.

As John and Josie rode into camp, the stares of all the people, young and old alike, fell on them, the weight heavy on Josie's shoulders.

Then, from the midst of the group, a young woman stepped out, her silky hair in a long braid. She too carried a papoose. Had Josie really been gone that long that Bright Star had gotten married and had a child?

Josie slid from Chariot and into Bright Star's arms. "Josie, you are really here. After all this time, you've come back. I almost did not recognize you. We are no longer children at play, are we?"

Josie wiped the tears from her eyes as she stepped back to drink in her friend's appearance. She had filled out and rounded out, much as Josie had during her own pregnancy. A light shone in her eyes, the light of love. "Tell me all about him."

A shy smile curved Bright Star's lips upward, and a dimple appeared in her cheek. "I married Soaring Eagle."

Josie laughed. "That scrawny boy."

"But he is no more a scrawny boy. Now he is a grown man, a proud warrior. He is strong but kind and loving. He takes good care of me and Blue Sky. He loves my daughter and me."

At the word *daughter*, a pain stabbed Josie like a knife to the heart. She swallowed hard so that her emotions wouldn't betray her. Instead, she leaned over Bright Star's shoulder and smiled at the infant with a shock of raven hair. "She is beautiful. She looks so much like you."

"Do you think so?"

"Of course. She's going to be almost as beautiful as her mother."

Bright Star nodded in John's direction. "And who is this you have brought with you? Is he your husband?"

"No. He is a dear family friend and our town's pastor."

"Ah, I can tell by the way you speak and your voice that you wish it to be more. You would like for him to be your husband."

Heat rose to Josie's cheeks, one she couldn't use the sun to explain away. "We will see what the Lord has in store for us."

By this time, John had hobbled the horses and led them to a patch of grass before joining Josie and Bright Star. "Hello. You must be Bright Star. I've heard so much about you. It is a great pleasure to finally meet you."

They chatted for a while as other village woman came to greet Josie. After a time, they drifted away to their chores. Life didn't stop for a visitor.

"Now you can tell me why you are here. Though it is very good to see you, I know you didn't come just to talk to me." Bright Star bounced, and Blue Sky's eyes fluttered shut.

"We need to speak to your father on a matter of great importance and a good deal of urgency. Already I'm afraid we've taken too much time."

Not long afterward, Bright Star escorted John and Josie into the largest teepee, the one with chevrons and deer and buffalo painted on the hides that covered it. She lifted the flap to allow them to enter. Seated on a pile of furs was a man Josie had remembered as strong and agile and capable. But this was an old man, his fingers bent, his hair gray, his eyes cloudy.

"Father, Josie is here to speak to you. She said it is very important."

"And who is it who has come with her?"

Bright Star made the introductions before bowing out. Josie sat in front of the chief and explained the situation to him. "I know it's asking so much, but without help, we will all be slaughtered like buffalo during the hunt. Our blood will run as theirs does."

John opened his mouth and inhaled, but Josie shot him a don't-say-anything look. The chief needed time to mull over her words. Pushing him would mean pushing him away. She nodded to him and then to John, and they slipped from the tent on silent feet.

As soon as they were outside in the bright sunshine, John grabbed her and pulled her back. "What do you think? Will they help us?"

"This coming from the man who didn't think it was even a good idea to come here."

John sucked in his lower lip. "I hope he doesn't take too much time to make up his mind. We could be with Houston, hurrying him on instead."

As if out of nowhere, Bright Star appeared. "Your horses are very thirsty, sir. I believe they require a drink from the river."

John eyed both women, dressed so differently yet so much the same on the inside. Then he harrumphed and left to check on their mounts. Bright Star wasn't wrong. If they were to return to the Alamo tonight, their horses would need to be fresh and ready to go. The day was wearing on, and it was anyone's guess as to how long it would take the chief to make his decision.

"Come with me." Bright Star dragged Josie toward a much smaller teepee. Blue Sky slept on a pile of furs, her little mouth drawn into an O as she sucked and smiled, dreaming a happy dream, the dream of childhood. A dream every human woke from far too soon.

"Tell me what happened. When Running Deer found you and brought you home, you hid away. You did not want to see me, and I don't understand. Why would you turn me away? You are my sister and can tell me anything." Even in the dim light, Bright Star's eyes shimmered with tears.

Josie fought against the rising tide of emotion in her own throat, threatening to cut off her breathing and choke her. "Are you happy?"

There came that slow smile of Bright Star's again. "Very much. At night, I lie in Soaring Eagle's arms, and I cannot believe my good fortune. You would say that your God brought us together. Why? Are you not happy? In your eyes, I can see you are sad, that there is someone missing."

"I'm glad to know Soaring Eagle makes you happy and that you have a beautiful family, but it will never be that way for me."

Bright Star crinkled her forehead. "Why not?"

For a long moment, Josie clasped her hands in front of her, squeezing them until the blood stopped flowing to her fingers as she stared out the hole at the top of the teepee where the smoke floated away on the light breeze. If she allowed the dam to be breeched, there would be no way of shoring it up again, of returning the water to the pond.

Then Blue Sky squeaked in her sleep. It was enough.

Josie allowed the entire story to burst from her lips like a spring overflowing.

When there was nothing more but a trickling stream remaining, Josie stopped, took a deep breath, and dared to focus her attention on Bright Star. At some point during the telling, she had picked up Blue Sky and had begun nursing her. Now she lifted the child to her shoulder to burp her, patting her back in a steady tempo. "I don't know what to say."

"There isn't much you can say. Unless you know where my daughter is, there are no words."

So Bright Star didn't offer any. Instead, she sat in silence with Josie, knee to knee on the animal fur, the pain radiating from Josie, the understanding flowing from Bright Star.

She didn't offer platitudes. She didn't suggest that time would heal Josie's wounds. She didn't tell her everything would turn out in the end.

The silence stretched on, even after Blue Sky fell asleep once more, her tiny hand clutching her mother's braid, an unbreakable bond, one that would last their entire lifetimes. A bond Josie would never share with her daughter because somewhere in Mexico another woman was forging that bond with the child Josie had birthed.

Yes, the child had not been born from love but from violence, but that didn't mean that Josie had not loved the life that grew within her. That unborn child had been with her through some of the darkest days of her life and had kept her from going insane.

And then had been ripped from her before she could even be placed in her arms.

Time marched along. Every now and again a tear or two leaked from Josie's eyes, but she no longer wept. At last Bright Star tucked Blue Sky among the animal robes and knelt in front of Josie.

"My sister, how I wish this had not happened to you. I am sorry you had to suffer such pain. You do not know where your daughter is. I do not know where your daughter is. But I imagine that your God knows where your daughter is. He sees her every moment of every day. That is what you told me you once believed."

"Very much so." Josie was hoarse from all the words that had spilled from her lips.

"Then you hold on to that as a man holds on to a tree branch when his canoe has tipped over."

Yes, God saw Naomi, knew where she was, what was happening to her, what she felt and thought.

But even that knowledge didn't ease the ache in Josie's chest.

CHAPTER TWENTY-SEVEN

*A*s night settled over the Alamo and Béxar, John and Josie led their horses through the woods to wait for the cover of darkness to return to the mission. Chariot snorted and tossed his head as Josie leaned against a pecan tree, more exhausted than she had ever been in her life.

John touched her cheek, the back of his hand cold but soft. "What is the matter? You were troubled even before the chief told us he wouldn't be coming to our aid."

She had never been very good at hiding her emotions. "I told Bright Star everything that happened to me when I was with Manuel, even about Naomi."

"It must have been so hard for you to see her with a child of her own. A little girl, no less."

"Yes and no." Josie stared overhead where the sliver of a moon rose above the trees into the not-quite-black sky. "I am happy for her. She is like a sister to me, and I want nothing but the best for her."

"But on the other hand. . ." John leaned against the tree next to hers, his gaze never leaving her face.

"On the other hand, it made me long for my daughter more than ever. My child and Blue Sky should be growing up together, the way Bright Star and I did, sharing secrets, giggling, imagining what the future holds for them. Not only have I been robbed of my child but so many others have been robbed of her."

Not too far from them, several frogs croaked their love songs to one another.

"You know I don't blame you for anything, don't you?"

Josie pushed against the rough bark and straightened. "What do you mean?"

"I was walking past the tent today when you told Bright Star that you would never have the happiness that she does. I didn't mean to eavesdrop. Deer hides don't hold in the sound very well. You shouldn't feel that way because of what happened."

What else might he have heard? Though she racked her brain trying to remember what she had said, the words had flown so unconsciously from her mouth that she couldn't bring them to mind.

He couldn't know how her heart beat faster around him or about the dreams she harbored deep inside of her, in a place where she only took them out when she was in private. Even then she refused to allow herself to believe them but only gave in to them to bring one bright spot of happiness to her dull life for a short moment in time.

"When any man discovers what happened to me, he will want nothing to do with me, and I refuse to lie to him or to present myself to him as something I'm not. If I were to marry, I would want it to be to someone I can share anything with. No man worth his salt would forgive me for what I have done."

"I have forgiven you."

Her heart fluttered.

"No, I take that back." He drew out his words, pulling her heart from her chest at the same time.

Of course he hadn't meant them.

"There never was anything to forgive. The person I blame, the man I would have to forgive, is Manuel. He is the one who murdered, violated you, and kidnapped your daughter. He is the one who will have to answer to the Almighty for his crimes. You were the innocent victims in all this—you, your mother and sister, and Naomi."

She turned to face the tree and hugged it, holding on to it lest she crumple to a heap on the leaf-littered ground. This couldn't be real. She had to be hearing things, or it must be a beautiful dream from which she wished never to wake.

Gently but firmly, he turned her to face him. "I do not look at you and see a sullied woman. I look at you and see a woman who is plucky and strong. A survivor. One who had to face tremendous adversity and, with the Lord's help, has overcome it. That is who I see."

"Thank you." The words rushed forth on a breath.

He leaned forward, his lips on a trajectory to meet hers. She hardly dared to draw in air. For an eternal minute, he hovered over her, so close that his breath was warm on her cold face.

And then he straightened. The moment was lost, evaporated like a light fog, never to return. It had been within her reach, but he'd snatched it back. Perhaps he thought better of what he was about to do.

"We need to get going. It is dark enough now for us to make our way back. Travis and the others need our report."

"Of course." With her shoulders squared, she grasped Chariot's reins, mounted him, and then rode toward the mission. John was beside her, but she didn't dare peek in his direction. Before long they were inside the walls, the gate shut behind them, Mr. Crockett and Mr. Travis and Father surrounding them, demanding John's attention.

She could stay and listen to him tell them how the chief had turned down their request for much the same reasons as John had said he would. She understood the chief's reasons. But it had been a long day, and her bed inside her family's cramped room called to her.

"Well, there you finally are." Charlotte's shrill voice shattered any illusions Josie may have had of enjoying a bit of peace and quiet. "You need to do the dishes. Thankfully, Senora Navarro and Susanna Dickinson brought over some food, or your father and I would have had to go hungry tonight. With my time so near, you can't be galivanting all over the place and leaving me to fend for myself. I need you."

Josie bit the inside of her cheek to keep from screaming. "I'll take care of it in the morning. I need to get some sleep."

"Don't you think we all do?"

"Charlotte, for once just leave me be. I'm worn out and weary. In the morning, when I'm rested, I'll clean up. And I'll be with you until your time comes. But for now, please let me sleep."

Father picked that moment to enter their room. "Josie, I've never heard you speak this way. Apologize to Charlotte this instant. I will not tolerate it. I have allowed you too many liberties. From now on, you will attend to her."

Couldn't he see? Couldn't he understand? At the moment, she didn't know up from down or left from right. "I beg your forgiveness, Charlotte. Good night to both of you."

Before Father or Charlotte could answer, she grabbed her blanket and quilt, spun, and fled out the door. She would sleep on the ground if she had to. The church, however, loomed in the almost nonexistent moonlight, and it was there she sought shelter. One of the small side rooms, the sacristy, held a few ancient pews. Here she huddled and at last was claimed by sleep.

⁂

Josie woke with a start and almost fell from the pew where she had fallen asleep.

"Everyone to your positions! Man the cannon and get her ready to fire! The wall's been breached! We have to hold them off as long as possible!" A chorus of shouts filled the church. Wrapping the quilt around herself, she stumbled from the sacristy into chaos.

Men ran around the church like mice attempting to escape from a large, hungry cat. There was no organization.

In the middle of it all was Father, trying his best to direct the soldiers where to go. She ran to him. "What's happening?"

"Josie, thank God you're all right. I've been sick with worry. Santa Anna has made his move. I'm afraid it's bad. Already they've made their way into the Alamo. Houston's men have yet to arrive, so we're on our own. Go to Charlotte. She's in need of you. Be careful."

While holding both her skirts and the quilt, Josie bolted from the church toward their room along the outside wall. Shots rang out in front of and behind her, from her left and her right. Men shouted, both in Spanish and in English.

The cannon boomed, sending her heart and her feet racing. She reached Charlotte in no time.

Charlotte's face was pale, and she bit her lip so hard it bled. "Josie, where have you been? Your father left me here alone, and the battle is going on, and oh!" Charlotte clenched her jaw.

Dear God, it couldn't be. Not now. This was the worst possible time. "Is the baby coming?"

"Yes. Yes. You must find your father. A midwife. Anyone. Help me. Please, Josie, help me."

When her own pains had started, Josie hadn't known what to do with herself either. She had only wanted someone by her side, to ease her agony and bring her through the ordeal. "Father is busy fighting the Mexicans. There is no midwife here. I am going to have to do."

Charlotte stared at her with wide eyes. "Have you ever delivered a child before?"

"In fact, I have." No need for Charlotte to know it was her own. She searched through her memories to recall what the midwife who had attended her had told her to do. "Breathe in and out, Charlotte. Stay as calm and relaxed as you can."

"There's a battle going on outside, and you want me to stay relaxed?" Charlotte screeched.

"Your focus now has to be on bringing this child into the world. Don't worry about what's happening around you. Focus on the babe you will soon deliver."

Though it was easy enough to say the words, it was much more difficult to live them. Each crack of the rifles, each reverberation of the cannons on either side drove home the fact that Charlotte was giving birth amid a battle.

Another pain had passed, and Josie mopped Charlotte's damp forehead with a soft cloth when a loud knock came at the door. Before Josie turned to answer it, Senora Navarro entered. "We have to go. The Mexicans have secured much of the mission. So many of our men have already been cut down."

Cold shot through all of Josie's limbs. Father. John. Were they among the dead? Not John. Not when there was that thin thread of hope that bound them together. Not Father. He was about to become a father again.

"Josie, help me up." Charlotte was struggling to get to her feet.

"Senora, you can see that Charlotte is about to deliver. I can't move her."

Charlotte grabbed Josie by the hand. "I am not going to stay here and allow those monsters to slaughter me. If there's a safer place, I will get to it. I just need a hand to stand."

As Josie assisted Charlotte to her feet, she turned to Senora Navarro. "Where are you going?"

"The church. I have sent Mrs. Dickinson there as well. The Mexicans haven't entered it yet. Right now they are making their way down the longhouse, searching for any soldier who might be hiding. We have to go."

"Let's hurry, before I have another pain." Charlotte lumbered through the door, Josie on one side, Senora Navarro on the other, her small children clinging to her skirts and crying.

Josie had a difficult time picking out the church, only flashes from firing rifles brightening the predawn hours. Twice she had to step over fallen Texans, turning her face away to avoid seeing their torn and bloodied bodies.

"My mother's quilt." Charlotte bent over as another pain racked her. They halted until the pain passed. "Josie, go back for it. I must have it. I must. It's the one item that brings me comfort in this life."

Senora Navarro nodded. "It's fine. I can get her inside myself. But hurry. And be careful."

Josie spun and scurried back to their small apartment. In the predawn darkness, she had to pick her way through their belongings until she found the quilt on Charlotte's pallet. A moment later, she was headed to the church.

Movement snagged her attention. From the corner of her eye, she caught sight of a man she knew to be Jacob Walker, his hands in the air. The Mexican soldier shot him, then bayonetted him as he lay on the ground.

Josie's stomach heaved, but she fought away the wave of nausea and entered the church, men shooting from the roof, the cannon firing from its place at the top of the ramp. Right beside it stood Father.

"George! George!" Charlotte called from just ahead of Josie, but Father didn't hear her above the battle's din.

"As soon as we get you settled, I'll let him know where we are." Josie followed Charlotte, the Dickinsons, and the Navarros to the small room where she had spent the night, her blanket still crumpled in a ball in the corner of the pew.

Senora Navarro shooed Josie away. "Senora Dickinson and I can help her get comfortable. Let your father know we're here. But be careful. Keep your head down."

Josie nodded and kissed Charlotte's cheek. "I'm sorry for last night. Don't worry. I'll be right back." Before Charlotte could reply, Josie was in the main sanctuary.

What had been a place of worship, hope, and new life was now a place of death. Bodies littered the floor, and the ground had indeed turned red from the men's blood.

John. Where was he? She scanned the room as fast as possible, but she didn't see him. Then again, it was difficult to pick out anyone. With the height advantage John had, though, he should be easy to spot. He must not be in here.

God, wherever he is, keep him safe. I can't lose him.

Just as she started toward Father, he clutched his chest.

Fell.

Rolled down the ramp.

A streak of red in the dirt marked where he had fallen.

CHAPTER TWENTY-EIGHT

From somewhere behind Josie came a scream. Possibly Charlotte. Or had the scream come from Josie herself?

Whoever it was, she propelled herself forward, her sight never wavering from Father. She squinted to discern the rising and falling of his chest. It was impossible to tell from this distance. He lay so still, so unmoving.

Just like Mother.

Just like Laura.

"No! No!" This time the scream did rip from her own raw, tender throat.

Hot pain seared the back of her leg, but she ignored it, closing the distance between her and Father.

As soon as she reached him, she dropped to her knees. "Father, can you hear me? Please tell me you're going to be fine." She glanced at the crimson circle in the middle of his chest and pressed her hand against it, much as she had with John, as if that could stop the flow of blood. Father's blood loss, however, was so much greater than John's.

He reached up and cupped her cheek. She turned to him to find his eyes open though hazy with pain. "My Jo. How I love you."

"Save your strength, Father. We'll get you to the room and take care of you there. Charlotte is laboring, and you will soon have another child. That child deserves to know you."

"Tell them I love them."

"You tell them. That's your job, not mine."

"Don't argue." He closed his eyes and winced before continuing. "Just tell them."

"Don't leave me. Father, I can't go on without you. Mother and Laura have left me. I will be all alone."

"Have faith, child. Protect them. I can't. It will soon be over. I pray they spare you."

"No, Father, no." Sobs shook her shoulders. She touched her forehead to his, her tears dripping onto his face.

"John."

"I don't know where he is. I haven't seen him since last night."

"Oh Josephine. If I could but stay."

"Then do. You don't have to leave."

"Do not sorrow for me. I go to a better place. This pain is temporary." His breathing grew shallower and shallower. "That joy is eternal."

"Father?"

"Hm?"

"I love you."

"Mother's ring."

"I have it here." She touched it to be sure. Yes, it still resided on her finger.

"It will be important."

"I know that. I know. I'm never going to take it off. Just say you won't leave."

"Must. Go. Jesus."

His breaths ceased, and his eyes glazed over.

Josie lifted her gaze to the ceiling, tears streaming down her cheeks and sliding from her chin. "God, why have you taken them all from me?" She screamed so the Lord couldn't help but hear her. "Couldn't you have left me one? Just one? That's all I ask. Is it too much?"

"Get back to the room." A very young soldier, one she didn't recall, pointed to the side.

"My father."

"Nothing more is to be done for him. Go, before you end up like him. Like we are all going to end up. And get your leg looked at."

Not until that moment did she have any pain. Her skirts had hiked up as she knelt beside Father, and her own spot of crimson stained her dark stocking. As soon as the soldier mentioned it, though, she sucked in her breath at the stinging of it. "I've been shot."

"Just a nick, but have it examined. Now get going." He helped her to her feet, and when she swayed he steadied her.

"Thank you." She hadn't gone more than two steps before a bullet whistled past her ear. She spun around. The young soldier, struck in the head, collapsed at her feet.

Biting her hand, she held back her scream and dashed for the relative safety of the sacristy.

Just as she entered, the wail of a child filled the small chamber, now crowded with women and children, including Susanna and Angelina Dickinson and the Navarros, and one dark-skinned enslaved man whom Josie recognized as Joe.

She pushed her way through the space until she was at Charlotte's side. Sweat dripped down her beaming face. "It's a boy, Josie, a boy. George Jr. What do you think? Your father is going to be so pleased. He has waited a long time to have an heir to carry on his name."

Senora Navarro handed a bundle wrapped in Josie's blanket to the new mother. "In all my days, I have never seen a baby come so fast, especially a first one. But the stress from the battle must have moved the delivery along."

"Are they both well?" Josie asked the question even though both Charlotte's voice and the child's cry had been strong.

"They are, *alabado sea el Señor*. Under such conditions, it's nothing but a miracle." Senora Navarro tucked Josie's quilt around Charlotte.

How could they praise the Lord under such circumstances?

"Where is your father?" Charlotte cradled the infant. "He must come meet his son as soon as possible."

Josie scrubbed her face. How did she go about breaking the news?

Charlotte raised herself on one elbow. "Your hands. They're red. Is that blood?" Her screech returned.

Josie nodded.

"Tell me that's not your father's blood."

Josie stood mute.

"Tell me. Tell me now."

"If only I could." Her airway closed, and she couldn't speak another word.

Charlotte's wails now matched those of her son. Pain pounded behind Josie's eyes, and she covered her ears. Too much noise. Too much. *Make it stop, Father. Please, make it stop. Let me wake up in my bed and discover this was nothing but a horrible, horrible nightmare. Please.*

But when she opened her eyes, the scene in front of her hadn't changed. The air stank of gunpowder and blood and death. The shooting continued. The cannon no longer boomed. With no one to man it, it had fallen silent.

Men's tormented screams seeped through the damp church walls, more chilling than even the weather. The retort of guns lessened.

The battle was coming to an end.

"In here." The words, spoken in Spanish, held a certain timbre to them. One that sent shivers up and down Josie's spine.

Manuel.

Let him take her. Let him kill her. She no longer had the energy or the will to fight him. Not now that everything she had ever held dear had been stripped from her.

He stood in the entryway, arms akimbo, like a conquering hero from Ancient Greece. An uneven grin revealed his mouth, almost devoid of teeth, but the smile didn't reach his dark, brooding eyes. "Well, what do we have here?"

Josie slunk behind Joe. The man was large enough to hide a cow behind. But she hadn't been fast enough, because Manuel slithered his way through the women, their children clinging to their skirts like burrs, and right up to the man.

He attempted to push Joe out of the way, but Joe was having none of it. He planted his feet to the ground like a live oak that had drilled its roots into a riverbank.

"That's right. You probably don't understand me. Here's a message that won't need any translation." Manuel punched Joe in the nose with a crack that churned Josie's stomach, followed by a punch to his gut.

Joe doubled over, exposing Josie.

"Aha, you little vixen. I thought I saw you try to hide from me. Don't you know you will never be rid of me? I will haunt you for the rest of your days."

"You have killed my entire family. You have stolen everything precious to me. Do with me what you will. I no longer fear you or what harm you can inflict. You can hurt me no more than you already have, even if you take my life too."

The room had fallen silent. Even from outside, the shooting had ceased. The raucous cawing of several crows was the only sound. Josie held her breath, and the rest of the world did so with her.

Manuel stepped closer, and she backed into the corner. There was no means of escape. Death was her only way out. She would embrace it and welcome it. Her chest heaved.

"My little bird." He stroked her cheek, his touch so different than John's. Yes, both elicited shivers, but these were not of pleasure. She could not revile the devil more than she reviled Manuel in that moment. "I would never hurt you."

"You wish to destroy me piece by piece, taking one thing away from me and then another and another until I'm left with nothing. You have even stolen my daughter from me. Sí, I know about what you did. Where is she? Just tell me that, and then you can kill me. All I want to know is where she is. Is she happy? Is she loved?" The Spanish-speaking women in the room now knew her secret, but that mattered little to her in the moment.

"You are crafty and wily, I will give you that."

Joe rose to his feet. Manuel must have caught sight of him out of the corner of his eye, for he aimed his bayonet at Joe's stomach. Josie motioned for him to back away.

"You didn't think you could hide the truth from me forever, did you?"

"You will never have her. You don't deserve her. She is payment for what your family stole from me." Manuel spit on the ground.

If the idea weren't so ludicrous and preposterous, Josie would have laughed out loud. Instead, she coughed.

"And I have killed your lover."

John? Josie's breath whooshed from her lungs as if he had also punched her in the stomach.

"Sí. I had the great pleasure of slicing him with my blade. He died a coward, cursing God."

Josie's knees went weak, and she slumped to the ground. John curse God? How could he do such a thing? His faith had been so strong.

"You do have one item I still want from you."

There was nothing more Manuel could take. He must be bluffing because Josie no longer had anyone. When he and those with him had killed Father and John, he had snuffed the life from her body too.

Manuel reached down and wrenched the ring from Josie's finger. Mother's ring, the cat's-eye one that Father told her she should never take off and never lose. The last promise she had made to him.

"No. Give that back." She lunged for the Mexican.

He jumped out of her reach and strode for the door. Once he reached the room's threshold, he turned around and stared straight into Josie's eyes. Dark red blood spattered his pale blue coat and not-very-white pants. Gooseflesh broke out on her arms.

Was it John's blood?

He waved the ring in the air. "This was the prize all along. You never knew it, but this ring is what I needed. Not your mother's life, though it brought a certain satisfaction to watch it seep from her. Not your purity, though there was a great deal of enjoyment in taking that from you. No, what I wanted, needed, had to have, was this ring. Your parents befriended and trusted the wrong person. My cousin entrusted this ring to them for safekeeping, and your mother, so bound by her honor, refused to give it to me. But this is the key to unlocking what I've wanted for a very, very long time."

"What? What is it that drove you to kill to possess it?"

Manuel sneered. "This ring that looks so innocent, so unbecoming, so unassuming, belongs to the rightful heir of the Garcia fortune. Without it, I could not claim the vast wealth that is mine. Not my cousin's but mine. When I took it the first time, I was able to claim my inheritance. With it once again in my possession, the money will be mine forever. I will never tell you Luisa's location. In this, I have my final triumph."

When he left, it was as if he removed all the air from the room with him. Time hung suspended. Then in a rush of sound, color, smell, it all came back.

Josie clutched her stomach. Joe and Senora Navarro and Susanna Dickinson surrounded her.

"Get her a drink." Susanna's words might as well have come from deep inside a cave.

One of the little children brought a canteen with cool water, and she sipped from it, unable to swallow, and most of it dribbled down the front of her. Joe knelt in front of her and patted her cheeks with hands the size of bear claws. "You all right, Missy? I don't understand him, but he shore is a bad man. That's for shore."

"I'm fine. Please, I just need a little air."

Senora Navarro shooed the crowd, which included many of her children, back several paces. Josie managed to draw several lungfuls of oxygen and revive herself a bit.

For a while, they all sat in the room in silence. Were they the only ones left alive in the entire mission? Had Santa Anna indeed made good on his threat and slaughtered everyone?

John. Josie shuddered. Her one hope, her one chance at happiness in this life. Little did she know when she left the meeting that would be the last time she would ever see him.

After a time, Senora Navarro came and dressed the wound on Josie's calf. It throbbed, but the pain in her heart far outweighed it.

There would never be sunshine in her life again. Not now that she had nothing left on this earth.

CHAPTER TWENTY-NINE

Present day

*M*orning, Mom." Kayleigh entered the kitchen where Mom sat nursing what was probably her fifth cup of coffee already today. None of it decaf. It was amazing that she hadn't flown here from Minnesota without the aid of an airplane.

"Good morning, sweetie. I hope you slept well."

"Fine." Not really. She hadn't slept well since... Well, she couldn't remember exactly. Not since all this business with the ring started. Up until Mom came last night, she'd kept the blinds down day and night and the doors always locked. She did change practices when Mom arrived. Kayleigh didn't want to alarm her.

No need in telling her something Kayleigh wasn't sure of herself. If she did, Mom would insist she move back to Minnesota.

"Well, that's good, because you looked like you really needed it. I hope you aren't working too much. I know spring is always such a busy time for you."

It was. That's when border crossings increased. Right now there was a severe shortage of housing. They were processing women and children as fast as possible, but it was difficult to keep up with demand.

"Why don't I make eggs for breakfast?" Mom slid from the barstool at the counter and opened the refrigerator.

"You're my guest. I'm the one who should be making you breakfast."

"I know you usually only have coffee. That's why you're so thin. A hearty meal first thing in the morning would go a long way in plumping you up."

"I don't need plumping up." Kayleigh pulled a pan from the cupboard because past experience had taught her that she would lose this argument. "I've worked hard to lose weight and keep it off."

"Men like their women with a little meat on their bones. That's what your father always said." Mom sighed and stared at the ceiling for a moment, as if she could see Dad up there in heaven.

That didn't require an answer. Instead, Kayleigh concentrated on preparing omelets for them. After prayers, Mom dug into hers with gusto. Kayleigh forked some into her mouth. "What would you like to do today?"

Mom sipped her tea. "You've never taken me to the Alamo. All the time we've visited here and driven past it, I've never been inside. I decided that was the one thing I wanted to see while I was here."

The day was looking up. Even though she would rather be at the market investigating the ring, Kayleigh nodded. Perhaps they could stop there afterward. "It's been a while since I've been. That sounds like fun."

A few hours later, Kayleigh parked in a public lot and they walked to the plaza where a large monument rose into the brilliant blue sky. At the base, at least two dozen carved statues stood, remembrances of the men who'd died in the battle here, the names of all the victims etched into the stone.

They picked up their tickets for the tour Kayleigh had somehow been able to book at the last minute and met their group at the far end of the park near East Houston Street. The guide scanned their tickets, and they took a bench while they waited for the tour to begin.

Mom grabbed Kayleigh's hand. "Can you believe all the history surrounding us? In Minnesota everything is so new. This has been here for hundreds of years. I can't wait to find out more."

"Me either." The one time Kayleigh had come was with a group of friends from work, and they weren't interested in much. They had wandered through the exhibits and seen all they'd wanted to see in less than half an hour before they'd adjourned to the Riverwalk for lunch.

After a few minutes, a swarthy gentleman dressed in breeches, a homespun shirt, and tall boots took to the raised dais, and the group gathered around him. "Welcome to the Alamo. I'm Brian, your guide for today, and I'm glad you were able to join us. Don't hesitate to let me know if you have any questions along the way.

"Imagine that it's 1836. The war for Texas independence has been raging for about six months. Santa Anna has had some success in beating back the uprising, but the Texans have had their share of victories as well, driving Mexican troops south of the Rio Grande.

"But in February 1836, Santa Anna has crossed the river again and besieged San Antonio de Béxar. The Texans are forced to give up the town and move into the mission known as the Alamo for protection.

"And then the calendar turns to March of 1836, a pivotal time in the Revolution, one that will not be forgotten or lost in history books."

Kayleigh gasped and grabbed Mom by the upper arm. "That's it. That must be it. I think I figured out part of it."

"Shhh." Mom waved Kayleigh away. Always the history buff—probably where Kayleigh got it from—Mom was the one who enjoyed historical tours and drank in every word the guide said. She also read every placard next to every display. By the time they finished here, it would be well into the afternoon.

But Kayleigh couldn't wait to share her findings with Brandon. Though it may be a bit impolite to do so when someone was speaking, she texted him.

COULD MAR36 BE MARCH 1836 WHEN THE BATTLE OF THE ALAMO TOOK PLACE?

She attempted to listen to what the guide was saying, but she couldn't keep her concentration on him while she waited for Brandon to answer.

She glanced at her phone, and three dots appeared in their text thread. Boy, did he type slowly. At last the message came through.

DUH. WHY DIDN'T I THINK OF THAT? I'M THE SUPPOSED HISTORY NUT. THAT FITS WITH THE RING'S AGE. NOW WE NEED TO FIGURE OUT THE CONNECTION TO THE ALAMO.

Even though Mom jabbed her in the ribs for not paying attention, Kayleigh didn't waste any time in texting back.

I'M HERE NOW. I'LL KEEP MY EYES OPEN.

This time he got back to her faster.

PERFECT. LUNCH ON MONDAY TO DISCUSS?

She accepted his invitation, and they set a time and place.

The guide finished his introduction and led the way to the long barracks that enclosed part of the area where the tours began.

"Was that work you were texting?" Mom always did have a rather nosy streak.

"A friend." No need to go into more detail than that.

Mom raised a plucked eyebrow. "You should have been paying attention to the guide. That was fascinating. I can't wait to hear what else he has to say."

"Look at this." Kayleigh slipped the ring from her finger. "I bought this several weeks ago at the Mexican market. Read the inscription."

"I don't have my glasses with me."

"Part of it says *MAR36*. I couldn't figure it out. Neither could anyone else. But then the guide talked about the battle of the Alamo taking place in March of 1836. The friend I was texting said that fits with the ring's age."

"So this friend is a museum curator, or what?"

"A jeweler. We're going to meet for lunch on Monday to see if that helps us in deciphering the rest of the inscription."

"There's more?"

Kayleigh nodded. She told Mom about the rest of the engraving. "I have a feeling we've only scratched the surface."

After the tour, they rested on a bench in front of the museum underneath the shade of a large tree. Apparently Mom was more interested in the ring than the treasures the museum held. "So tell me what you know about it."

Kayleigh shared how she'd come across it and what Brandon had told her about it. "That's it. We're stumped as to the rest of the puzzle."

"It makes sense that MAR36 refers to the battle of the Alamo. I just can't believe you're holding a piece of history in your hand. I wonder if it was here at the time. Maybe it belonged to one of the men who fought and died a hero."

Kayleigh stared at the ring on her finger as goose bumps popped up on her arms. If that was the case, what a story the ring would have to tell, even beyond the connection to her birth mother.

"When we're in the museum, we can ask if the curator is in. Maybe he has some ideas. Perhaps there's even a legend about it. You might have made quite the discovery." Mom's green eyes sparkled in the dappled sunlight. She hadn't been this animated since Dad died last year. Caring for him during his cancer battle had taken everything out of her. If this gave her a spark of life, then Kayleigh would go along with it.

"We can ask. It would be pretty cool if I discovered a long-lost piece of history or something that Alamo buffs have been searching for a long time."

They meandered through the small museum, drinking in every word printed on the cards beside the displays. None of them mentioned a ring. At last Kayleigh spied a docent near the display of weapons used in the battle. "Excuse me. I believe I may have a ring from around the time of the Alamo. Is the curator available or can I leave a message?"

The middle-aged woman frowned at a child who had his nose pressed against one of the glass cases. "I'm afraid the curator was involved in a serious car accident last night and will be out for a while. I can leave a message for his assistant. She's on vacation, but she'll get back to you when she returns."

Kayleigh supplied the docent with her contact information, and she and Mom left the museum. "I'm so disappointed no one was around to answer our questions."

Mom gave her a grin, a rare sight but a welcome one. After months of darkness and mourning, Mom was getting back to her old self. "This just means we'll have to do some sleuthing on our own. Between you, me, and your friend, we're sure to solve it."

"This isn't one of your mystery novels, Mom. This might be an enigma that will remain hidden forever."

"Come on. I've never pegged you as someone who gives up so easily. When you came to us, you were a fighter. You had to be to survive all you did."

"Fine. We'll keep investigating."

They moved on to the church. Other than the long barracks, it was the only original remaining part of the mission, and it was barely standing. There was nothing inside of it other than different signs indicating various points of interest, including a sacristy where the mission's women hid.

The little placard in front of the room mentioned that among the survivors were Susanna Dickinson and her daughter Angelina, Charlotte Wilkins, her children Josephine and George, as well as several Tejano women and an enslaved man named Joe.

Josephine Wilkins. Kayleigh sucked in a breath. That matched the initials on the ring.

"What is it, honey?" Mom squinted at the printed words.

"Josephine Wilkins. JW is one of the set of initials on the inscription. But this says she was just a child, so it can't be her. Can it?"

"That doesn't seem to fit. It sounds like a man gave this to his sweetheart. And there's nothing I've seen all day about a ring."

Maybe they'd been wrong about the date after all.

Despite the breakfast she'd had, Kayleigh was famished by the time Mom finished scouring every inch of the old mission. "Why don't we go to the Riverwalk and find something to eat? I'm ready to be done here."

Mom raised one penciled-on eyebrow. "Already?"

"We've seen just about everything there is to see. We can come back later if you want. I'd just like a break."

Less than fifteen minutes later, they had chosen a restaurant and were seated at a table overlooking the water, the boats coming and going, churning up the otherwise calm river.

Mom sat back with her glass of half-sweet tea, something she'd discovered on one of their trips south when Kayleigh was a kid. "Tell me what's driving you. Why do you want to find out this ring's story so much?"

Kayleigh nursed her Diet Coke. "I dunno." There was an invisible force driving her forward, to find out more about the ring's history and how Mama had come to have it.

That wasn't something she was going to discuss with Mom, the woman who had taken in a scared and scarred child, loved her with fierce determination, and watered her so she would blossom. Mom would only be hurt if Kayleigh spoke about her birth mother.

"I think there are things you aren't sharing with me. You know you can tell me anything." Mom's words were warm, like sunshine after a spring rain.

"I know." Just not this. Nothing would diminish Kayleigh's love for Mom, but she'd lost so much so recently that Kayleigh wouldn't do anything to cause even a tiny sliver in her heart.

Their food arrived just then, and Mom dove into her hamburger with gusto. How she could eat the way she did, especially when other women her age complained about how difficult it was to maintain their weight, was beyond Kayleigh. Every now and again she envied Mom her genes.

She picked at her own salad. Trouble was, Mom was right. Yes, Kayleigh was enthusiastic about the topic, but she geeked out about anything historical. Now her interest in it was more than the history aspect.

So very much more.

CHAPTER THIRTY

*A*t the stroke of noon on Monday, Kayleigh entered Brandon's jewelry shop, two subs and two Cokes in her hands. He came to the counter a moment after she entered. Thankfully, there was no one else in the store. "Sorry it's nothing fancier. Busy day. Mom had a ridiculously early flight out, and I had to make a run to Karnes County."

"That does sound busy. You amaze me with all your energy."

She shrugged and glanced around the vacant store.

"It's not always like this." A little red had the audacity to grace his fair cheeks.

Heat flamed in hers as well. He had caught her staring. Too observant for his own good. Or maybe she needed to learn a little subtlety. She flipped her ponytail over her shoulder, unwrapped the subs on the glass display case, and sat on the stool that Brandon had pulled over for her. "So, we have a possible lead." Best just to get down to business. "Tell me where we go from here."

"If the ring is tied to the Alamo, it's possible that JG or JW could be a man who was killed there."

"Very possible. And perhaps it's possible that JW is Josephine Wilkins, though unlikely." With Mom in town, she hadn't had time to research that lead. She reached down, pulled her laptop from her oversized purse, and opened it. Once Brandon gave her the store's Wi-Fi information, she typed *men who died at the Alamo* into the search bar. The first result led to an Alamo website. She sucked in her breath. "Here's the complete list, as far as they know, of those who died there."

He came around the counter and leaned over her shoulder. "Let's start with JG since he or she is listed first."

She scrolled to the *G*'s. She bit the inside of her cheek, then blew out a breath. "There are eight of them. Eight. How are we supposed to figure out which one is which?" She bit a piece of cheese that overhung her sandwich, and sipped her pop.

Brandon hummed a tune she couldn't identify as he gazed over her shoulder. "Since your birth mother and her family had the ring in Mexico, why don't you start with José Guerrero? Are there any other Hispanic names?"

She shook her head. "He's the only one." She inhaled long and slow as she clicked on his name. Her browser took an impossibly long time to load the webpage, during which time she couldn't breathe.

At last, the page opened. When she read the first line of José's bio, however, her heart sank. "Little is known about him."

Brandon's shoulders slumped. "Does it say anything else?"

She read a few more sentences. "Okay, they do have a few details about him. He was Tejano, apparently, so not Mexican. From Laredo, from what they can tell. He came with William Travis. And his commander, Juan Seguin, listed him as one of the Alamo's fallen. That's it."

Brandon bit his lip. "That really isn't much to go on."

"Tell me about it."

"Let's see if any of the others with the initials JG hold out any more hope."

Heads bent together over the small screen, they perused the catalog of the dead. She clicked on John Gaston. "Oh, look at this one. He was only seventeen."

"Wow. To give your life for such a cause at such a young age. I can't imagine being called on to do something like that."

But little other information was given about him either. None of the biographies listed anything about the men other than their place and date of birth, if known, their military service, if any, and that they all died on March 6, 1836.

Even when they searched through census records and the like, they found no information on any of the men.

Kayleigh sighed. "I don't have too much time before I have a meeting, but maybe we need to focus on JW." She scrolled down the page until she came to those names. "Here's a Jacob Walker." She clicked on his name.

Brandon let out a whistle. "Would you look at that? He married Sara Ann Vauchere, so I don't think he has a connection to our ring, but read what it says about him during the battle."

"He was shot and bayonetted to death in front of 18-year-old Josephine Wilkins." She turned to Brandon, whose eyes were shining. "JW. She wasn't a child but a young woman."

"I've heard the name Wilkins talked about in my family. Something about us being descended from them."

Ice shot through her veins. What if Brandon was the rightful owner of the ring? She clutched the hand with the ring on it to her chest.

If Brandon noticed her discomfiture, he didn't mention it. "I know we're both busy with work this week, but if you can manage to get away during your lunch hour on Friday, let's try the Béxar Heritage Center and see what they can tell us."

She nodded, stiff and wooden. "Fine." In the meantime, she was going to research Josie Wilkins.

Kayleigh had curled up on the couch with a tub of ice cream and a sappy old movie when her phone rang, Paula's name greeting her on the screen. She pushed PAUSE on the TV remote and answered it.

"I've been thinking about you all day. How are you?"

"Honestly? I don't know. My nice, neat, ordered life has been turned upside down ever since I bought that ring. Now someone is after me because of it. At least, that's what I think."

"Don't forget that this started about the time Jason was released, so it could be him."

"The police don't think so. They questioned him, and he had alibis for the car incident and the one at my apartment. Plus, it's just not the way he operates. Or not how he operated before. He showed up in weird places and sent me flowers and creepy text messages and emails, but that was it. He never broke my car windows or slashed my tires, especially not in broad daylight. Who does that?"

"Someone desperate for a ring, that's who. It's a good thing Brandon could be there for moral support."

"Yeah, funny how that works. He manages to be around just about the time my stalker strikes again."

"What are you saying?" Paula drew out each word.

"Nothing." Before continuing, Kayleigh savored a creamy bite of chocolate chocolate-chip ice cream. She and Paula often had "dateless" nights where they watched movies together over the phone, so her friend was used to Josie's lip-smacking in her ear. "I mean, I don't know much about him. He comes into my life just at the time it goes haywire."

"Don't go getting paranoid."

"I know. I know. But we have a lead on who JW might be. Josephine Wilkins. And he said there's a legend in his family that they're related to Wilkins in some way or another."

"Wilkins is a common last name. I think you're reaching at moonbeams. You, ma'am—" Paula would be poking her finger in Kayleigh's chest if they were in the same room— "are afraid of commitment."

"That's the most ludicrous thing I've ever heard. I have half a mind to hang up on you."

"Come on. Who else dates ten different men over the course of a year?"

"I only do that because you keep foisting them on me. Otherwise, I'd be quite content with my life."

"Really?"

"Really." Kayleigh ran her fingers over the buttons on the remote in her hand. Maybe that wasn't one hundred percent true. During the times she wasn't busy with her job, she was lonely. She missed Mom. It would be nice to come home to someone with whom she could share her day. While Mom was still a relatively young woman, who knew how long Kayleigh would have her? Look at what happened to Dad.

"You still there?" Paula made a slurping sound.

Kayleigh got up to get a Diet Coke. "Yeah." She opened the fridge and pulled one from the shelf. "Maybe you're right."

"Oh, I'm going to circle this date on my calendar in red marker."

"Stop it. But you do have a point. I'm afraid of losing another person I love. I've lost three parents already. Three. Most people have only two, but I've already lost three." She sniffled.

"I know, sweetie, I know. No one's blaming you for that. At some point, though, you have to take the leap."

"Says who? I'm content. Please, let it be. I have enough problems right now without a man complicating my life." Although one already had. "Plus, you're a fine one to talk."

"One of these days, Mr. Right will walk into my life, and I won't hesitate to pull the trigger."

"We'll see who beats who to the altar."

"We can make it a bet."

"I don't gamble."

"You know I don't either, but—"

"Give it up." Paula had this knack for making Kayleigh smile, no matter how badly her day had gone. Anyone she ended up with would have to be able to do the same.

Could Brandon? She shook the thought away like a pesky mosquito. "Anyway, we're going to the Béxar Heritage Center on Friday if I can get off work a little early."

"See, you do like him."

"Or maybe I'm just using him for his knowledge of the ring."

"I thought you didn't want to get too close to him in case he had some claim on it."

"Who said I was going to wait until Friday to go?"

"Very, very sneaky. I like this side of you."

The idea hadn't popped into her head until the words flowed from her mouth, but why couldn't she see what she could find out earlier in the week? She didn't need Brandon to tag along and do all the work when she could manage it herself.

CHAPTER THIRTY-ONE

*E*arly in the week, Kayleigh contacted the curator of the small museum situated within the county courthouse. By Wednesday the woman called her to let her know what she'd found. Kayleigh didn't have much time to spend there as she needed to check up on Elias, but he was still at school, so she had a few minutes.

The very pregnant woman who greeted her couldn't be more than five years older than Kayleigh. Red curls spilled over her shoulders, and freckles dotted her face. Then again, this wasn't a large museum. Just a few displays, but it did tell the story of Béxar and the Texas Revolution. "Thank you for allowing me to research such an interesting topic."

"Thank you for taking the time."

"I've been doing some digging and some thinking since you called. As I'm sure you're aware, the Texas Revolution was much more than just the Alamo. So I allowed myself to disregard the March 1836 date. That's when it hit me. The SA in the note could well stand for Stephen Austin."

"Stephen Austin?" So Brandon's hunch about him at the very beginning looked like it could be right.

"Since it was obviously used for spying, it makes sense that it would go to one of the leaders of Texas."

"I suppose."

"Then I did some digging into JG. You mentioned there wasn't much information on any of the men who died at the Alamo with those initials, so my thought was he might not have died there."

Kayleigh held back a gasp. Why had the idea never occurred to her or Brandon? Or if he had thought of it, he hadn't mentioned it to her. "You, Avalon Windsor, are a genius."

"Just a history detective, that's all. Let me show you what I found." She led Kayleigh around the corner and through a door marked EMPLOYEES ONLY. In one of the offices on the right was a desk with a book opened on it. "Have a seat." Avalon motioned to the couch along one wall.

That's what Kayleigh needed in her office, a place to make herself and those who visited her comfortable. Especially the kids. Instead of the

Mexican market on Saturday, she and Paula might have to head to a thrift store and see if they could find a decent one. Then again, her office was so small, it might not fit.

She settled herself on the comfortable blue-gray sofa, and Avalon sat beside her, pulling her hair into a ponytail before picking up the book. "The first battle of the war was the battle of Gonzales."

"I've been reading about that."

"Okay, so then you know about the Old Eighteen."

"Yes, I've heard of them."

"This is a list of those men, the eighteen who banded together to begin the quest for independence, although they weren't interested in breaking away from Texas at the beginning. They just wanted to keep their cannon." Avalon pointed to a name in the list. John Gilbert.

"JG." Kayleigh leaned forward. "He's the only JG listed."

"That's right. Apparently he was a leader of the group, at least until Captain Moore arrived."

"Why wasn't he at the Alamo?"

"There wasn't an organized army at the time. The men who were at the Alamo came in mostly as volunteers or stayed with the group from the original eighteen who were at Gonzales. He was also the town's pastor, even though Mexico had barred Protestants from the territory. It could be that he was busy seeing to the town's spiritual needs."

"And what about Josephine Wilkins, the woman who survived the Alamo? Could she be related to the ring and, in some way, to John Gilbert?"

Avalon twirled a curl. "I haven't had much time to get very far in my research, so I can't say either way. What I have is what I've told you. It shouldn't be very difficult to look up the census records and see what you can find."

"It's so much more information than I possessed when I came. So you don't know what happened to him after Gonzales?"

"Not yet. I can do a little more digging when I get a chance, but I don't know when that will be." She rubbed her expanding waistline. "If I'm not too exhausted, I might get in a little reading during maternity leave."

"Oh, I hate to make you work while you should be enjoying your new baby. Now that I have this to go on, it might be the catalyst for more discoveries."

They said their goodbyes, and Kayleigh, after a brief inspection of the museum's displays, exited. As soon as she was on the walk in front of the large redbrick building, she dialed Brandon.

She could hardly wait until he answered before blurting out the news. "Guess what?" That earned her several stares from passersby.

"You sound excited."

"I am." Wait, why had she called him? Something held her back, kept

162—LIZ TOLSMA

her clutching those cards close to her chest. Perhaps later, when she knew more, when she was sure she had a connection to the ring, she would share the information with him. In the seconds since she'd placed the call, she'd changed her mind. It was time she struck out on her own.

"I, uh. . ." Great. Now she couldn't even come up with a good way out of this or an excuse not to meet him on Friday. "You know, I think I've decided to give up the search for the meaning of the ring. It's brought me nothing but trouble. It's a beautiful ring, what I believe to be a family heirloom, and that's enough. Thank you for all your help."

"Are you sure? You sounded so happy at first."

"I am. It's a good thing to be rid of whoever is after the ring."

"How are they going to know you've given up trying to figure out what it means?"

She was never the best liar. Mom always told her that was a good thing, but every now and again, being able to tell a fib would come in handy. Just then her phone beeped. It was work. "Listen, I have the office trying to reach me on the other line. I have to go. Thanks for everything." She switched to the other call.

They had a new batch of kids coming to Karnes County later today, so she needed to get over to check on Elias before she headed there.

She strolled to where she'd parked her car and took a minute to search John Gilbert on her phone.

The site where she looked up census, birth, marriage, and death records had many John Gilberts that could be the one. One had kept over twenty enslaved people. She shuddered. Another had married three times, once to a Jane Worth. That was in 1840, so it could be a possibility, though it wasn't Josephine Wilkins. Maybe she didn't have a connection to the ring.

Another was living with his son in 1870. No mention of a wife, though he did have a granddaughter named Josephine. Perhaps the ring was meant for her.

She glanced at her watch. Whoops. It was too easy to get lost on those sites. She would have to do more searching for John Gilbert on her own time, if he was the right one. But if he wasn't involved in the Alamo, why have the date of March 1836 on there? Unless it was coincidence that they married in the same month as the massacre took place.

She started her car and left the parking garage. The shade had kept it cool, but now it was quite warm, so she blasted the air conditioning and the radio, an upbeat country tune coming on the station.

Good. It would drown out her thoughts. Particularly how she would manage to keep Brandon from discovering what she knew about the ring.

CHAPTER THIRTY-TWO

March 6, 1836

$\mathscr{T}$ime lost all meaning to Josie as she huddled in the corner of the church's sacristy. Sunshine streamed through the window high above her, but nothing could illuminate the darkness deep within her soul.

Like the gentle lulling of a ship, the voices of the women and children remaining in the room with Josie rose and fell. Every now and again her little brother's cries or the cries of one of Senora Navarro's children filled the air. She shut her mind, her heart, her soul to it all.

She focused on the darkness and allowed it to consume her.

Sometime later a commotion awoke her from her sleep or brought her out of her stupor, whichever she had been in. Before her stood a Mexican soldier. Like Manuel, he too was covered in blood. Crimson stained the sword at his side and even his hands.

From the tilt of his chin to the puffing of his chest, he exuded pride. This could be none other than Santa Anna himself.

A smaller, less dignified soldier stood beside him. Blood also covered him. How much had been shed on this day?

"Only women and children in here, sir. One Negro."

"Bah. He's nothing to us. We will allow him to live, and these others as well, for if we do not, who will ever tell of Santa Anna's great victory at the Alamo? This day will become legend, and I will be considered one of the greatest military minds of all time, there is no doubt."

"No doubt, sir, none at all."

Josie understood every word the general spoke. So did Senora Navarro and the other Tejanos with them. Only Charlotte and Joe and Susanna wouldn't know. It was best they didn't.

When none of the other women stirred, Josie wiped her already-dry eyes. She stood, dusted off her red-stained skirt, and marched to stand in front of the Mexican general. "What is the news of our men?"

He tsked. "Ah, you are well acquainted with our language and speak it almost like a native. But you are naive. Don't you remember the red flag flying over the camp? It was my promise to destroy any and all who fought against us. That is exactly what I have done. They are dead. All dead." He spat the last word.

"*Por favor, señor.*" Josie swallowed hard. "Allow us to bury our deceased. And one of your soldiers, Manuel Garcia, has stolen something from me I wish to have returned."

Santa Anna stroked his chin as if he were contemplating the idea. He turned to his comrade, who shrugged his shoulders. "No to both of your requests. This is what I want you to do. All of you here, each and every one of you, the last survivors of the Alamo, are to leave at once and make haste in going to Sam Houston. I know he is marching here with reinforcements, but he is too late. Still, I desire to battle such a worthy foe. When you meet him, give him a message from me. Tell him to prepare for Santa Anna."

"Sir, I beg of you. Our requests are small. All we want is the bodies of our loved ones, and I need to retrieve my possession from Senor Garcia."

"No!" Santa Anna's shout reverberated throughout the church. "This will not become a memorial. The ground here will not remember the dead. The only remembrance will be in your hearts for the rest of your lives. Go now. There shall be no further delays."

Even as Josie stood in front of the murderer of her father, the man she loved, and countless others, the Tejanos in the room scurried past them and out of the church. Senora Navarro and her brood came last, the woman assisting Charlotte along.

With a single glance, Josie stopped them and stared straight into Santa Anna's soulless black eyes. "This woman has just given birth. She cannot be expected to make such an arduous journey at this time. She must recover."

"I care not about that. It isn't my concern. This mission is now under my control. Unless you desire to be my prisoners, you must leave by daybreak tomorrow. In a show of good faith, I will give each of you two pesos and a blanket. I want you out of my sight now. After dawn tomorrow, I cannot guarantee your safety."

"Josie, please." Charlotte jostled her slumbering newborn. "We must go now." Senora Navarro must have translated the general's words for her.

Then again, even though Charlotte didn't speak Spanish, Santa Anna's delivery made it clear to everyone what he was commanding.

Joe turned back and swept Charlotte from her feet. "I's able to help Miz Charlotte. No worries, Miss Josie."

Josie and the others left the sanctuary and filed out of the church. Already the Mexicans were gathering the bodies in wheelbarrows. Santa Anna ensured that even in death, there would be no dignity for those he had conquered.

On stiff limbs, the women and children moved toward their rooms, Joe still carrying Charlotte. "She weighs less than a baby bird, Miss Josie. Ain't no problem for me."

They passed the bodies of Davy Crockett, William Travis, and Jim Bowie leaning against a stone wall, bayonet wounds visible in their chests.

No mercy. Santa Anna had promised such, and he had delivered.

Throughout the day, they packed their few household goods and clothes. Joe located a wagon, the one Father had used to transport Charlotte here, and at first light, he managed to get Chariot hitched to it. What was amazing was that the Mexican soldiers now in charge of the garrison hadn't stopped him from doing so. Santa Anna had full control of his soldiers.

Soon Josie had Charlotte and the infant tucked under quilts, and the procession of the handful of Alamo survivors trickled through the gate the Mexicans had breached. A horrendous, gagging odor struck them as they dragged themselves away. Dark smoke rose into the air, giving off the noxious fumes.

The funeral pyre.

Father.

John.

Josie clutched her chest to keep her heart from breaking into tiny pieces.

She turned back for one last long gaze at the crumbling, cannon-pocked walls of the crumbling mission, tears gliding down her cheeks unchecked.

"I love you, Father. I love you, John. I shall miss you with a vengeance."

March 9, 1836

Little by little, the band of women and children, led by the ever-faithful Joe, trod eastward, toward Sam Houston and the reinforcements that hadn't arrived in time. If only the troops had hurried more. If only the commanders at the Alamo had gotten the message sooner.

John had been correct. Instead of going to the Indians, they should have found Sam Houston and urged him to make haste. It was her fault they hadn't hurried and hadn't been there to relieve the troops caught in the Alamo.

She didn't gaze into the cloud-streaked sky. She didn't watch as the hills gave way to plains as they lumbered toward the rising of the sun. Instead, she kept her attention on the ground beneath her moccasins, trampled by the feet of those who went before her as she tarried behind them.

For three days, they tramped onward toward Gonzales. No one said much. Each of them had lost at least one loved one. A father. A brother. A husband. For all of them, the weights on their shoulders were heavy. There was no banter, no laughter. Even the children were silent.

Joe came beside Josie. "Miz Charlotte wants to see you."

"I don't want to talk to her." They had a shared grief, but at this point, it was a grief that was to remain bottled inside of her until she had the time and the privacy to take it out and deal with it.

"You gots to talk to her. What you doing ain't no good. And Miz Charlotte needs you. She just had a baby and is awful alone."

Father would want her to be with Charlotte and to help her in her time of need. Josie sighed. Nothing in life was easy, not a single thing. "For Father, I'll go to her."

"He'd be right proud of you, miss."

"You're a good man, Joe. After all of this is settled, I hope you manage to find a place in this world where you can be your own person."

"That's what I'm planning. Mexico don't hold to slavery, so people may talk 'cause of all this with the Alamo, but for me, it's a safe place. So that's where I be heading. The promised land."

Perhaps for him some good would come of all this.

Josie picked up her pace until she intercepted the wagon carrying Charlotte. One of the older Navarro boys was driving it and slowed so that Josie could climb aboard.

"Your brother misses you." Charlotte handed the baby to Josie.

She cradled him close to herself in a vain attempt to shield herself from the pain. There were too many emotions to name. She closed her eyes and allowed her tears to drop onto George's tiny face.

"I miss him too. He should be here for his son. What was he thinking, going to that place and dragging us there with him?"

Josie snapped to attention. "He couldn't have predicted what happened. No one could. What he did, he did out of love and concern for us. All he wanted to do was to protect us. He gave his life so we could be safe, so his son could grow up without fear. Don't you ever, ever question what Father did."

"How dare you speak to me in such a way. I'm a brand-new mother and a brand-new widow. I need your comfort, not your condemnation. Perhaps this conversation was a bad idea."

It had been, but Josie couldn't alienate Charlotte. George, after all, was her brother. "I'm sorry. Grief is a strange bedfellow."

"You should be used to it by now. After all, you had already lost two of your loved ones to the Mexicans."

All Josie could do was stare at Charlotte, at her thin, pale face. "This isn't anything you get used to. I lost my father, and I lost John, the man I love. My grief is as deep as the deepest ocean, as high as the highest stars, as wide as the widest valley. It knows no bounds. What am I to do? What are we to do?"

"Oh Josie." Charlotte rubbed Josie's shoulder, the touch, for once, tender and filled with compassion. "I didn't know. I should have suspected that you fancied John."

"I did. I loved him. I still love him and always will. Nothing will change that. If this hadn't happened, if God hadn't snatched him away from me, I believe we would have been married by summer. He was everything to me."

"As was your father. He was a good man, kind and considerate." Charlotte worried the hem of the multicolored quilt over her lap. "I wasn't always the best wife. I should have treated him better. But despite my shortfalls, he never raised his voice or said a cross word. Now I shall never have the chance to make it up to him."

The babe in Josie's arms stirred and whimpered. She handed her brother back to Charlotte. "He loved you and saw the good in you, just as I do." If nothing else, her stepmother was devoted to little George.

"Where do we go from here?"

"First things first. We will meet Mr. Houston in Gonzales. We have a home there and can take time to figure out what our future entails." For a brief, shining moment, that future had included John. Now that light had been extinguished. "Let's trust our future to the Lord. He tells us not to worry about tomorrow because each day has enough trouble of its own. How true that is."

"Amen."

The wagon wheels continued to turn, taking them farther from the scene of the massacre and closer to help. Sam Houston might be able to give them some advice. They still owned the house in Gonzales and the *sitio* Father had farmed. Perhaps they could do something with that.

Right now her head hurt too much to contemplate anything more. She lay down among the blankets and quilts and willed herself to sleep. Without success. Each time she closed her eyes, all she could see was Father's body and those of the other men.

"We's found them. We's found them." Joe's shouts from the front of the ragtag band brightened all of them. Josie sat up, then kneeled in the wagon bed. Indeed, on the horizon came a large group of cavalry. In the not-too-far distance was Gonzales. As the troops approached, Josie picked out the man leading them. Sam Houston, if her guess didn't miss the mark.

Even under the brim of his hat, there was no mistaking his wide forehead. With eyes deep set under bushy eyebrows, he examined their little group, his mouth slightly downturned. He scratched his sloping nose and approached them.

And. . .

Josie rubbed her eyes.

It couldn't be. Her exhausted, grief-stricken mind had to be playing tricks on her.

Then again. . .

CHAPTER THIRTY-THREE

*F*or the rest of the day, Kayleigh ignored all of Brandon's texts and calls. Each time he came up on caller ID or on text notification, it served to befuddle her more.

Part of her ached with missing him. Since she had walked into his jewelry shop, she had either spoken to him on the phone or through texts or other social media almost every day.

The merest thought, though, that he could have a claim to Mama's ring chilled her to the tips of her toes.

So what was she supposed to do about the entire mess? On the drive to Elias's house, new tires and windows installed on her SUV, the question was her constant companion. Her mind swung from one side to the other, like a pendulum with its regular rhythm. There was no way out of this mess except to keep going as she was.

With a sigh, she turned into the Cliftons' driveway, shut off the ignition, and sat for a moment. What a day it had been, and what she had to tell Elias didn't make her day any easier. After a deep breath and a quick prayer, she strolled up the walk lined with roses toward the red front door. The flowers' sweet fragrance filled her, motivating her, giving her strength. She could do this.

Soon she was seated in their HGTV-inspired living room, two gray sofas with bright throw pillows accenting the space, all open to a white kitchen with gray and white marble countertops where something that smelled of garlic and oregano bubbled on the stove. She sipped from the glass of ice water Tina had offered her.

But she couldn't sit back on the overstuffed couch. Instead, she perched at the edge of the cushion. Tina, Dan, and Elias did the same on the couch opposite her. Talk about being able to cut the tension with a knife.

She spoke to Elias in Spanish so he would be able to understand every word of what she was about to tell him. "We found your uncle, the one whose address you had."

Elias's dark eyes lit up and a wide grin crossed his face. "Really? Do I get to go live with him? It's not like going home, and I don't remember him much, but he is family."

Better to rip the Band-Aid off as soon as possible before Elias's hopes rose too high. "I'm afraid I have some bad news. Your uncle has not obeyed the law while he was here, and he is in prison." She refrained from informing him that as soon as his uncle was released, which wouldn't be for a few years, he'd be deported. That might put ideas into Elias's head of how he might make it back to Mexico.

"Jail?"

"*Sí*. I am so sorry."

Elias stared at the new, hardly broken-in blue jeans he wore. "What happens to me now?"

"I'm not sure about that. The Cliftons and I and some other social workers and people from the government will talk about it."

He looked up and stared at her. "I want to go home. Tell the social workers and the government people that is what I want more than anything. I miss my parents. I didn't care how poor I was. We loved each other. At least I thought we did." The hardness left his big brown eyes, replaced by tears.

She went to him and knelt on the light hardwood floor in front of him, grasping him by both hands. "I wish things were different and that you never had to make this trip at all. Your parents love you. They did this because they believed it was best for you. They wanted to give you the best life possible, even if that meant that life was without them."

"But without them, my life is empty. Isn't family worth more than money?"

Kayleigh swallowed hard. She'd been blessed with two wonderful families. Still, if they had never left Mexico, she might well still have her birth parents. No doubt life would have been a struggle. God worked all things together for good, but couldn't He have worked them for good with Mama and Papi?

"Just never stop believing in their love for you. I'll pray that you get to the place God means you to be." The cross over the couch gave her the courage to speak those words to Elias, even though she wasn't supposed to be talking about the Lord when she was working.

Elias swiped away the moisture from his still-hollow cheeks and nodded. "I will pray too. I will pray that God sends me back to my family."

"If it's okay, I would like to speak to Tina and Dan for a few minutes."

Tina sniffled, her own brown eyes shimmering. "Why don't you take the dog out and play fetch with him for a while?"

"I do like the dog." Elias bounced out of the room.

Dan sipped from his water bottle. "That's such a shame about his uncle. But where does that leave us? And Elias?"

"I'm afraid the situation is complicated." Kayleigh bit the inside of her cheek. "If the US sends Elias back, it's possible his parents would try to get him here again. The trek is dangerous enough once. I shudder to think what might happen to him if he attempts it another time."

Tina leaned forward, over her knees. "We want to respect his wishes."

"I understand. We also have to take into consideration what is best for Elias. If it's returning home, that's what will happen. If it's remaining here, then I'll ensure that occurs. Just so I know—I'm not saying this is what will take place—but if he can't return to Mexico for whatever reason, would you be willing to consider providing a home for him?"

The Cliftons gazed at each other in that way married people did, speaking without words. Dan smiled, then turned to Kayleigh. "Of course. He needs the love and stability that we can provide him. And he's such a pleasure."

Kayleigh made a few notes in her computer about the situation, then closed her laptop. They chatted for several minutes more about how Elias was doing at home and in school.

After a quick stop in the backyard to say goodbye to him, Kayleigh headed for her car. She turned it on but leaned against the seat before pulling out of the driveway. Just a moment to regain her composure and get her swirling emotions under control.

Nothing about this was neat or clean. When the public heard the headlines on the news, what they often forgot was that there were real people involved, some of them young children like Elias who didn't ask for any of this to happen to them, who got hung up in bureaucratic red tape.

The music on the country station cut out, and the announcer came on the air. "We have a breaking news bulletin we want to pass on to you. A pipe bomb has exploded at the Béxar Heritage Center, right outside the museum's entrance. Details are just coming in, and we have a reporter on the way to the scene, but what we can tell you is that ambulances have been called. We'll keep you posted as soon as we have more information."

Kayleigh covered her mouth, her hands shaking. She'd been there only two hours ago or so. She riffled through her memories, searching the pictures inside her mind for suspicious packages in front of the door or anywhere on the grounds. Unfortunately, she came up empty.

Before she left the Cliftons', she dialed the number the police had given her when her car had been vandalized. After a few transfers, she reached the officer familiar with her case. "This is Kayleigh Hewland. I think I might have some information on the bombing at the courthouse."

"What do you know?"

"I was there only two hours before this, doing research."

"When did you decide to visit the museum?"

"A couple of days ago."

"Who knew you were going there?"

"Only my friend Paula."

The officer typed what she could assume were her answers in a computer as she gave them. "I'll need her information. And I'd like you to come in so we can talk some more."

"I have an important meeting in just a short while. Would it be possible for me to come in tonight?"

"The nature of this crime makes time critical. The longer we wait, the farther away the suspect might get. This may or may not be related to what's been happening to you, but the sooner we figure that piece out, the better."

"I'll be there as early as possible." She hung up the call, informed her saintly boss what was happening, and headed for the station. All the way, the reporter on the radio continued updating the situation and providing details about the crime.

One person was dead. Dead. Black and purple spots danced in front of Kayleigh's eyes, and she worked to keep her concentration on the traffic in front of her. Passing out while driving wouldn't be good. By gripping the steering wheel with all her might, she managed to stay in her lane, brake when needed, and make all the correct turns to get to the station.

Before long, she was seated next to the officer's desk, though he was busy in another part of the station. The place was a beehive of activity with officers coming and going and cell phones ringing in stereo. Not too long after she arrived, so did Paula.

She adjusted her ponytail. "What's going on? All of a sudden, I get this call that I have to come down here and I couldn't even wait until after work."

"Neither could I. And it's my fault. Did you hear about the bombing?"

Paula dropped into a nearby chair, then scooted it to face Kayleigh. "Were you there?"

"About two hours before. I had to call them because it could be the person who's after me."

"Let's focus on something else right now. Like, did you find anything out at the museum?"

Well, it was still talking about the museum, but it was a different aspect of it. All Kayleigh could do was pray that Avalon wasn't one of the injured or the one who was killed. She was pregnant, after all. Kayleigh rubbed the chill from her arms. "I did. The curator believes that JG is John Gilbert, a member of the Old Eighteen who fought at the battle of Gonzales. And that SA could be Stephen Austin."

"That's exciting. Steven Austin of all people. Your ring might very well be famous. So what about the other set of initials?"

"Nothing on that yet. I spent a few minutes researching on my phone, but I'm going to need a block of time for that, time I don't have right now.

There's no proof one way or the other that JW is Josephine Wilkins."

No more going to museums and involving other people though. Risking other people's lives wasn't worth finding out about the ring. But she wouldn't be able to rest until she knew everything there was to know about it.

This search was now up to her and her alone.

CHAPTER THIRTY-FOUR

March 9, 1835

There was no mistaking the tall man in the saddle. His sharp cheekbones and long sideburns. His angular nose. His soft eyes, in stark contrast to the rest of him.

Josie covered her mouth, her entire body shaking. "I have to be seeing a vision."

Beside her in the wagon, Charlotte chuckled. "I'm having the same vision."

"You are?"

"I am."

"But it can't be. No man who fought against the Mexicans escaped Santa Anna's wrath. He made sure of it. Manuel told me he'd killed him himself."

"Did you ever see John's body?"

Josie shook her head. "But every other man died. What else was I to believe? The last time I saw him, he was in the mission. How did he ever escape?"

"God has given you a gift." Charlotte drew in a deep breath. "Go embrace it and hold on to it with everything you have. Enjoy each minute that the Lord gives you together. Every second is precious and is to be cherished."

Josie leaned over and kissed Charlotte's cheek. Her eyes widened and softened. Perhaps she had a heart after all. "Thank you. You are a wiser woman than I ever gave you credit for."

"Go, go." She swatted Josie away. Back to the old Charlotte.

Josie slid from the halted wagon and grabbed handfuls of her skirts. The tall figure dismounted and raced toward her. In the middle of the field, surrounded by soldiers and tired, dirty, defeated women and children, John grasped her in a tight embrace.

"John, oh John." She stroked his cheek, his chin, his chest to confirm that he was real, that this was more than a beautiful, wonderful dream.

He kissed both cheeks and held her at arm's length. "To what do I owe this enthusiastic greeting?" He bent lower and whispered in her ear. "Not that I mind."

She stepped from his hold. "I thought you were dead. They all are." Her voice cracked, and she wobbled on her feet. Good thing he held her fast. "Father included. Santa Anna made good on his threat."

All the color gushed from John's face, and he stumbled backward. "What? We're too late?"

All she could do was nod. "It was awful. We"—she gestured to the women and children behind her— "all hid in the church's sacristy while the Mexicans slaughtered every man in the mission. Only Joe survived. It was brutal." She shuddered, wiping the images from her mind. "It lasted maybe ninety minutes."

"Oh Josie, I am so sorry. If only I had been there."

"No, no, don't feel sorry. If you had been there, you would be dead too. They wouldn't have spared you. One gun more or less wouldn't have made a difference."

"What is that you're saying, young lady?" Sam Houston had dismounted and strode in their direction, his dark brows drawn into a V.

She relayed the entire story to him. By the end, he bowed his head, his hat in his hands. All the soldiers with him followed suit. For a while, there was no noise but the wind through the prairie grasses and the nickering of the horses.

When Houston returned his hat to its rightful spot on his head, he turned his attention to his men. "Remember the Alamo!"

They shouted in unison, "Remember the Alamo!"

Josie wiped away her tears. They could never forget, not the sacrifices all those men had made. Jim Bowie. William Travis. Davy Crockett. Father. Each of their names would be immortalized, no matter what Santa Anna said. At least in her own heart, she would always remember.

Mr. Houston bowed over her hand. "From what young John has said, you are a remarkable woman. I have to agree."

"I come bearing a message from Santa Anna himself."

Once again, Mr. Houston cocked an eyebrow.

"He says to prepare to meet him."

Mr. Houston gave a single nod. "You can be sure that we will be ready for him."

❦

Evening had fallen, and Mr. Houston and the rest of the troops had made camp in the military plaza in Gonzales. So much had changed since Josie was here last. Father had been with them. They had a sturdy house, and Father had a good business and a farm.

Now the house was empty without him even though his presence touched every surface. His chair at the table. His clothes in the wardrobe. His pipe on the mantel.

Because Manuel took her from her home, she hadn't had to deal with such memories when he'd killed Mama and Laura. They assaulted her now. She couldn't stay in here, so she fled to the porch, gulping in the chilly evening air.

A shadowy figure approached, and there was no mistaking who it was. "Miss Wilkins?" John climbed the single step and bowed over her, the hand holding his hat over his heart.

All in all, the gesture elicited a rare smile from her. "Good evening, Preacher Gilbert."

"Would you care to take a turn about the village with me?"

Here, surrounded by men and soldiers, she relaxed for the first time in days. Father was gone, and she had survived a horrific nightmare, but John was by her side once more. A slight bit of light shone in the dark recesses of her soul again.

She rose from her spot and brushed off her filthy gown, then took his arm. If only she had changed into clean clothes. She likely wasn't the most pleasant creature to behold in that moment. With nothing else to do, she smoothed back a stray lock of hair. "Thank you, kind sir. I should be delighted."

He led them to the edge of the military gathering. Firelight flickered against the darkness of the night. "How are you holding up?"

"Now that I know you're alive, so much better. I just can't believe. . ."

"I will miss him too. He was a good man."

"In all the excitement of seeing you and relaying the story of the Alamo, then the business of the evening meal, I haven't had the chance to ask how you managed to get away from the fray. Where were you?"

"After you left the meeting, Travis sent me out again to try to reach Sam Houston. As you can see, it took me a bit of time to locate him and more time to mobilize the troops and start heading for Béxar. I take it you didn't know I'd been sent out."

"No. I didn't see anyone else that evening, and by dawn the next morning, the Mexicans were attacking. Manuel told me he had killed you. It was a valiant defense, but we were at a disadvantage from the beginning."

"That man is despicable for leading you to believe such a falsehood. I thank God that He spared you and the rest of the women."

"Even that ruthless dictator knows better than to harm innocents."

The way John tipped his head said he didn't agree.

She bit her lower lip. "There's more about Manuel." She leaned against John.

He halted and pulled Josie so she faced him. "Tell me he didn't hurt you."

She swallowed the lump in her throat. "Not physically." She blew out a breath. "He took Mother's ring from me and said it was the prize he'd been seeking all along. Whoever possesses the ring can claim the Garcia fortune. I don't care about that. We never knew its connections to wealth, but now the ring is gone." A fresh round of tears wet her face. Would they ever stop?

"Oh Josie, I'm so sorry that happened. I know how much you cherished it."

She brushed the dampness from her cheeks. "I'm trying to keep in mind that it was nothing more than an object. People are far more precious than the rarest of all stones. I have lost far too many who are worth more than rubies, sapphires, or diamonds, but I am so very grateful to God that I have you with me. That somehow the Lord brought you back from the grave."

"I was never dead."

"To me you were. I believed you slaughtered. Because the Mexicans were burning all the bodies, I never got the chance to search for you, so I took Manuel at his word."

He drew her close, his cheek brushing hers. "I am not going anywhere. As long as God gives me breath and sees fit to keep me on this earth, I'm going to stay by your side."

"Even if I want to search for my daughter?"

"No matter what you want to do, I'll support you. But I want you to think long and hard about that. Where would you look?"

She leaned against John. "I don't know. Manuel's letter wasn't addressed to anyone, nor to a specific place."

"And think about your daughter."

Oh, she did. She thought so hard about the little girl that her childish laughter rang in Josie's ears. Her sweet smile was like a painting in front of her eyes. Her skin was soft and smooth underneath her fingertips. "Do you suppose she's happy? I pray every moment of every day she is."

"I do too."

"But to have Manuel as a father. How am I supposed to leave her in such a situation? I would be a horrible mother if I allowed my daughter to suffer."

"Manuel isn't there right now."

Josie shook her head. "You're correct, I'm sure. He never went to Mexico much. Of course, now he is here fighting."

"So for most of the time, she's away from him."

"Even if that is the case, it rips me apart inside to think she has to spend even a moment in that man's presence."

"We can see what we can discover, but don't get your hopes up. You may have to entrust her to the Lord and to His providence and protection."

"That is so difficult."

"I know, but that's how faith and trust operate."

He tilted her chin and forced her to stare into the bottomless blue of his eyes. Grief and joy swirled together inside of her until she couldn't separate one from the other. Strange how they could be so intertwined.

"I love you, my dearest Josephine." He kissed her forehead.

The words, so long in coming, fell like rain on her battered soul. More time would be needed, more comfort and encouragement until she sprang to life once again, but it was a start. "I love you too, my darling John."

Hoofbeats shattered the beautiful moment. A scout approached them. "Santa Anna's on his way. He can't be more than five miles from here." The scout spurred on his mount and made haste for the encampment at the edge of town.

John broke away from her. "I must go and see what Mr. Houston wants to do. Let me walk you home first."

"There's no need." She stood on her tiptoes and kissed his chin. "Go and bring me a report as soon as you can. Promise you won't leave for the battle until you have said goodbye."

He drew her close once more, leaned over, and traced a path from her ear to her mouth with his lips. Such tingling sensations filled Josie, ones she'd never experienced before. Her head spun, and heat from his body seeped through her gown, warming her. She responded to him, deepening the kiss.

He broke away, breathless. "If I don't leave now, I'll never be able to go."

"Part of me wants to make you stay, but I understand your duty. Make haste, or I will make good on my threat."

With a last peck on her cheek, John disappeared into the darkness.

Josie returned to the quiet house. Charlotte must have gotten George to go to sleep. She peeked in the door. Charlotte lay fully clothed, snoring on the still-made bed. Josie pulled off her shoes and tucked a blanket around her. George slumbered sweetly in the cradle Father had made for him. It was a good thing they had left it behind.

She had just splashed cold water on her face from the white pitcher and basin in her room when a shout came from outside. "Get ready to leave. Get ready to leave."

Josie scuttled to the porch. "What is it? What's going on?"

The young man on a light brown horse pulled up in front of her and the other women emerging from their homes. "Houston feels we aren't ready to meet Santa Anna yet. He wants to wait until we're in a better strategic position. We're heading toward Galveston and burning the town behind us."

"What? But why?"

"To be sure no spoils go to that despot. Gather your belongings and hurry. We leave in thirty minutes."

They had only just arrived and had had almost no rest. Poor Charlotte had just fallen asleep, and now Josie would have to wake her. There was nothing else to be done though.

Thank goodness Josie hadn't had any time to unpack. She roused Charlotte and explained what was happening.

"They can't do that to us. We'll lose our home and George's business. We'll be left destitute."

Charlotte's words rang of truth. Almost everything they owned was tied up in this town. Without it, they only had the land to sustain them. "We can't think about that right now." She pushed her own thoughts to the very back of her mind, an exercise she was well versed in. "We must make our preparations as swiftly as possible."

In no time, they gathered a few more belongings and mementos of Father and Mother they'd left behind before. They were better prepared. By the time Josie left to fetch Chariot, John had arrived to help. Together they hitched the stallion to the cart once again and loaded Charlotte, George, and their belongings inside.

In no time, their band, now swelled by the ranks of soldiers, had pulled out of the town Josie claimed as home. As she held the reins and urged Chariot forward, she turned and looked behind her.

Red colored the dark sky, flames leaping toward the clouds.

An ominous chill swept through Josie, and she shuddered.

March 10, 1836

Following the noon meal, the band of soldiers, women, and children clustered together, the March sun warming them, though many of the women wore their black, embroidered shawls over their heads, just as Josie did.

Charlotte stood beside Josie, cradling little George in her arms. All Josie had to do was to gaze into his cherubic face to find Father's reflection there. God had sent this little gift from above so that Josie would never forget what Father looked like. *Thank You, Lord.* They may have lost much, but they had this reminder of God's goodness and faithfulness.

Many of the women sobbed, a few in silent mourning, many of them with heart-tearing wails. Not one of them had gone untouched by this massacre.

John stood on an upturned vegetable crate, his Bible in his hands, the leather cover worn from a great deal of use. He hardly needed the raised dais, but he used it nonetheless. Because of his commanding presence, he had no need of calling for quiet. The crowd fell silent in front of him.

"Brothers and sisters in Christ, we have gathered here today in remembrance of those courageous men who died in defense of the Alamo. They were our sons, our fathers, our husbands, our friends. Their absence has left a gaping void in our lives."

The loud weeping resumed. Josie's own tears dripped on the ground, and she drew Charlotte into an embrace.

"We cannot fathom the Lord's ways. They are too great for us, too far above our understanding. In this life, we may never understand why He snatched our loved ones from us in this manner. But rest assured, brothers and sisters, in the knowledge that God's plans and purposes are perfect. He sees and comprehends what we cannot see nor comprehend. He loves us with the compassion of a father, one that outstrips every earthly father. His word assures us that He will never leave us nor forsake us. Lo, He is with us to the end of the age."

A chorus of "amens" rang out among the congregation. The Tejano women crossed themselves.

"It is to this faith that we must cling in our hour of need and in our time of trouble. Faith that our loved ones are now in His presence, feasting at the Lamb's table, free from worry, sorrow, and pain. And if you place your faith in Him, the time will come when He will also seat you at His table, and you will rejoice in His presence forevermore."

John completed the short service with a prayer, and the gathering scattered. The time had come for each of them to return to their own homes, if they had any left, and for the troops to prepare for their encounter with Santa Anna.

John had entreated the group to remember that God loved them and would never forsake them. With all her might, as one who clings to a shipwreck's debris to keep from drowning, Josie clung to that.

CHAPTER THIRTY-FIVE

*W*ith the air conditioner and her smart speaker blasting, Kayleigh stood under the stream of hot water in the shower in a vain attempt to wash away the day's troubles.

The police had questioned her and Paula for about two hours, going over every detail of anyone who might have it out for Kayleigh, searching for any connection to the bombing at the heritage center.

It was a security guard who had been killed when he was examining the package left at the museum's entrance. At least Avalon and her child were safe, but what a tragedy for the security guard's family. The experience left Kayleigh as limp as a plant that had gone weeks without water. No wonder criminals cracked under the pressure.

When she had exhausted her supply of hot water, she left the shower and dressed in a super soft pair of leggings and a long T-shirt. The ice cream in the freezer was calling her name. Better yet, a Coke float. And a chick flick. Something brainless.

No sooner had she settled on the couch and started Netflix than the doorbell rang. Mom always wished she would live in a secured building or that she would at least get one of those doorbells where you could see who was outside.

Much as Kayleigh hated to admit it, at this point, Mom was right. Maybe if she ignored the ringing, whoever was there would give up and go away.

They didn't.

"Kayleigh, I know you're home. It's me. Brandon. Please, can we talk?"

A pounding started behind her eyes, intensified now because he switched to knocking.

He wasn't going to leave her in peace, so she might as well let him talk to her through the door.

She pulled the door open until the chain was taut, her drink in her hand. "It's been a long day. I was just getting ready for bed."

"By having a float? Coke, if I'm not mistaken?"

"Say what you've come to say and then leave me in peace. I'm exhausted."

"What did I do?"

"Nothing."

"You haven't answered my calls or texts or anything, so you're ignoring me at best and pushing me away at worst."

She'd lean against the door if it wouldn't close. Then again. . . . No. She owed Brandon some kind of explanation.

"And you were very weird on the phone earlier this week."

"Thank you. That's a nice compliment to pay a woman."

He blew out a breath, the wind of it ruffling the curl falling over his eye. "You know what I mean. Just tell me what mistake I made."

"It's not you." She huffed herself. "It's this entire situation. People around me are getting hurt. This bombing at the heritage center might even be connected. I haven't seen Paula much either, so you aren't alone."

"But you could take my calls or text me back."

"I've been busy and stressed. Having a conversation with anyone isn't high on my list of priorities. When I get home from work, all I want to do is chill out and unwind."

"Can I come in?"

She had to give him bonus points for persistence. "This isn't a good time."

"You found out something about the ring you don't want me to know. I don't understand why you would keep that information from me. I thought we were a team."

A bubble that had been building deep in her chest burst. "Do you want the ring for yourself? It's legend in your family." The words spewed from her lips before she had a chance to check them.

"Is that what you believe?" Brandon paced around the tiny concrete step. "That's the furthest notion from my mind. Yes, I'd like to find out what connection, if any, there is to my family, but it's yours. I have no intention of taking it from you. I promise. Please, have faith in me."

Could she? Did she dare? So far he'd proven himself to be true to his word. Faith. It meant taking that giant step and putting herself in someone else's hands. She'd had to do it with Mom and Dad. Have faith that they would take care of her and have faith that they wouldn't hurt her.

Brandon hadn't given her any reason to mistrust him. And she did have the ring. Wasn't possession nine-tenths of the law?

If Paula were here, she would be telling Kayleigh to take the leap, would be pushing her off the cliff.

"I did discover who I believe JG was. And possibly even JW."

He slapped his thighs. "But you aren't about to share that information with me."

An out. She took it. "What if I promise to inform you if either of them has anything to do with your family? Will that be good enough for you?"

In the silence that followed, the crickets sang their bedtime songs. A car whooshed past, and a motorcycle hummed by. "I don't have any other choice, do I? There's nothing I can do to force the information from you. But don't think I'm going to give up on trying to solve this mystery. If you can discover JG's identity, so can I. I just wish you could believe me. And don't worry about me or my safety. It's up to me if I want to pursue it. It's you I worry about. I care about you." He spun on his heel and strode away, eyes fixated on the concrete walk, his tennis shoes making very little noise.

She had hurt his feelings, and that had never been her intention.

His leaving sent a pain to the middle of her chest.

❧

Ever since the bombing at the heritage center a few days ago, Kayleigh hadn't slept well. Here it was, three in the morning, and she was prowling about the house like a cat burglar. Maybe a little warm milk would help. Mom swore by it.

She paced in small circles as the glowing green numbers ticked off the time and the microwave beeped that time was up. As she pulled her mug out, a loud boom cracked nearby, and the house shook. What in the world was that? There weren't storms in the area. A firecracker, maybe? But at this hour?

And that smell. Gasoline.

Adrenaline shot through her, and she raced toward her bedroom, mug still in her hand.

Her window was broken, shards of glass shining in the red-orange light from flames licking at her curtains and her bedding.

If she hadn't gotten up, she would have been injured.

Or worse.

The mug fell from her hands and shattered on the tile floor.

Her phone was on the bedside table. Each second, the flames intensified. There was no way she could get it.

Her heart stuck in her throat and cut off her breathing. She had to get out of here. Clad only in her nightshirt, she slipped on a pair of flip-flops that were by the door and raced to the neighbor.

She pounded on the door. "Help! Help! Fire!"

It took a few moments for the young mother to open up. "Kayleigh, get in here. What's going on?" In the background, a baby wailed.

"Call 911. Someone just threw something through my bedroom window and started a fire."

"No." Yvonne covered her mouth.

"Yes. Please, hurry. Or give me your phone while you get your family out. You have to leave. The fire is spreading fast."

Yvonne raced from the room and returned moments later with her screaming son on her hip, her husband following as he spoke on the phone.

Adam took control. "The fire department is on its way. Let's go. Yvonne, grab the diaper bag on your way to the door." He herded them outside, then went to wake the other neighbors.

Yvonne jiggled the baby, and he snuggled against her. "How did this start? What's going on?"

Kayleigh's throat burned, and not from smoke. "I wish I knew. Someone has it out for me and tried to really hurt me tonight. I just want it to stop." This search for her roots wasn't worth her life. Why would someone resort to such means to try to harm her?

Though to Kayleigh it was an eternity before the fire trucks raced to the scene, it was probably only mere minutes. The police also arrived, along with an ambulance. One of the paramedics gave her a blanket to wrap herself in, and the firefighters got to their work while the police came to interrogate her.

This was getting to be too much of a pattern. At least it wasn't the same officers as the other day. This crew was the overnight shift. They'd probably seen it all.

By rote, she answered their questions. What happened? Who would do this? What else can you tell us?

Due to their great skill, the firefighters managed to knock down the flames in short order, though the acrid odor of burning wood and fabric and the thick smoke lingered in the air. The head firefighter, the one who had ordered and organized the others, came to the police officer still attempting to draw information from Kayleigh.

He held a curved piece of glass in his hand. "We found this and others like it and a metal bottle lid. It's early in the investigation, but it appears this was a Molotov cocktail. Maybe two. Rudimentary but effective."

The officer, a haze of dark whiskers covering his cheeks and chin, peppered her with more questions.

By the time the questioning ended and the officer told her she was free to go, the sun was peeking over the horizon. Her condo was a crime scene. Thank goodness it hadn't spread to any of the other units and her neighbors were allowed to return home.

Because of the ongoing investigation, the authorities forbade her from entering her home. Even if she could have grabbed a few clothes, they would have reeked of smoke, so there was no use in asking to get some.

"Do you have a place to stay?" The officer gave her a small smile. To his credit, he had been kind to her.

She nodded. "My friend is out of town, but I have a key to her place, and I know she won't mind me staying there. Not that I can call her and ask. My phone was next to my bed. It's probably toast."

"More than likely."

"And my keys are on a hook by the door to the garage."

"We can get those for you, and it's no problem for you to take your car. Some of the other officers swept it, and it's clean."

She didn't even want to ponder what he meant by that.

"The only problem is. . ."

Of course there would be a problem.

"We don't want you to be alone. There's strength in numbers. Do you have anyone else you can call?"

She ran through her list of coworkers and friends. The ones she would call didn't have room for her. Others, she wouldn't think of burdening. With the danger nipping at her heels, she hesitated to name anyone in case that meant putting them in harm's way.

She shook her head.

Just then, a red pickup truck pulled up.

Brandon. Just what she needed.

He approached her, hair disheveled, dressed in sweatpants and a Van Halen T-shirt with a hole in it. "What happened?"

She bit back the lump rising in her throat. "How did you know what was going on?"

"Sometimes when I can't sleep, I listen to the police scanner. Strangely enough, it relaxes me." He shrugged.

"O-kay." Kayleigh drew out the word.

"So what's this all about?"

"Another bombing. This one directed straight at me. If I hadn't been up getting some warm milk, I might be in the hospital now."

The officer beside her nodded. "At the very least."

Brandon opened his arms, and she couldn't resist their draw. However he managed to find his way here, he was here. Before she knew it, she found herself buried in his chest, sobbing. He stroked her back and her loose hair, speaking something into her ear that she didn't try to hear. Just the cadence of his words was soothing.

Finally, her tears subsided, and she stepped away. She'd left a big wet spot on his black shirt. "Sorry about that."

"You have nothing to be sorry about. If I ever get my hands on the jerk who did this to you. . ."

"Where am I supposed to go? I have no clothes, not even my phone. They won't let me back inside, and my phone was right where they threw the explosive. It was either blasted to smithereens or melted."

"Right now, you need some tender care. While I'd love to be the one to provide it, I have to get to work, and I won't compromise your reputation by having you stay with me. Noreen, my pastor's wife, is known for her compassionate heart. She'd love to pamper you."

"I don't want to have anything happen to her because of me."

"You have to go somewhere. I'll call her and ask her before we go if it would make you feel better."

"It would."

So long as the woman didn't preach at her. That was the last thing she needed—someone hawking at her about how good and loving God was.

Judging by the smoke-smudged hull of her house, He was just the opposite.

CHAPTER THIRTY-SIX

April 18, 1836

True to his word, John had remained by Josie's side almost every minute of every day. She and Charlotte had traveled with the army as they marched east. Many of the soldiers weren't happy with Mr. Houston's refusal to engage Santa Anna.

He must have a plan though. That's why he sent John and Josie out today to scout. Chariot and John's horse slogged through the mud, even as more rain fell. Underneath her soaked wool coat, Josie shivered. "This is madness. Why doesn't Mr. Houston turn around and fight?"

"He's afraid his troops aren't seasoned enough to stand against the Mexicans, though they aren't that well trained themselves. He's going to have to take action soon, or else he'll have a full-on mutiny on his hands."

Josie was no military mind, but right now, according to all they knew, they had the numbers advantage on Santa Anna. Delaying might allow reinforcements to arrive and swell their enemy's numbers. If that happened, the fight might turn into another Alamo. Already there had been the massacre at Goliad. More men had died there than at the Alamo.

It was unthinkable.

As Chariot sloshed through the marsh, tall grasses grazing Josie's legs, she leaned over his withers and rubbed his neck. "My faithful companion. What would I do without you? I know this is difficult, but you must keep going. It's what we all must do."

"Wise words."

John's compliment dissipated her shivering, even if only for a moment. "Words I've been striving to live by these past few weeks, though I don't know how much longer Charlotte can keep up the pace. Perhaps we should go to Galveston where the government is and await the outcome."

"Even wiser words."

"How I wish, though, that I could stay with you." Forever. He had yet to ask her to be his wife. But he'd told her he loved her. That had to count for something.

So she waited, much like the Texan army.

When she glanced up, she caught movement in the distance. "John." She pointed toward the horizon straight ahead.

He squinted and leaned forward. "From the looks of it, I would say a lone rider, but it's impossible at this distance to tell if it be friend or foe. Whoever it is, they are headed straight in this direction."

She reined Chariot toward a stand of oaks not far from the swamp. If nothing else, it would provide them some protection from the rain while they waited for whoever was riding toward them.

John followed suit.

They found cover under the round-edged leaves, rain pattering above them, the leaves dancing with each drop. One hit Josie square on the nose, and she wiped it away.

The rider approached, larger and closer each moment. He wore the uniform of a Mexican private.

John leaned over to whisper to Josie. "When he comes, we'll jump out and take him by surprise. I'll go in front of him, you pen him in by the rear. Don't shoot. Since he's alone, he's likely a courier. We'll want him alive. I've no taste for taking another man's life."

The rider approached, his Mexican pony struggling in the mucky swamp, his pace slow. Perfect for them to intercept him.

She turned her attention to John, studying his strong profile. What a wonderful silhouette that would be to hang in her house.

No, thoughts of John couldn't distract her. She had a job to do. At his nod, she dug her heels into Chariot's flank, and he bounded forward. John and his horse were right beside her.

Once they broke through the trees, they parted, Josie moving behind the gaping courier, John approaching him head-on. Josie drew a borrowed gun and trained it on the Mexican's backside.

If Manuel were in front of her, what would she do? Just the idea of him, and she was squeezing the weapon for all she was worth, her finger twitching over the trigger. "By orders of Sam Houston and the Texan Army, I command you to halt."

The man raised his hands in surrender, never even reaching for his rifle or his sword. "I will give you what you need. Just don't hurt me, *por favor*. I beg you to spare me."

Just like they had spared Father and the other men at the Alamo? He deserved no mercy.

John's eyes, however, softened, though he continued to point his gun at their prisoner. "Josie, tie him up."

She reached in her saddlebag for Chariot's lead and used that to bind the

Mexican. Even though he could have overpowered her without a problem, he offered no resistance. Tales had reached them that Santa Anna had conscripted soldiers as he chased the Texans toward the east. Perhaps this man had little to no loyalty to the dictator.

Each turn of the lead brought another memory to mind, of Manuel binding her hands and feet and slinging her over his saddle. This turn of the lead was for killing Mother and Laura. This turn was for stealing her innocence. This turn for was ripping her child from her life.

"Josie." John's soft call of her name snapped her to attention. "That's enough."

She shook her head. What was she thinking? She loosened the lead and mounted Chariot once more.

All the while they were taking him to Mr. Houston, John and Josie didn't speak. She followed his lead, behind the prisoner, and together they brought him to their camp.

A grin broke out across Mr. Houston's face when they presented their captive to him. "Well done." He motioned an aide forward. "Search this prisoner and bring me whatever you find on his person."

John loaned Josie a hand in dismounting. "Is anything bothering you?"

She shook her head.

"Be honest with me."

Her legs trembled, and if not for John's supporting arm around her, she might have collapsed in a heap. "The memories overwhelm me from time to time."

"This is too much for you. Go and pack. I'll escort you, Charlotte, and George to Galveston and then rejoin Houston. Once this is over, I will come to you. I long for you to be safe and well."

She nodded, but before she had gone three steps, Senora Navarro ran to meet her. "I'm so glad you're back. Senora Wilkins has fallen ill. She needs you."

Josie scurried ahead of Senora Navarro to the tent where Charlotte lay on the pallet, pale and sweating.

"Josephine, there you are."

"What happened? What's wrong? You were fine when I left."

"I don't know. Such pains, such pains in my stomach. And then I woke up in the tent. How is George?"

Senora Navarro peeked in. "I have him with me, senora. Do not worry. He is fine."

Charlotte nodded and drifted back to sleep.

"She is burning with fever, senorita. She grabbed her middle, cried in pain, and fainted. I have been bathing her with cool water, but I don't know what else to do."

Neither did Josie. She knelt beside Charlotte's pallet, removed the warm wash rag, and replaced it with a cooler one. "It's too late for childbed fever, isn't it?"

"I think so. I don't know."

Josie leaned over Charlotte. "We may not have seen eye to eye in the past, but we are all we have now. You have little George to think about. He can't be left without parents. For him, you must recover. Please, please, fight for your son."

Throughout the rest of the afternoon and into the evening, Senora Navarro came and went, along with one or two of her older daughters. To Josie, they were background fog. She focused her attention on Charlotte. If possible, her fever spiked higher, and her breathing slowed.

"No. Do you hear me? You can't give up. Your baby needs you. I need you." Together she and Charlotte could keep Father's memory alive. They could care for George and remind him what a wonderful father he had. It was wrong that he lose both parents the way Josie had.

As the shadows deepened, the tent flap opened a tiny bit. "May I come in?"

John. For the first time since she'd arrived, Josie allowed herself to relax her shoulders. She stretched her aching back. "Come."

He ducked low to enter and had to almost waddle across the small shelter. "How is she?"

"Not very good, I'm afraid. I can't believe how fast this happened. She was fine this morning. A little tired, maybe, but George had fussed a good part of the night, nothing out of the usual. She urged me to go with you." The words *If I had stayed* dangled on the end of her tongue, but there was nothing she could have done to prevent this.

John sat beside Josie, grasped her by the hand, and intoned the words of a prayer. To her they didn't make much sense. She couldn't comprehend them or focus on them. But the rhythm of them flowed over her like water over parched land.

At one point, an infant cried in the distance. Manuel was there, leering at her, his face contorted, his bulbous nose growing until it consumed his face.

Then the child ceased crying.

Josie jolted awake.

She lay on her own pallet, and Senora Navarro bent over Charlotte. A thin stream of sunlight wound its way into the tent. Josie rubbed her eyes. "Is it morning?"

"*Sí*. You slept, and that is good."

"How is Charlotte?"

"Holding her own."

"Praise the Lord."

"I have been praying all night."

Josie rose and went to the woman's side. *"Gracias, mi amiga.* You have been so good to us. We can never repay you."

Senora Navarro straightened the rough blanket around Charlotte's thin shoulders. Josie hadn't noticed until now how much weight Charlotte had lost. Perhaps she'd been ill for some time and hadn't told anyone.

"Go freshen up and get something to eat." Senora Navarro sat back on her heels. "Then you can relieve me. It is almost time for George to feed. I have enough milk for my daughter and him."

"I never even thought about that."

"Because you are not yet a mother yourself. That day will come."

Little did Senora Navarro know how wrong her words were. Oh, the tears she'd cried when her milk came in a few days after what she believed was her child's death. How had Manuel fed Naomi?

Josie exited the tent, the bright sunshine an unusual event these days, almost blinding her. She took several steps before almost running into someone.

He grabbed her and held her from falling on her backside in the mud. "I was coming to check on you."

"Good morning, John. My apologies for falling asleep while you were praying last night."

"Part of my prayer was that the Lord would provide you what you needed. That proved to be sleep, and I'm glad you were able to enjoy some."

"Charlotte remains very ill."

John shook his head. "I will double my efforts, though our heavenly Father knows what we need. A piece of good news now. The papers the courier we apprehended yesterday was carrying detailed Mexican troop movements and Santa Anna's plans for engagement. Very valuable information."

"I'm so glad."

"He appears headed toward Lynchburg, so he's close."

"You'll go after him there, then?"

"Yes. We leave immediately." He pulled her behind a stand of nearby trees. "I know this is all very untoward, especially since I am a minister of the Word, but. . ." He bent over and kissed her, soft and slow at first, then deep, full of passion, full of love, full of promise.

A tingle rushed from her lips to the tips of her toes, like sunshine sparkling on water. She leaned into him and relished the feel of his lips against hers, his arms encircling her. Like a cloth to a slate, the goodness, pureness, and love in this kiss erased all of Manuel's rough, possessive kisses.

So she savored every moment, the rhythm of her heart the beat of a song. A song of love. Of desire.

All too soon, he broke away, both of them breathing hard.

She traced the outline of his jaw. "Please, just promise to come back to me."

CHAPTER THIRTY-SEVEN

Present day

*N*ow you just enjoy that nice, hot shower, and when you get out, I'll have this bed all made up for you with some fresh sheets." Noreen bustled to the linen closet in the hall.

"You don't have to do that. I can make the bed myself." What Kayleigh needed, maybe even more than a shower, was a Diet Coke. But she couldn't ask Noreen for that. "Especially since we woke you up in the middle of the night." She shot a glance at Brandon, who leaned against the hallway wall.

His face was unreadable.

"Nonsense, it's not the middle of the night. I was already up for the day. You've been through an ordeal. I can't even imagine what it must have been like. Great heavens, I'd still be shaking if I were you."

Precisely why she needed that Coke. She trembled more than San Francisco during an earthquake.

"Go on, now." Noreen flicked her away. "Things won't look so bleak after a good rest. And you can sleep well knowing you're safe in God's hands. Unless you're uncomfortable because my husband is out of town." She busied herself with snapping sheets across the bed in the simple but pretty blue and white room.

"No. Not at all." Anywhere with anyone was better than alone. Kayleigh moved to help her, but Brandon stopped her with a touch to her elbow. He led her from the room.

She spun the ring on her finger. At least she'd been wearing it. At least it was safe.

For now.

"You have to tell me what you know."

She blew her smoky bangs from her eyes. "I don't want to throw around accusations, but I can't fully trust that you won't swipe the ring from me. I've put my trust in too many people, only to have them prove untrustworthy. Just understand that it's difficult for me to have faith in anyone, especially under these circumstances."

"It's entirely possible this has nothing whatsoever to do with the ring. Perhaps it's your work, unpopular to say the least, that's provoking this."

"So it's my fault?"

Brandon turned in several circles before facing her again. "This isn't the time to be getting into this. It's late, or early, depending on your point of view. You've been traumatized. It's better that we speak later when we've both calmed down and had some sleep. Tell Noreen goodbye for me."

"Thank you." Her words stopped him in his tracks. "I've probably come off as ungrateful and rude, but you've been kind and helpful. I do appreciate that."

"I understand. Maybe a little more than you know."

Even though Noreen was gracious and accommodating and had provided Kayleigh with everything she would need, between replaying the firebombing and Brandon's last words to her, Kayleigh got very little sleep.

⁓⊱✤⊰⁓

Kayleigh rose about noon, and the rest of the day was filled with speaking to the police and purchasing new items for herself. It wasn't until much later that she was able to return to Noreen's and sit and take a breath.

Noreen cooked a wonderful pan of lasagna and homemade French bread. The tanginess and slight spiciness hit the spot. No wonder they labeled it comfort food.

Brandon sat across from her. He had been so kind to her. How could she even entertain the idea that he might want to take the ring from her? Perhaps it was a good time to tell him what she'd discovered. She finished the bite of cheese and noodles, swallowed, and sipped her water. "I went to the Béxar Heritage Center, and I think I know who JG might be."

Brandon leaned forward in his chair. "You did what? You do?"

"Yes. The curator there told me about a man who fought with the Old Eighteen at Gonzales but who wasn't at the Alamo. His name was John Gilbert."

At this, Noreen dropped her fork, and it clattered to the floor. "Did you say John Gilbert?"

"I did." She had told Noreen about the ring this morning at breakfast but nothing specific about the inscription. "The engraving has the initials JG and JW. From what we gather, the ring may have belonged to John Gilbert at some point. And when Mom and I visited the Alamo, we discovered a Josephine Wilkins who might be part of the story. She also survived the battle."

"May I see the ring?" Noreen scooted forward on her chair.

Kayleigh slipped it from her finger and handed it to Noreen. "The inscription is old and difficult to read." She told her what it said. "We don't know what *Fe* is, and we have no way of knowing for sure who either of the initials might be."

A broad smile crossed Noreen's face, crinkles appearing at the corners of her eyes. She pushed back from the table and dropped her napkin beside her plate. "You wait here. I have something you may be very interested in."

CHAPTER THIRTY-EIGHT

April 19, 1836

The long, dark night pressed on Josie, a heavy mantle on her shoulders. She and Charlotte weren't alone in the camp. There were many other women and children and a few men who were too old or too sick to fight. Mr. Houston had wanted the Tejanos to stay back and guard them, afraid they would be mistaken for Mexicans, but they insisted on going to the battle and Mr. Houston relented.

Charlotte remained very ill. Every once in a while, Josie managed to get her to sip a bit of broth or a swallow of water, but nothing more. She grew weaker by the hour.

After nursing George for his middle-of-the-night feeding, Senora Navarro came in to relieve Josie. Before she could settle down for a rest, she needed a bit of privacy. The blackness of the night and the clouds scuttling the moon provided her cover for her business.

As she walked, she prayed for Charlotte's healing, for John's safety and the success of the battle, for peace for her still-grieving heart. By the time she stopped to take stock of where she was, she discovered herself much farther from camp than she had intended, beyond the scope of the guards.

No sooner had she turned to head closer to safety than someone grabbed her from behind and covered her mouth so she couldn't scream.

The odor of tequila and cigars was heavy on him. And familiar enough to gag her.

"I have you at last, little vixen."

She fought against Manuel, stomping on his foot. His heavy boot prevented her from doing much damage. On the next try, she aimed higher, and this time, Manuel let out a primal howl and released her.

She spun around and picked up a rock. Thank goodness they were near a river, swollen though it was. Mud covered the stone, and it was slippery. She needed both hands to hang on to it. "What do you want? That day in the church, you said the ring was the prize you sought. Now you have it. Keep it.

Déjame en paz. Don't ever bother me again."

Her pulse pounded in her ears and thrummed in her wrist.

"*Sí*, that was the prize, but I miss your companionship. I need a woman like you to warm my bed at night."

The world around Josie spun. She locked her knees to remain upright. "Never. Never. You will never have me like that again."

"Even if I would give you Luisa?"

Tremors shook her entire body. Luisa. Her daughter. Manuel was offering her the chance to mother her own child, to be able to hold her and kiss her, to tell her that her mother loved her deeply and always had.

Why would Manuel do that? There was only one explanation. "You're lying. I know it as well as I know my own name. If I would go with you, you would never allow me access to my daughter."

"But wouldn't you like to see her face, even once, for a moment? To gaze on her long, dark lashes."

She had long, dark lashes, just as Josie always dreamed she had. It was to that thin thread that she clung. "I am not up for sale. Not even for my daughter."

"Such a shame." Manuel reached behind himself for his gun. "Because you are mine, I cannot allow another man to have you. Especially not that tall one you are in love with."

Just as he withdrew his rifle, Josie flung the stone at him with all her might, striking him in his shoulder. The weapon dropped to the ground as Manuel backed away.

As quick as a deer in flight, Josie snatched the rifle and pointed it at him. This was the moment she'd been waiting for, dreaming about. She clenched the gun's butt and fingered the trigger.

In her mind, she watched him fall, the life oozing out of him as it had out of Mother, Laura, and Father. Directly or indirectly, he'd had a hand in all their deaths. And her daughter was as good as dead to her.

"You wouldn't shoot me. I know where she is. You need me."

"I don't need you." She pinched the words through clenched teeth. She rested the gun's butt on her shoulder.

Justice must be served. Manuel needed to pay for his many, many crimes. God demanded blood for blood, didn't he? Her pulse pounded in her ears, her cheeks, her entire body on fire.

"Love your enemies."

Not those that slaughtered your family and stole everything valuable to you.

"Pray for them."

She would pray that his soul would suffer in eternal torment.

"Love your enemies."

This was too much. God was asking too much from her.

"Pray for them."

She couldn't.

"Pray for them."

How could she forgive him for all he had done? He'd stolen her entire family from her. She had so little left. She couldn't allow him to get away without serving the penalty for his sins.

The penalty for his sins. The words rattled around Josie's brain. The penalty for sins.

"If you forgive men their trespasses, your heavenly Father will also forgive you."

How can I do that, Lord? How can I just let it go?

"Faith, child. Just have faith."

I am of such little faith, Lord. Help my unbelief.

"Faith."

The word that John admonished her with. Just have faith. Believe there is One higher and greater than yourself. Faith meant putting her trust in Him. As a deer longs for a drink on a hot summer afternoon, her spirit longed for that faith, that all-consuming, all-powerful faith.

Lord, take away my anger and my hatred. The seething heat in her chest eased a slight bit.

"Vengeance is mine. I will repay. Have faith that I will accomplish what I have promised."

I leave him in Your hands, then, Lord. As You have just shown it to me, may He know Your love and mercy.

The bands that had wound themselves around her rib cage the moment Manuel entered their cabin the very first time loosened. She drew in the deepest breath of her life. When she released it, she released all her resentment and bitterness.

She breathed free, like stepping from a smoky house to the fresh outdoors.

Little by little, she lowered the rifle but not her guard. *"¡Váyase!* Don't ever bother me or anyone I know again."

Manuel started forward, and she raised the gun once more. "You will not touch me. Now go, before I pull the trigger."

Behind her, branches broke. Whatever was there was enough to send Manuel scampering away into the inky night.

For a long time, she stood stock-still in case he returned. He never did. A deer bounded from the thicket, its eyes shining even in the darkness. It drank from the stream and skipped away.

At last Josie made her way back to camp. *Thank You, Lord, for keeping me from pulling the trigger. I would have been no better than him. I truly do pray that You would work in his heart and show him Your love, that in You, he may find forgiveness for all his sins.*

April 22, 1836

As the sunbeams streamed through the clouds, turning the bottoms of them pink and yellow and orange, Charlotte breathed her last. Josie held George in her arms as tears streaked down her cheeks. "Your mama loved you so." She kissed her brother's soft cheek. "She and Father would want you to grow up to be a strong man, kind and thoughtful and loving toward all. They will be proud of you."

George fussed, then settled into the crook of Josie's arm, his dark lashes sweeping his fair cheek as he slumbered, his mouth puckering in his dreams. He would never remember the mother or father who gave him birth, but as far as it was up to Josie, she would make sure he never forgot.

Josie left the tent and allowed Senora Navarro and the other women to come in and prepare Charlotte's body. For her part, Josie was numb to it all. Too much loss had hardened her heart.

John wasn't here to perform the funeral. Perhaps even as Josie stood facing east, toward the dawning of a new day, he was locked in a battle for Texas independence and his very life.

Protect him, Lord.

If she had to face the death of yet another loved one, she would shatter into a million pieces. Yet two that she had thought had passed to their eternal rest—John and Naomi—still lived and breathed. One she prayed would return to her.

She peered at George, his forehead wrinkled like that of an old man. "I won't leave you, I promise. You have no one else to raise you, to teach you, to protect you. We'll find our way together. For you, and only for you, I will allow my dream to die so you can have yours."

With an infant to care for, she couldn't conduct a search for her daughter. Even if she knew where to begin looking, George demanded her time and attention. He had no one else. Naomi did. At least that's what Josie prayed and believed. "I give her to You, Father. You must be the One to take care of her because I can't. She is and always has been Your child before she was ever mine. I give her back to You. For me, take very good care of her."

Like the eagle that soared high above the sky and disappeared into the dawning morning, so her dreams for her child took flight to the heavens, where she vouchsafed them.

Two tears, just two, flowed from the corners of her eyes. That was all she allowed herself. If she truly meant what she had told the Lord, then she couldn't weep.

She turned her face away and lifted George to her shoulder. Like a wooden soldier, she went about the tasks that needed to be done. Senora Navarro continued to act as George's wet nurse—one function Josie was unable to perform. Other than that, she fashioned a papoose for him and carried him much the way Bright Star carried her own infant.

Her brother was her gift. Not a replacement for Naomi, but a gift nonetheless, and one that eased her heartache and brought her a small measure of joy.

Around the noon hour, a disturbance rose around the camp. Women gasped and, clutching their children in one hand and their skirts in the other, raced to the east.

Josie turned, and over the ridge rode John, as tall and proud as ever. So many other men came with him. Had they even fought the Mexicans? What had happened?

Swept in the tide of other women, Josie forged her way toward John, George still strapped to her.

The soldiers rode into the camp, each sliding from his mount's back and into the arms of the woman he loved.

John was no exception. As soon as his boots hit the ground, he gathered Josie and George and pressed them close. Closer than propriety allowed, but then again, what did it matter?

He swooped her up and spun her around. "We did it. We beat them good and sound. Some are off hunting down Santa Anna and his right-hand man, General Cos, but I have no doubt that the once high-and-mighty Mexican dictator will be more than willing to take our terms. Within days, I expect Texas to be a free country."

"And the casualties?"

"Only a handful. Nothing compared to the losses they suffered."

"Praise the Lord."

He set her on the ground once more. "But you aren't as joyful as I expected you to be."

"Charlotte passed into glory this morning."

"I am so sorry, Josie, more than you will ever know."

"I've made my decision. George is now my responsibility to raise. There is no one else. He will be my first priority. That means I've had to give Naomi into the Lord's hand. I will never know where she is or who is raising her, but He does. He will watch over her and bless her."

"She won't have Manuel for a father. That much I can tell you."

She jiggled as George fussed. "What do you mean?" She should understand what John was saying, but she couldn't fathom it.

"Manuel was killed in battle today. I saw his body myself."

She reached out for John. "Are you sure?"

"There is no doubt in my mind."

"Did you search him? Did he have the ring?" Did she dare to hope? "Any information about Naomi?"

"I'm afraid not. There was nothing on his person other than what he needed for the fight. He took a ball to his stomach, though it appeared he also had been injured on his shoulder at some point."

"I pray he made his peace with his Maker before that shot found him."

John searched her face, his gaze as intense as the summer sun. "Truly?"

"Truly. I have forgiven him. God has different plans for me, ones that include George and making a life for him. That's why He brought me to this place, and I am happy I can be here."

"Do you know how much I love you?"

"If it's half as much as I love you, that's a great deal."

"It certainly is. Enough that I want to spend the rest of my life with you. This isn't the time or the place, but one day, very soon, I'm going to ask you properly to be my wife."

"I don't need anything fancy or elaborate. You don't need to find another time to make an offer to me, because my answer will be the same then as it is today. It would be the greatest pleasure of my life to be joined to you in matrimony."

From the trees along the riverbank, birds sang out their songs of joy, more melodious than a thousand church bells. "I love you, Josephine Wilkins, and I always will."

"I'll love you forever, John Gilbert."

CHAPTER THIRTY-NINE

May 21, 1836

GALVESTON, REPUBLIC OF TEXAS

*I*n the cool of the early morning, before the sun scorched the day and put everyone into a foul mood, Josie donned a lovely pale blue gown with lace around the neck and hem and large sleeves. Senora Navarro helped her to braid and coil her hair. When she held the looking glass for Josie to see, it was as if her eyes deceived her.

Soft, dark waves of hair fell along the sides of her face. Her eyes shone, and a pale pink dusted her cheeks. She bit her lips to give them a touch of color.

Senora Navarro kissed Josie on the cheek. "You are very lovely, senorita, though I won't be able to call you that for much longer."

A salty breeze blew in off the gulf. Josie licked her lips. "Do you think John will be pleased?"

"You could wear a flour sack, and he would not be able to take his eyes from you. Your mother and father would be so proud of you, the way you love George and John. I pray God will bless your little family and enlarge it."

The heat in Josie's cheeks had nothing to do with the temperature of the room. To be held in John's arms tonight was a delight she didn't allow herself to anticipate. If so, she would rush through her vows and leave the breakfast the women had prepared.

"And do not worry about George. I will take good care of him tonight. Enjoy being a married woman."

"Enough." Josie giggled. "You'll embarrass me and have me in a tizzy before the ceremony even begins."

"Then let's find John and have the minister unite you."

From the single trunk of belongings that Josie possessed, she pulled out Mother's small Bible. The pages were thin and fragile, the cover worn by many years of daily use. Mother and Father couldn't be here with her, but this was the next best thing. She and John would base their marriage on the commands and wisdom found within this book.

She and Senora Navarro traversed the short distance from the house where they were staying to the pastor's home. The plump pastor's wife opened the door and escorted them inside. Would that be Josie in twenty years?

It was a simple abode, but pleasant with cheery furnishings and homey touches like a clock that ticked on the large fireplace mantel. John stood in front of one of the windows overlooking the water, staring out.

When her shoes tapped on the floors, however, he spun around. His eyes widened and his grin stretched as large as Texas itself. He approached her and took her by both hands. "You are the loveliest creature I have ever beheld."

He had trimmed his hair and smoothed it back. He wore white trousers and a long, dark morning coat with a dark red vest that highlighted his fair features. "You are a most handsome man. I am blessed to become your wife."

The pastor called them to stand in front of him. The middle-aged man with round, red cheeks opened his Bible and began the covenant service.

Josie couldn't concentrate on anything other than the man beside her, the man who was promising to stay beside her for the rest of his life.

"Repeat after me." Josie focused on the pastor. "I, Josephine Faith Wilkins. . ."

"I, Josephine Faith Wilkins, do pledge and covenant before God and these witnesses to be your faithful and loving wife; to honor, cherish, and obey you for richer or poorer, in sickness and in health, for as long as we both shall live. This is my solemn vow."

"Do you, John Peter Gilbert, accept this woman as your wife?"

"I do."

John placed a simple gold band on her finger. It wasn't quite like having Mother's ring, but the meaning behind it made it all worth it.

"By the power vested in me by the church of Jesus Christ, I now pronounce you husband and wife. You may kiss your bride."

Though soft and gentle, John's kiss was lingering and filled with promise.

Senora Navarro and Sam Houston cheered the new couple and then disappeared into the dining room where the pastor's wife had prepared breakfast.

John held her back. When they were alone, he resumed the kiss, this time with much more pressure on her lips, more passion, more love. All of it left her desiring more, desiring that the breakfast would not last long, that evening would come soon. At last he pulled away, but not far. "I have a gift for you, Mrs. Gilbert."

"You didn't have to get me anything." She hadn't a thing for him. What little funds she possessed before their marriage went to George's needs.

"It isn't much, but I hope it means something to you." He reached into the pocket of his morning coat and pulled out a piece of paper, which he handed to her.

She unfolded it. *Fe/JG2JW/MAR36*

"It's what I had engraved on the ring when your father took it from you. I have been planning for a while to ask you to be my bride. He gave us his blessing."

She blinked away the moisture that gathered in the corner of her eyes. "It's beautiful. Thank you so much. I may not have the ring, but I will always have the promise that was engraved on it."

"A promise I intend to keep to the very end of my days."

And so, as Mr. and Mrs. Gilbert, they left the room to begin the rest of their lives.

CHAPTER FORTY

Present day

*K*ayleigh turned to Brandon and raised one eyebrow. He raised one back. So then, neither of them knew what Noreen was getting.

He toyed with the napkin at the side of his plate. "How are you really doing?"

"Hanging on by a thread. I'm exhausted and overwhelmed. There's so much going on with the authorities and the insurance, not to mention all I have to replace. And my job. Even though I took the day off, my phone, once I got a new one, keeps ringing. Tomorrow I have to go into the office and get some work done."

"And emotionally?"

She hadn't allowed herself to feel anything since the entire incident occurred. There was too much else to do. If she talked about it, she would unleash a torrent of tears she may not be able to stem. "Scared. Angry. All the feels." Her cheeks dampened as a few tears leaked out.

Before she knew what was happening, Brandon was at her side, gathering her into his arms, allowing her to weep.

"Don't worry." He spoke the soft words into her hair, his breath brushing her ear, sending goose bumps up and down her arms. "You'll see how it turns out all for good. That's how God always operates."

She dried her tears and sat back. In a way, her parents' deaths had turned out for good. She'd had a loving family who taught her about the Lord and provided well for her. Everything so far in her life had led her to this point.

Looking back with more than twenty years of hindsight was one thing. It was difficult to see the good in the circumstances when she had no home and was being threatened by an unknown enemy.

Still in his arms, she touched his cheek. "How did you get to be so wise?"

Noreen picked that moment to enter the room. Kayleigh jumped from Brandon's embrace and dabbed at her eyes with her napkin. A moment later, Noreen set a large book in front of Kayleigh. The title read *One Hundred Years of Faith Church: 1836–1936.*

She shook her head. "I don't get what this has to do with the ring and everything else."

"Didn't you see the date of the founding of the congregation?"

"1836." The lightbulb clicked on. "The year of the Alamo. The year engraved on the ring."

"Exactly. Now open to the first page."

Kayleigh followed Noreen's instruction and discovered a list of all their pastors. The first few were drawings or paintings. It wasn't until later in the 1800s there were photographs.

She studied the faces of the men who had presented the gospel to the people of the area for a hundred years at that point. Almost two hundred now. She gazed at the first one and caught a glimpse of the name below it.

John Gilbert.

She sucked in a breath. "Is this our John Gilbert?"

"I believe he is." Noreen sat at the table and sipped her coffee. By this time, it must be lukewarm at best. "If you read further, you'll find it says he established the church in San Antonio after the battle of the Alamo, once Texas became a republic. His biography is a few pages in."

Kayleigh flipped the pages until she came to one labeled *Our Pastors.* It proceeded to give biographies of all the ones they'd had up until that time, beginning with John Gilbert.

It spoke of how he valiantly fought at the battles of Gonzales and Concepción during the Texas Revolution, of how he was at the Alamo until the night before the battle when he rode out of the mission to Sam Houston to urge the reinforcements to hurry.

Brandon had been reading over her shoulder, and she tapped the book at that section. "So he did have ties to Sam Houston. And now we know how he could have been at the Alamo and yet escaped."

He nodded. "Fascinating, absolutely fascinating. Imagine sneaking out in the middle of the night to undertake such a dangerous mission, only to return to discover everyone was slaughtered."

"No." Kayleigh returned her attention to the book. "Remember, there was that group of women that Santa Anna sent to take a message to Sam Houston, so they would have known of the defeat before they ever reached the Alamo."

"And I thought I was the history nerd." Brandon chuckled.

Kayleigh joined him. "I've out-nerded you."

"Seems you have."

"Keep reading." Noreen leaned across the table. "You haven't even gotten to the good part." She motioned for Kayleigh to continue reading.

"He married Josephine Wilkins, a survivor of the Alamo, on May 21, 1836." Kayleigh couldn't breathe. This was the biggest break they'd had yet. "Josephine Wilkins. JW is for Josephine Wilkins."

Brandon gave a single clap of his hands. "We've almost deciphered the entire ring."

Kayleigh had to finish reading the story. "'They raised her half brother after her father was killed in the Alamo and her stepmother died soon after childbirth.' How sad. So tragic. 'They went on to have seven children of their own. They both always said how it was faith that saw them through the toughest times of their lives.'"

She couldn't stop the smile that spread across her face. "They had their happy ending. I'm so glad to know that the owner of this ring had a beautiful life. But how did it come to be in my family's possession back in Mexico?"

"That remains the great mystery." Brandon shook his head.

"Not such a great mystery." Noreen handed them another sheet of paper. "This is very old and was written by Josephine Gilbert herself. We found it hidden in the walls of the original part of the house when we were doing some renovations a few years ago. Yes, John and Josie Gilbert built this house themselves. She was a remarkable woman who led a remarkable life."

With a great deal of care not to rip the yellowed paper, Kayleigh set it between her and Brandon. The faded script was difficult to make out but clear enough that with a little work, they were able to decipher it.

> *This is my true and accurate witness to the events of my life, so help me God. When I was but fifteen, I was kidnapped by a band of ruffian Mexicans after one of them slaughtered my mother and my younger sister, all to wrench my mother's cat's-eye ring from her finger. This ring was key to securing a vast fortune in Mexico, though we were unaware of it at the time my mother took possession of it.*
>
> *Though we were not married, the leader of the group, the man who held the grudge against my family, got me with child. I believed my daughter had died and didn't learn that she lived until two years later. By then, she was in Mexico, in a place I never knew. Because my husband and I raised my half brother and then the other children God blessed us with, I was never able to search for her.*
>
> *Not a day passes that I don't think of my child and pray for her health, her well-being, and her spiritual maturity. By now she is likely married with children of her own. Does she know about me?*

As for the cat's-eye ring, I repossessed it at one point. John took it and engraved it for me, but when the battle of the Alamo occurred, the same ruffian cruelly ripped it from my finger, though I had just lost my father in the fray. I never saw it again. The inscription inside read: Fe/JG2JW/MAR36.

Fe is the Spanish word for faith.

Kayleigh straightened. "Of course. That's it. How could I, fluent in Spanish, not know that? The answer was staring us in the face this entire time. Do I ever feel stupid."

"You weren't thinking Spanish," Brandon said. "You had no reason to believe that would be its meaning."

Then, of course, our initials. I was Josephine Wilkins before I married John Gilbert. And lastly is March 1836, when John was going to make me an offer of marriage. The battle delayed that, but it serves as a good remembrance to all the fine men, many of whom John and I knew, who were killed that day, including my beloved father. With his dying words, he told me to never lose faith.

I haven't. Through the many joys and many sorrows of this life, faith has been my constant, my stronghold. Now, as I near the end of my life, it is my hope for my eternal future.

Wherever my ring is, wherever my daughter is, I pray she holds to our precious faith and finds this hope for herself.

Signed by my own hand,
Josephine Faith Wilkins Gilbert
October 9, 1867

Complete silence engulfed them as Kayleigh struggled to absorb the words. Imagine having a daughter ripped away from you and never knowing her fate. But the ring. It had belonged to this woman. Perhaps, because it was taken by the child's father, it did pass to her. Could this mean. . .?

"Wow." Brandon shook his head. "I can't believe the ring held so much history and meaning. And to think, you're a descendant of that woman."

"So you think it too."

"How else could your family have come into possession of it?"

"Who knows? Two hundred years is a long time for something to happen to it. It could have been sold for food, or it could have been stolen. We may never know the truth."

Brandon picked up the letter and scanned it again. "She doesn't name the father of her child, which makes things more complicated. Do you remember your birth parents' names?"

"Armando and Juanita Garcia."

"How about their birthdates or where you were from?"

"Why do you want all this information?"

"I don't want to get your hopes up, but if I have the information, I may be able to do a little more research."

"I don't know their birthdates or where we were from. It's not in any of the paperwork my parents saved from the adoption, so I think that's an unknown. They were young, that's all I know."

"It's something. Let me see what I can do."

"This is so exciting." Noreen clapped her hands. "Here I've had this letter all along and just thought of it as a sweet story that found its way into this book. But there was so much more to it. I never thought I would see the ring."

Brandon took a picture of the letter and stood. "I'm going to get going. I'll check back in the morning." With a quick peck on Kayleigh's cheek that tingled her skin, he was gone.

Noreen finished the last dregs of her coffee. "That boy. When he gets something in his head, he doesn't give up. I'll bet you're going to get all your questions answered and then some."

Kayleigh could only pray that would be the case.

CHAPTER FORTY-ONE

"Good morning." Noreen stood at the stove, the heavenly aroma of bacon wafting from the pan, as Kayleigh entered the kitchen.

She was far too cheerful for so early in the morning. "Good morning." Kayleigh managed not to mumble her greeting too much. Instead of heading for the coffeepot, though, she made a beeline for the fridge and pulled out a Diet Coke.

Just a few sips in, and she was much more awake. "That smells amazing."

"Bacon, eggs, and hash."

"You do know that they're going to have to roll me out of here when I leave?"

Noreen gave a hearty chuckle. "No worries about that. You're so slim. I envy you young ladies who manage to keep trim. Just wait until you hit forty or fifty. Then things change."

"I won't pry about your age, but whatever it is, you look fantastic. You have nothing to worry about either."

"Keep that up, and I'll have to feed you doughnuts for breakfast tomorrow."

Kayleigh got a couple of plates and some cutlery and set them on the table. As she was going for the salt and pepper, her phone dinged with a text from Mom.

Flight arrives at 3:15 this afternoon. I have a hotel for us near your place. Don't worry. Renting my own car. See you between 4:30 and 5.

Kayleigh drew her eyebrows together. She and Mom had never talked about her coming. Unless, in the fog of all that was happening, she had somehow missed it. She scrolled backward through the string of texts between her and Mom. Nothing about her coming. She texted back.

Wait, what? Did I miss something?

Of course I would come and be there for you. There must be so much that needs to be done.

What about work? I've taken some vacation time. No worries.

Some vacation time. No specified length of time. "Well, it looks like you're losing your houseguest. My mother has just announced that she's flying in this afternoon, so we'll be moving to a hotel."

"A hotel?" Noreen shook her head and tsked. "I'm sure they won't serve you breakfasts like this."

"Probably not. More likely it will be congealed eggs, floppy bacon, and packaged pastries, but it will be much more hip-friendly."

"You're both welcome to stay here. I really wouldn't mind."

"No, thank you. We wouldn't want to impose. Besides, I spoke to the condo manager yesterday, and he said he might be having a unit coming open soon that I can rent for a short while. We'll see. Everything is still so up in the air."

"You do what you and your mom are comfortable with. No pressure. I understand the need you two might have to be together right now. Just know that my door is always open for you."

"Thank you. I don't know how I would have been able to manage these last thirty-six hours without you." Kayleigh downed the rest of her Coke and threw the can into the recycling bin. "I'm going to head over to what's left of my place and see what, if anything, I can salvage. With the police investigation, I didn't get over there yesterday."

Noreen turned from the stove. "Be careful. I hate the thought of you out there alone."

"It's far too early in the morning for criminals." Kayleigh laughed and grabbed her car keys and phone. "I'll be back when it's time to check into the hotel to pick up the rest of my stuff. What there is of it."

"No worries. I'll see you later." Noreen gave her a big grin, then returned to her breakfast preparations, humming a hymn under her breath.

A short time later, Kayleigh pulled up in front of the burned-out shell of her condo. The front part, where the living room and bedrooms were located, was done for. The back part where the kitchen and laundry were had survived. At least she wouldn't need all new pots and pans. Little consolation when everything of worth was in the living room and bedrooms.

She ducked under the yellow police tape and tiptoed around her scorched living room. The cabinet underneath the TV was relatively unscathed, and when she peeked inside, the scrapbooks Mom had made of her growing up were not damaged.

She took them to her car, then returned to see what she could find in her bedroom. Her swimming trophies were of little consequence, but the stuffed bear that Dad had given her when they had first met her. . .

Crunching footsteps sounded behind her. Her arms and legs weak, she spun. A man dressed in jeans and a dark green T-shirt approached her, a crooked grin on his round face. He finger-combed his dark hair.

She was being silly. Neurotic. Wasn't she?

He kicked his way through the debris. "Miss Hewland, we meet at last."

Though his voice was deep, it sent shivers through her, the tone of it gruff. "Who...Who are you?" She reached for her phone in her back pocket, but it wasn't there. Great. She'd left it in her car.

"That's not important. Just give me what I want."

"I...I don't know what you mean." She still had her smart watch. Because of Jason, she'd learned how long to hold the crown before she could swipe to call 911. She could do it with her eyes closed. So that's what she did now.

"The ring." He stepped toward her, and she backed up. "Just give me the ring, and this can all be over."

"I don't know what you mean, but you need to leave. You're scaring me. You don't belong here. Please, don't hurt me. Just leave." Hopefully that was enough that the dispatcher on the other end of the line could figure out what was going on. "I'm not okay with you being here."

"You know exactly what I mean. That ring with the inscription. It belongs to me."

"It was my mother's." Whoops. She spoke before she thought.

"She had no right to it, and neither do you."

"What's so special about this ring? Why are you after it?"

"Like you don't know." He made another move in her direction. This time she sidestepped him.

"I don't. I truly don't. Please, leave me in peace. I don't have the ring. It's gone."

"Gone?" The man's voice wavered for a moment.

"I lost it when you firebombed my house."

Red rose in his face like the brightest of dawns, and he whipped a pistol from his waistband. Pointed it at her.

"Put that gun away!" *And please, Lord, let the dispatcher understand they need to send someone as fast as possible.*

"Find that ring. I don't care if you have to sift through every piece of this rubble, just find it."

She dropped to her knees, her hands shaking as she sorted through the ashes of what had been her dresser.

Thankfully, the ring was at Noreen's house, tucked away in a drawer in the guest bedroom. "Just tell me why it's so important."

"Ha!" The laugh was not one of amusement. "You know. You want the Garcia fortune for yourself. Well, I'm going to make sure you don't ever see a penny of it. Your mother wasn't the heir. My father, her brother, was. She denied him his birthright by accepting the ring from their mother."

This was her cousin?

"And then I saw it on the internet, but the man sold it to you before I could get it. I watched you walk away with it the day you bought it. I've been watching you ever since."

In the distance, sirens blared. Kayleigh let out a breath she hadn't realized she'd been holding. As long as this man, her cousin, didn't panic.

"Hurry up!" His screams should be enough to wake the entire complex.

"I'm trying. I'm trying. It doesn't seem to be here." She caught sight of a squad car screeching to a halt in front of her unit. The man took off, but officers jumped from the car and gave chase.

One of them stopped by as she squatted, panting.

"Are you okay, miss?"

She nodded. "Just get him. Get him."

Her head spun, and she bowed it so she wouldn't pass out. Though she fought to stem the torrent of tears that threatened, she was unsuccessful. They burst from her in great, heaving sobs.

Mama and Papi gone because of a ring. Because of money. When would money stop being more important than human life? So many had died because of it. How many others had in the past? All for wealth. Temporary. Fleeting. Worthless in the end.

Her tears hadn't stopped before the officers returned with the man between them, his hands cuffed behind his back. As they led him to the car, she stared him in the eyes.

They were as dark as her own. Somehow, though, they managed to be cold and lifeless. Steeled. Had he no heart, this man who shared her DNA?

She shook away the thought. Genes were all they shared. There was much she didn't know about her birth family, but if he was indicative of what they were like, she wanted nothing to do with them.

The next hours passed in a blur. More chats with the police. She'd had enough to last two lifetimes. Her glass was full to overflowing. As if by rote, she answered their questions.

By the time she was finished with them and was released to return to Noreen's, Mom had been texting her for a while, each one more frantic than the other. All Kayleigh had the will to do was to text her Noreen's address and tell her she'd meet her there.

At last she arrived and saw what she assumed to be Mom's little white rental car on the street in front of the stucco house.

Mom was at the door when she opened it.

Mom. The one who had raised her and given her everything she'd needed and who had loved her with a selfless love.

She fell into her open arms. "Oh Mom. I love you. I love you."

CHAPTER FORTY-TWO

$\mathscr{K}$ayleigh had grabbed a shower, and Noreen had insisted that she and Mom stay for dinner. With her husband still out of town, Noreen would be alone otherwise. Mom and Noreen hit it off so well, like they were long-lost sisters, Kayleigh gave in and agreed.

They had just said grace over their meat loaf when Brandon arrived, a brown accordion folder in his hand. Noreen poured him a glass of iced tea, Kayleigh introduced him to Mom, and he settled at the table, smiling at Kayleigh the entire time.

"What? What is it? You're grinning like the cat that swallowed the canary."

"Okay. This is what I have."

"Wait. Before you do that, I have to tell you what happened today." She relayed the incident at her condo and informed him of what she had learned about the ring,

He whistled. "Imagine that. Wow. Your cousin of all people. That's amazing. Do you think you'll talk to him? See if your grandmother or aunts or uncles are alive?"

She glanced at Mom, whose expression was neutral. That was the great thing about her parents. They had always allowed her to take the lead with anything to do with her adoption or her past.

She shook her head. "When I looked him in the eyes, I didn't like what I saw, what greed had made him into. I always knew, deep in my heart, that God had given me a gift in my parents. In that moment, I truly understood and fully appreciated that gift."

Mom sniffled and dabbed at her eyes with her napkin. She squeezed Kayleigh's hand.

When everyone's eyes were dry again and they had settled into dinner once more, Brandon pulled some papers out of the folder and spread them across the table. "I spent a good bit of the night last night working back your genealogy. It's a history nerd kind of thing. Any chance I have to get on one of those sites, I take it."

"So you know if my grandmother is still alive."

"No, I don't. Recent information isn't always public. I managed to get names, and that was it. Anyway, this is what I came up with."

She set her plate to the side as he took her back through her mother's side of the family to a child, Luisa Garcia, born in 1834.

"Her father was Manuel. He fought in the Texas Revolution, including the battle of the Alamo. The mother is simply listed as deceased. As I did a little more digging, though, I found this." He withdrew a paper from his folder and slid it across the table to Kayleigh.

It was no larger than a composition notebook piece of paper. Across the top was typed in old-fashioned type TEXAS REPUBLICAN and the date July 5, 1834.

She scanned the single-paged copy of a newspaper. "What a gem."

"There were many short-lived papers in Texas beginning way back in 1819. This one I found on the internet. It fit the date I was searching for. This was its premier issue. It ran until about the time of the Alamo. And you're right. It's rarer than any of the gems in my store. But read that bottom article in the right corner."

She shifted her attention to the headline Brandon pointed out.

RESCUED FROM MEXICANS
More than a year has passed since young Josephine Wilkins was kidnapped from her home after the brutal murders of her mother and infant sister. This grisly crime was committed by a rough and hardened Mexican by the name of Manuel Garcia, a ruthless soldier in Santa Anna's militia, intent on stealing a ring belonging to Josephine's mother, Mrs. George Wilkins.

The rescue was conducted by Running Deer, an acquaintance of the Wilkins family and a member of the friendly Tonkawa tribe. Our gratitude to them for returning a young woman to her grieving father. Our best wishes to Miss Wilkins as she settles in at home in Gonzales.

Kayleigh gripped the edge of her seat. "So Luisa Garcia was Josephine Wilkins's child?"

"Yes, that's what my research led me to."

"This is our Josephine? I'm related to her?"

Brandon nodded.

She clasped the hand that wore the ring. Josephine's ring. Her four times great-grandmother.

Brandon poured ketchup over his meat while she processed this news. This was a past she could cling to, the story of an extraordinary young woman of deep faith who endured more than any person should have to. And Kayleigh was her descendant. Josephine's blood ran in her veins.

The thought robbed her of her breath. To be related to such a woman was remarkable. This was going to take some time to come to terms with, how her three-times great-grandmother was conceived and born.

"So that's how Luisa ended up in Mexico instead of San Antonio. Josephine mentioned in her letter that the man who got her pregnant took the baby away."

That would make sense and match what the newspaper said. Kayleigh grasped her cold pop can, almost crushing it. "What an evil, despicable man." Yet she was his flesh and blood. Better to focus on the fact that she was also the descendant of a very courageous young woman. "Did Luisa ever know the circumstances of her birth?"

Brandon shrugged. "We may never know. But there's more."

"More? I'm not sure I can take any other revelations today. I've already learned so much. To think I'm related to men who fought on opposite sides of the battle of the Alamo.

Brandon produced more papers from the folder. He also spread these across the tabletop. "This is my genealogy. I'll just skip to the good part." He pointed to a couple at the top of his tree.

John Gilbert and Josephine Wilkins. Kayleigh's mouth fell open, and she couldn't shut it.

"They are my four times great-grandparents."

"So we're related?" She squinted at the printed words on the page.

"A little bit, and only very distantly."

Her ring. He had equal claim to it. They were both descended from Josephine Wilkins Gilbert.

He covered her hands. "Don't worry. I'm not going to take the ring from you. As a descendant of Josephine's oldest child and as someone who has had it in her family for all these generations, it's yours by right. I never wanted it."

She stared at him, her mouth puckered.

"Okay, maybe I did want it, at least to verify the legend in our family, to find out if it was true or not. Boy, did I ever find out it was true. I've seen the ring with my own eyes and can put my family's questions about the veracity of the story to rest."

She blew out a breath. "I'm so relieved. Thank you. Just so you know, I was prepared to fight you for it."

He laughed, rich and full. "I have no doubt about it. But especially since it's all you have of your birth mother, I could never take it from you."

"That means the world to me."

He gave her a tender, wide-eyed gaze that almost said he felt the same way.

When he broke off eye contact, he picked up his papers, squeezed her hand, and kissed her cheek. "I have to get back to the store, although I doubt I'll ever have such an interesting, intriguing customer as you walk through those doors again."

She managed a small smile. Would they see each other again? If she hadn't happened into his jewelry store, they would never have met. Now, the thought of him walking out the door and out of her life forever was too much. "I hope we can catch lunch or dinner one of these days soon."

"We'll see." With a wink, he was gone.

In between meeting with the condo manager, the insurance company, and the police yet again, Kayleigh managed to slip in a quick lunch with Paula. Mom had decided to go for a pedicure, and Kayleigh had declined.

"Howdy, stranger." Paula slid into the booth across from Kayleigh, balancing a salad and her lemonade on a tray. "Nice to see you again. You had quite the adventure while I was on vacation." She sobered. "How are you doing?"

"Pretty well. But you won't believe what Brandon discovered."

When Kayleigh finished the story, Paula leaned forward, her dark eyes wide and sparkling. "Wow. Imagine that. How cool to know that you did find your family's ring. What are the chances?"

"When God is involved, I'm learning that they aren't all that far out as you might imagine."

"Why do I have a feeling you're talking about Brandon now?" Paula popped a bite of lettuce and chicken into her mouth.

"I mentioned having lunch or dinner sometime. He was noncommittal."

"Basically, asking him out was a mistake?"

"Probably. I mean, it was fun figuring out this mystery with him, and even though we're related, it's very distant, so no problems there. It wouldn't have worked out anyway."

"Why do you say that?" Paula picked the tomatoes out of her salad. And the cucumbers. It was amazing the girl was as healthy as she was.

"That's how it always ends up."

Paula leaned forward. "Because you keep them all at arm's length. You don't open yourself to anyone. Hardly to me. You have trust issues. You're afraid to lose another person you love."

The knife in Kayleigh's heart twisted just a little bit. Mama and Papi. Dad. Yes, she'd lost a lot. And it hurt. A hurt she never wanted to experience again. But love? Did she love Brandon?

Not yet.

Someday?

That remained to be seen.

"Open up, Kayleigh. Don't miss out on the future because of what you lost in the past."

"It's not as easy as you make it seem."

"Just promise me you'll try. Please. He's a good guy. Don't lose him too."

Kayleigh bit into the apple that came with her bowl of soup and chewed. "You're not going to get off my back until I do, are you?"

"Not a chance." Paula tipped her head and grinned.

"Fine, then. I promise."

⁂

Kayleigh had to laugh as the waiter brought the dinners to her and Brandon. "I don't think I've ever seen so much meat in one place in my entire life."

"That's what Brazilian steak houses are all about."

"I should have expected it."

They chatted while they consumed copious amounts of beef, delicious as it was. When she couldn't fit in another bite, she sat back, as did Brandon.

"How are you doing with the discovery we made a few weeks ago?"

"It's hard to wrap my mind around the fact that something awful happened to Josephine. I can't imagine what she must have gone through. I hope she found support and love, that John truly took care of her and was good to her."

"If not for that bad thing that happened to her, if not for Manuel, you wouldn't be here. So to me, something good did come from it."

"Without John coming into her life, neither would you."

"God does have this way of bringing good out of evil."

"Do you believe my five-times great-grandfather was an evil man?"

Brandon shrugged. "That's not for me to say, but the killings at the Alamo were brutal. It's pretty clear he had a hand in the murder of our five-times great-grandmother."

Kayleigh shuddered.

"Remember what Josephine wrote? Always have faith. I believe she truly lived that and that she experienced it. With faith, you can endure anything, because there's the hope that God is working out everything, even when you can't see it."

"At least my so-called cousin is behind bars."

"That man isn't going to bother you for a very long time."

"I can sleep again."

"Hey, we wouldn't have met if not for the ring. I'm awfully glad I got the chance to meet you."

"Me too." Paula's words rang in Kayleigh's head. *Open yourself up.* "I hope we get the chance to know each other even better." She held her breath, waiting for his response.

"I would like that."

She blew out the air from her lungs.

"You beat me to the punch. I was going to ask if you would like for us to be an exclusive couple. I want to see where this relationship goes."

"Maybe this will be Josephine's happy ending."

"I think it will be ours." Brandon came around to her side of the table and gave her a soft kiss on the lips.

Their first kiss.

One that sent a tingle from her mouth throughout her heart and down to her toes.

Hopefully, it wouldn't be their last.

Brandon might just be right. Like the promise engraved on the ring, she would have faith. Faith that God would work healing and happiness in her heart, with Brandon by her side.

ACKNOWLEDGMENTS

So many people came together to make this book possible, there isn't room here to thank them all. First of all, thank you to my son, Brian, for opening your house to me so I would have a home base in Texas while I did my research. I still think of that steak dinner you made me. It was worth the trip just to spend that precious time with you.

Thank you to everyone at the Alamo, including my tour guide and the docent at the museum for answering all my questions about the mission and the battle and especially about the church, including what happened in the sacristy where many of the women and children hid.

Thank you to the team at Barbour Publishing for all you do. Becky, Shalyn, Abbey, Laura, and everyone else there, you rock. What a fun and educational book it proved to be to write. I so appreciate the opportunity.

A huge shout-out to my editor, Ellen. You took my first attempt at dual timeline and made it work. Thank you so very much! I'd be lost without you—and so would my readers.

Thank you to my nephew-in-law, Isaac, for your help with the Spanish phrases. I really appreciate your willingness to step in and help me make sure it was accurate.

Thank you so much to my beta readers, Jessica and Stacey. You guys were awesome. Your encouragement and insights from the point of view of readers was huge to me. I can't say enough good things about you both.

A big thank-you to everyone on my launch team. You guys are the best! Thank you for spreading the words about my books, for all the reviews you write, for the great graphics you come up with, for cheering me on and helping me overcome my doubts. Your prayers mean the world to me.

I have the deepest appreciation for my agent, Tamela Hancock Murray. Thank you for encouraging me to write this book and for making it happen. You're the best, and I'm thankful that I get to call you friend.

A huge thanks to my family, for putting up with me while I was busy with my writing and editing. Doug, my awesome husband, where would I be without you? Definitely not a published author, that's for sure. Thank you for doing laundry and dishes, for taking care of Jonalyn so I could concentrate, for even allowing me time by myself so I could get some uninterrupted work done. I love you so much.

To my fans, a huge round of applause. Without readers, I couldn't be a writer. Thank you for picking up this book, for reading it, for telling others about it. I pray that the words inside here make you think, draw you closer to God, and bless you.

All the praise goes to God, the giver of all good gifts. Thank You for blessing me and providing for me and my family. Thank You for never leaving me or forsaking me. May You receive all the glory.

HISTORICAL NOTES

The Wilkins family, John Gilbert, and Manuel Garcia are all made-up characters. Senora Navarro is a compilation of the Navarro sisters, both of whom survived the Alamo. One was unmarried at the time, though she went on to have eight children. The other was married with one child. The rest of the characters are historical, including the Dickinson family. Susanna and her daughter Angelina were the only two white females to survive the Alamo. They, along with the Tejano women with them, hid in the sacristy. Santa Anna did visit them and give them twenty-four hours to leave. He did speak the words about the Alamo not becoming a memorial to the dead, which is why he burned all the men's bodies. Such an irony that today an obelisk stands in what would have been the middle of the mission, each of the murdered men's names carved into the marble.

There were spies coming and going in and out of the Alamo during the Mexicans' thirteen-day siege of it, so it was not out of the realm of possibility for John and Josie to go for help. Some men survived because they did just that. Santa Anna did raise a red flag over San Antonio de Béxar, as it was known at the time, indicating he would take no prisoners. The only man who survived was an enslaved man named Joe, who didn't fight in the battle but hid in the sacristy. It is believed that he returned to Mexican territory after the war where slavery was outlawed.

Santa Anna had invited settlers from America to Texas, then a Mexican state, promising them free land and the same liberties they had enjoyed as US citizens. They did have to convert to Roman Catholicism to immigrate, though many continued to practice their Protestant faith. Tensions rose in the years after Santa Anna threw out the Mexican constitution and ruled the country as a dictator. Stephen Austin even spent time in a Mexico City prison because Santa Anna didn't take kindly to his comments about the government. Santa Anna demanding the cannon back was the tipping point.

While I don't include every battle that was fought, the ones I do include are as factual as possible. Manuel shooting John at the end of the battle of Gonzales was fictional. No shots were fired. The Mexicans fled without their cannon.

The Texans did win the battle at Concepción by hiding below the river-bank, which offered them a strategic position, though they did indeed get showered with pecans. Sam Houston did burn Gonzales to the ground when he fled ahead of Santa Anna, not yet ready to engage him.

I found a detailed map of the town of Gonzales as it was in 1835, which was a great help. I used the location of Almaron Dickinson's home for the Wilkins's house because I knew there was a dwelling at that location. There was a blacksmith's shop where I said it was, as well as the military plaza.

Rings were used for many years to pass messages, including during the Revolutionary War and the Mexican-American War. While there was no specific mention of one being used during the Texas Revolution, it is possible that one could have been used.

There is a cat's-eye ring in the museum at the Alamo, and it's what first gave me the idea for the item that linked the past and the present. Legend says that William Travis, the Alamo commander, gave it to Angelina Dickinson as he was dying. Whatever the case, it was amazing to go to the museum, see it in the display case, and wonder what might have been.

LIZ TOLSMA is the author of several WWII novels, romantic suspense novels, prairie romance novellas, and an Amish romance. She is a popular speaker and an editor and resides next to a Wisconsin farm field with her husband and their youngest daughter. Her son is a US Marine, and her oldest daughter is a recent college graduate. Liz enjoys reading, walking, working in her large perennial garden, kayaking, and camping. Please visit her website at www.liztolsma.com and follow her on Facebook, Twitter (@LizTolsma), Instagram, YouTube, and Pinterest. She is also the host of the *Christian Historical Fiction Talk* podcast.

Doors to the Past

Visit historic American landmarks through the **Doors to the Past** series. History and today collide in stories full of mystery, intrigue, faith, and romance.

HIGH-WIRE HEARTBREAK
By Anna Schmidt

A successful historical mystery writer, Chloe Whitfield comes to Ca' d'Zan to research her next novel. Chloe's fascination with the circus is rooted in family stories of her great-grandmother Lucinda Conroy, who reportedly was a trapeze artist of some renown. She's heard hints of scandal—and perhaps larceny, but no details. Chloe's grandmother—rumored to be Lucinda's only offspring—was raised in an orphanage and never knew her mother. Intrigued as she is, Chloe has no intent of writing about Lucinda until she sees a poster featuring Lucinda as the star performer for a seventieth birthday gala for John Ringling in May 1936. From there the trail goes cold. Who was Lucinda, and what happened to her?

Paperback / 978-1-63609-137-2 / $12.99

LOVE'S FORTRESS
By Jennifer Uhlarik

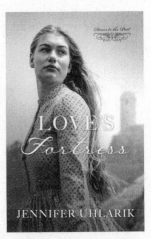

Upon receiving word that her long-estranged father has passed away, Dani Sango inherits the former art forger's entire estate. Among his many pieces of artwork are a series of obviously Native American drawings and paintings, which lead her to research St. Augustine of 1875. Broken Bow is transported to Florida to join other Cheyenne braves already being held in Fort Marion. Sally Jo Harris is at the fort teaching the Indians. When a friendship develops between them and false accusations fly, it could cost them their lives. Can Dani discover how their story ends and how it shaped her own father's life?

Paperback / 978-1-63609-181-5 / $12.99